It had been a long time since he'd been tempted to kiss a woman.

Being burned by Abby and Gillian had done a number on him and his desire to get close to anyone, and this was the longest he'd ever gone without female companionship. He wasn't here in Moose Falls to establish a romantic connection. Being here was purely a business move to enable him to truly pursue a career in acting. If they sold Yukon Cider, he could use his share to bankroll his life as an aspiring actor in Los Angeles.

He tried to distract himself with something else other than Sophia's lips, but there was nothing up here but boxes and boxes of stuff. A light floral aroma rose to his nostrils. His chest tightened at the feminine scent that hovered in the air.

Was it getting hot in here or what?

FLIRTING WITH
ALASKA

FLIRTING WITH ALASKA

BELLE CALHOUNE

FOREVER

New York   Boston

Forever
Hachette Book Group
1290 Avenue of the Americas, New York, NY 10104
read-forever.com
@readforeverpub

First Edition: December 2024

Forever is an imprint of Grand Central Publishing. The Forever name and logo are registered trademarks of Hachette Book Group, Inc.

The publisher is not responsible for websites (or their content) that are not owned by the publisher.

The Hachette Speakers Bureau provides a wide range of authors for speaking events. To find out more, go to hachettespeakersbureau.com or email HachetteSpeakers@hbgusa.com.

Forever books may be purchased in bulk for business, educational, or promotional use. For information, please contact your local bookseller or the Hachette Book Group Special Markets Department at special.markets@hbgusa.com.

ISBNs: 978-1-5387-5822-9 (mass market), 978-1-5387-5823-6 (ebook)

Printed in the United States of America

BVGM

10 9 8 7 6 5 4 3 2 1

For my father, Fred. For teaching me about classic movies and so much more.

PROLOGUE

The Arizona heat bore down on Caleb Stone with a ferocity he had never experienced in his eight years of life. Heat shimmered off the blacktop of the playground like sequins glittering on his mother's fanciest dress. He had heard folks say it was so hot one could fry an egg on the sidewalk. He'd never heard that expression before now, but then again he had never lived in a warm climate in his life. Folks were saying that it was the hottest October on record here in the Grand Canyon State. Just his dumb luck!

"It's an inferno out here," Caleb muttered to himself. "No one told me we were moving to Death Valley." So far Arizona wasn't anything his mother had promised it would be. Instead of Arizona being awesome, all he'd experienced were scorching temperatures and stupid kids. Moving from Alaska had been a total fail.

None of the boys in his class who were shooting hoops during recess wanted to give him the time of day. Caleb was the new kid at school, transplanted from Moose Falls, Alaska, after his parents split up. Did he smell or something?

Did they think he had cooties? He hadn't been asked to join in even once.

His older brother, Xavier, didn't have a problem making friends. He was already on the football team and making a name for himself. Everyone loved him. Back home in Alaska Caleb had also been popular. As far as he was concerned, Arizonans had no taste whatsoever. Didn't they appreciate charm, pee-your-pants jokes, and handsome good looks?

Landon, his younger brother, had found a group of nerd-balls like himself to hang out with. They did dorky things like work with microscopes and specimens. Landon had found his tribe, even if they were dweebs. Birds of a feather flocked together, he supposed. But where was his posse of like-minded kids? Ones who were cool and funny and liked to play jokes. It wasn't fair that he was the odd person out. What had he done to deserve this? Not a bleepity-bleep thing. He was so mad he wanted to cuss, but the thought of it getting back to his mother stopped him. She was already going through enough heartache. Caleb hated seeing her with red-rimmed eyes in the morning after crying herself to sleep.

He never wanted to make anyone hurt the way his dad had made his mom ache. Caleb wanted girls to like him, but he wasn't sure about the love part. As far as he could tell, it was a lot of trouble.

The girls here in Arizona were different from back in Moose Falls. They liked him. A lot.

In class they kept passing him notes filled with red hearts and smiley faces. They would write down their phone numbers and ask him to call them. So far he hadn't called a single one. He was only eight years old, and he didn't need or want a girlfriend. Plus, he didn't have a cell phone. His mom and dad thought he was too young for one.

He felt a sharp pain in his chest at the thought of his dad. He was back home in Alaska probably wishing they hadn't left. Things had been bad at home for a long time with lots of shouting and slamming doors. He'd hated his father at times, even though he really loved him. He kept that love way down deep where no one could see it. He didn't want Xavier to be mad at him for still loving their dad, not when he'd done so much to hurt their mom.

Sometimes it just made his head hurt. Why couldn't he just have a normal family? That way he wouldn't have had to leave Moose Falls in the first place.

"You're special, Caleb. And don't you ever forget it."

His grandmother Hattie had whispered those words in his ear before they'd left Moose Falls. Just thinking about it made his eyes fill with tears. *Don't cry*, he told himself. If the fellas saw him crying, they would probably think he was a baby and call him names. He needed to be strong like Xavier. He never cried.

"Hey, Caleb. Do you want to push me on the swing?" Denise Hall was standing next to him fluttering her eyelashes. She was pretty, he supposed, with long, curly hair and a nice smile.

Caleb shrugged. Honestly, he'd rather be playing hoops with the boys. He didn't understand girls or what they wanted from him. But for some reason they were drawn to him like a magnet.

"I was going to ask Caleb to play jacks with me." Another girl—Samantha, maybe—stepped in between him and Denise. "So, do you wanna?" she asked, pressing the point.

Suddenly, he was surrounded by five girls, all of them pestering him with requests.

"You're the nicest-looking boy in the whole school," Shayna Lockett whispered in his ear. "I have a crush on you."

He felt his cheeks getting flushed. The girls swarmed around him, all trying to get his attention. He felt like a member of a famous boy band. Caleb wasn't sure what to do in the situation. There was only one person on the planet who could handle this.

He channeled his father, Red, the coolest dude in the universe.

Caleb held up his hands. "Ladies, I appreciate the warm welcome, but if you could give me a little space I'd appreciate it."

With smiles and apologies, the girls backed away from him and headed over to the swings, giving him exactly what he had requested. It was as if he had special powers or something.

"I could get used to this," he murmured. He could feel a huge grin stretching from ear to ear.

"Hey, Alaska."

Caleb rolled his eyes and turned toward the squeaky voice coming from behind him. Hal Tanner was standing there gawking at him. With a head of red hair, round cheeks, and a face full of freckles, Hal looked like a Cabbage Patch Kid. Hal was in Caleb's class, and he seemed to think him being from Alaska was hilarious. He kept making jokes about Caleb living in an igloo and eating raw fish for dinner. He was incredibly lame, but for some reason he was popular.

Clearly, he didn't know the first thing about Alaska or how cool it was to live there.

A powerful wave of homesickness washed over him. He missed Moose Falls and the huge mountains he could see from his bedroom window. He missed wearing cable-knit sweaters and going tobogganing with his brothers. And he missed having a best friend.

"Yeah. What do you want?" Caleb asked Hal. He was

tired of trying to make inroads with him and the rest of the guys. If necessary, he would simply be a lone wolf and go his own way. He could make it on his own, especially since he could still hang out with Xavier and Landon. He would never be alone.

"How do you get all the girls to pay attention to you?" Hal asked with his head cocked to the side. "You draw 'em in like bees to honey."

Caleb jutted out his chin. "Wouldn't you like to know?" It felt nice to get some of his mojo back.

Hal stepped toward him and grinned. "I would like to know. I've had a crush on Denise since first grade. She won't give me the time of day."

"Maybe your breath stinks," Caleb quipped. Why should he be nice to Hal after he'd given him so much crap about Alaska? He had to show him he wasn't a pushover.

Hal sucked his teeth. "It does not. I'll have you know that I brush my teeth twice a day, and I use mouthwash. Scope, matter of fact," he said, puffing out his chest.

"Your pits then," Caleb said, enjoying the sight of Hal squirming. Caleb wanted to laugh out loud when Hal tugged at his shirt and sniffed his underarm.

"My pits are fine," Hal said. "I don't smell."

"Whatever," Caleb muttered.

"You want to come to my birthday party on Saturday?" Hal asked, causing shock waves to wash over Caleb.

"You're inviting *me*?" Caleb asked. "I don't get it. You don't like me. You've made it pretty obvious." Caleb stood his ground, folding his arms across his chest and sticking his chin out in mutinous fashion.

"You're cool, Alaska," he said with a nod. "If all the girls think so, then you must be all right." It took Caleb a few moments to process what Hal was telling him. On his own he was a weirdo from Alaska, but when surrounded by a flock of girls, he was suddenly a hot commodity.

Because where he went, the girls followed. And it gave him street cred with the boys at school. Suddenly, he had value. Caleb puffed out his chest. He was a chick magnet. He was somebody!

Caleb might not be athletic like Xavier or a smarty-pants like Landon, but he was pure gold in the getting-girls-to-like-him department. All this time he'd been clueless about his own superpower, and here it was. It had fallen right into his lap, right out of the blue. And now that he'd discovered it, he was going to work it to his advantage for as long as he could.

CHAPTER ONE

"Are you really going to marry this guy?" Caleb asked his future sister-in-law, his voice sounding incredulous as he posed the million-dollar question. He was far from serious. He was punking his older brother, Xavier, and trying to get a reaction out of him. Although he was teasing Xavier, the truth was that his big brother getting married hadn't been on his Alaska bingo card. When they had arrived in Moose Falls four months ago, Xavier had been wary of all women and any romantic entanglements because of being betrayed by his ex-fiancée. Honestly, he could relate due to his own experiences. Now, Caleb had fully accepted that Xavier had found love everlasting with True. They were endgame.

The Stone family was moments away from celebrating the happy couple, along with a host of friends, at their engagement party. He was playing with Xavier, but pushing his brother's buttons was a habit he couldn't quit. Doing so had been a way of life in their household growing up. Why would he stop now?

Xavier let out a sigh. "Yep, she's marrying me. Unless you know something I don't."

"We're *definitely* getting married," True said, correcting him.

Xavier leaned over and brushed a kiss on her lips. "That's right, baby. We're getting hitched."

"As in walking down the aisle married?" Landon asked, adjusting his glasses as he spoke. "With an actual official marriage license and everything?" Landon looked over at Caleb and smirked. They were tag-teaming Xavier, who remained oblivious to their joke.

True made a face. "You two are making me nervous. Why the shocked reaction? You've had weeks to get used to the news." She leaned forward and whispered, "Is there something you're not telling me? Blink twice if the answer is yes."

Xavier stood up from the couch, throwing his hands in the air. "Okay, guys, I understand you might be surprised by this turn of events, but you've been grilling us for the last twenty minutes at our very own engagement party. The answer isn't changing. True and I are getting married."

"And I for one couldn't be happier." The sound of their grandmother's voice caused all three Stone brothers to turn toward the dining room threshold. Looking resplendent in a gold ensemble and with her gray hair styled in a fancy updo, Hattie Stone always knew how to make a grand entrance.

She had a habit of appearing without making a sound. These days it was a little harder for her to pull it off due to her electric scooter, but at the moment she was walking under her own steam with the help of a fancy cane. Due to a terminal diagnosis, Hattie was "living with an expiration date," as she liked to say.

Caleb quickly got to his feet and went to her side. He took Hattie's arm and led her over to a velvet love seat. After she was seated, he lifted her hand and kissed it. "You look stunning tonight, Grandmother," he drawled.

Hattie nodded her head slightly in his direction. "Thank you, my sweet charmer. It's not every day that my oldest grandson gets engaged." Caleb sat back down in his seat and looked over at the happy couple. Xavier and True were now snuggled up on the couch, whispering to each other and tightly holding hands.

Caleb and his two brothers, Landon and Xavier, had returned to Moose Falls four months ago after a nearly twenty-year absence. Granny Hattie was dying, and she wanted to make sure her company, Yukon Cider, was inherited by her grandsons. The catch was, they had a year to decide whether to keep the company and stick around Moose Falls or sell it to the highest bidder. The decision had to be unanimous or they would forfeit their inheritance.

Xavier had always been skeptical of staying in Alaska, but now that he was engaged to True, all bets were off. Since the three brothers had to be in agreement on the decision, he and Landon had some sway in the situation. Caleb could still go to Hollywood and pursue his dreams. Caleb knew there had to be a way to make casting agents forget about his disastrous appearance on the reality show *Love Him or Leave Him*. He wasn't ready to give up on his dream. Not by a long shot. He was down, but not broken.

Caleb and Landon burst into laughter at the irritated expression etched on Xavier's face. Seconds later Xavier caught on. "You two are messing with me, aren't you?"

"Of course we are. For old times' sake," Caleb said, grinning.

"Call it an engagement present," Landon told him.

Xavier shook his head. "Two knuckleheads." The corners of his mouth were twitching with amusement.

"Enough of this nonsense. It's almost time for the guests to arrive," Hattie announced, clapping her hands together in a gleeful gesture. "Look alive, boys," she barked, tapping Caleb's foot with her cane.

"Yes, ma'am," Caleb said, sitting up straight. His brothers hid their laughter behind their hands. They all had the habit of reacting to Hattie's reprimands. At this point it didn't bother Caleb. He knew Hattie was old-school and meant no harm whatsoever.

"Has anyone seen Jacques?" Hattie asked, looking around the room as if her man were going to pop up out of thin air.

A chorus of nos ensued.

Jacques was Hattie's boyfriend, or paramour, as she liked to say. He was also her chauffeur and majordomo. A jack-of-all-trades, so to speak. He was a good man who was in love with Hattie and treated her well. Caleb's own parents' divorce had been traumatic and life-altering as an eight-year-old. Nothing in his life so far had shown him that true love was attainable. At least not for him. So why not focus on becoming the next Idris Elba?

Suddenly, Jacques was standing in the entryway, looking dapper in a black tuxedo, a red cummerbund, and a crisp white shirt. Hattie let out a sharp whistle of approval at the sight of him, which caused a huge grin to overtake Jacques's face. He made a beeline to Hattie, leaning down to press a lingering kiss on her lips. Their love story was opening up Caleb's eyes about the meaning of love and relationships.

"Get a room," Landon muttered, looking away from the couple and wrinkling his nose.

"Jealous?" Caleb asked, jabbing his little brother in the side. He tended to tease Landon about being perpetually single, since he'd never had a significant other. Maybe Landon wasn't finding the ribbing so funny these days, judging by the fierce expression on his face.

Landon glared at him and rammed his elbow into Caleb's side, causing him to let out a grunt of pain.

"That hurt," Caleb said. When had Landon gotten so buff? He must be lifting weights in his spare time.

"Good to know," Landon said, a smile of satisfaction spreading over his face.

"Come on, boys," Hattie said, her tone full of disapproval. "I expect you to be on your best behavior tonight in the happy couple's honor. After all, you're representing the Stone family."

Representing the Stone family was of the utmost importance to Hattie. Ever since arriving in Moose Falls, he'd felt the weight of her expectations on their shoulders.

The doorbell pealed, heralding the arrival of the first guest. Within seconds servers were in place, holding trays of champagne and hors d'oeuvres. A harpist was gently playing in a spot next to the fireplace. Caleb stood up from the couch and moved toward the entryway, ready to greet their guests as they trickled in to the great room. He loved the rush of excitement pulsing in the air. Caleb thoroughly enjoyed working a room and socializing. Moments like this allowed him to shine. Schmoozing was good practice for his future in Hollywood. He was more determined than ever to make a big splash as a professional actor.

Caleb reached for a bacon-wrapped scallop from one of the serving trays and popped it into his mouth. He had the feeling this was going to be a long night. As the rooms began to fill up, Caleb found himself feeling a bit out of sorts, which was unusual for him, since he loved parties and being in the spotlight.

With Xavier getting hitched, nothing in their lives would ever be the same again. He felt it acutely. True was the perfect woman for his brother, and Caleb thought they made a great pair, but at the same time it felt as if he was losing something. He and his two brothers had always been the Three Musketeers—all for one and one for all. That dynamic would shift now with Xavier becoming a husband and a surrogate father to True's younger brother, Jaylen.

Suck it up, buttercup, a voice buzzed in his ear. *This is life. He's your brother, and he also happens to be your best friend. Be supportive. Stop acting as if the sky is falling in.*

Caleb looked around the room, determined to distract himself from his feelings, and caught sight of a flash of red— all curves and hips—snapping photos with a professional-looking camera. Her vibe was intense as she zeroed in on the guests to take their pictures. She looked vaguely familiar but he couldn't immediately place her. She was walking on the highest heels he had ever seen, and for a moment he held his breath as she appeared a bit unsteady on her feet.

Why did women put themselves through such torture? Especially at the risk of falling on their butts. But she was defying the odds by staying upright. He couldn't look away from her. The woman was smoking hot with a curvy figure and long auburn hair. Her skin was the color of mocha. She was radiant.

Easy there. Remember your vow.

Women were off the agenda, especially while he was here in Moose Falls. He still wasn't over the public humiliation of being branded "the Love Rat" on a reality television show. Caleb had believed that starring on the show would give him a leg up in Hollywood. Instead, he had been caught in a love triangle and had his dirty laundry aired for all the world to see. Or at least the show's seven million viewers. His version of events had never made it on-air, and he'd been left to twist in the wind by the woman he'd fallen in love with. That betrayal still burned, and he couldn't even fathom the idea of pursuing another relationship.

But there's no harm in looking. Surely that couldn't get him in any trouble, could it?

He was in Moose Falls for about another eight months, and working at Yukon Cider without any extracurricular activities was getting old. All work and no play made Caleb a very dull boy. He smiled directly at her, giving her his million-dollar grin. Caleb then raised his champagne glass to her. It was his go-to move at social gatherings, and usually women responded quite well to his flirty vibe. He wasn't used to being subtle when it came to women. And if history was any indication, they loved his swagger.

Wait for it, he told himself. She would be swarming him at any moment now. *Ten, nine, eight, seven . . .*

She gave him an icy look followed by an eye roll. She then turned her back on him and faced a completely different direction. *Ouch!*

Shock washed over him like a bucket of ice-cold water. He wasn't used to a woman responding to him with no interest. This had to be a first. Had he lost his touch?

Why did the Stone brothers have to be so freakin' hot? Sophia Brand asked herself for the tenth time that evening as she walked around taking pictures of the guests. Especially the middle brother, Caleb. Things would be so much easier if he were cross-eyed and homely instead of looking like Webster's definition of the word "fine." Super fine, in fact. Honestly, jaws in Moose Falls had dropped the moment these three men arrived in town.

No wonder Caleb had made hearts melt all over the country during his stint on reality television. Thankfully, she knew enough about him from watching *Love Him or Leave Him* to never see him as anything other than a complete jackass. That had made it easy for her to resist his come-hither look from across the room. She wasn't going down that road with him . . . or anyone else, for that matter.

The Love Rat. She stifled a snort. And, boy, had Caleb earned the nickname by hooking up with the twin sister of the woman who had selected him as her final pick. What a disaster! He had cemented his bad boy reputation in reality show history with his antics. She almost felt bad for him. Even at his brother's engagement party, Caleb was trying to flirt up a storm.

This wasn't her first time seeing Caleb Stone in action. About a month ago he'd winked at her from across the room at Northern Exposure when she was talking to True. The gesture had been overly flirtatious and downright cheesy. Maybe if he'd walked over to her and introduced himself, she might have been receptive, rather than getting the ick. Maybe she hadn't been fair in her assessment of him. After all, as a huge reality TV junkie, Sophia had known all about Caleb before he'd ever stepped foot in Moose Falls.

Clearly, he was the type who thrived in social environments.

Sophia didn't enjoy going out, even though she loved her hometown of Moose Falls, Alaska, and the townsfolk. She didn't normally attend social functions on weeknights. Or actually on any nights of the week, if she was being honest. Not that Moose Falls had a hopping night life to speak of, but in the last few years she had been a bit of a homebody. Having a child did that to a person, not to mention being drop-kicked by her baby's daddy.

Do not think of him. Don't even breathe his name.

Donny. Ugh. His name popped into her head before she could stop herself from conjuring it. Well, it wasn't as if she could pretend he didn't exist, even though it would be nice if he went up in a puff of smoke or fell into a mine shaft. She still had to deal with him until Lily turned eighteen. Since her daughter was only four, it felt like a life sentence.

Tonight she was celebrating her friend True Everett's engagement to one of the gorgeous Stone brothers. She was marrying Xavier, a former NFL player who seemed super sweet and perfect for True. A small part of her acknowledged that happily-ever-afters did exist, even if they were few and far between. She didn't believe that one was in the cards for her, which was okay, since she had her sweet Lily. Her daughter was her happy ending. It was difficult being away from her, but this evening was about work.

As a professional photographer she needed to grab jobs as they came her way. She was barely getting by as it was. Due to Moose Falls being a small Alaskan town, Sophia had to hunt down assignments, which tended to be frustrating and very competitive. So when the inimitable Hattie Stone had asked Sophia to take pictures at her grandson's engagement party, Sophia's answer had been an enthusiastic yes. Hattie was an icon here in Moose Falls, not only due to her company, Yukon Cider, but also thanks to her lively personality and her philanthropy.

"Sophia, it's time for you to take a break." Hattie's voice came from directly behind her. Sophia whirled around and greeted Hattie with a kiss on the cheek. "You've been a whirl of activity since the party started."

"That's how I like it," Sophia admitted. "Once I get in the groove, it's hard to get out of the groove."

"Well, grab a glass of champagne and some of those crab bites." Her face lit up. "Oh, and don't let me forget the camera in the attic. I've been meaning to give it to you for ages now."

Hattie had told her about a vintage camera that was simply gathering dust in her attic, and she'd offered the camera to Sophia. She could barely hold back her excitement at the idea of acquiring such a rare item.

"Since I'm taking a champagne break, I can run upstairs and get it now," Sophia suggested. She could use a little pause from the action. Maybe she could even sneak in a phone call to Patience and find out how Lily was doing. She was missing her little girl, even though she knew that her daughter was in great hands.

"I can send one of my grandsons," Hattie said, looking around the room. "One of them must be nearby."

"It's not necessary," Sophia assured her with a pat on the shoulder. "I've got muscles too, you know." She winked.

"Well, the box is right by the door, so it won't be hard to find." Hattie looked down at Sophia's heels. "Are you sure that you won't twist an ankle in those clodhoppers?"

Sophia chuckled. "At this point I'm a pro," she said. She turned away from Hattie and made her way toward the grand staircase. She grabbed the hem of her dress and pulled it up so it wouldn't be a tripping hazard. Maybe Hattie had been right about the shoes. When she reached the top of the stairs, she took off her heels and placed them to the side before proceeding up the last flight toward the attic.

She huffed out a relieved breath when she reached the final three steps.

"I should have listened to Hattie," she muttered. Why was she always so stubborn? It was a terrible trait that always seemed to land her in trouble. She could be sipping champagne right now instead of getting a workout and a run in her pantyhose.

Sophia fumbled with the doorknob that didn't want to budge.

"Hey there. Let me get that for you," a deep voice said from behind her.

Sophia didn't need to turn around to know who was standing there. She had listened to him for months on *Love Him or Leave Him*. The tone of his voice was rich and silky, perfect for charming the panties off unsuspecting ladies.

Little did he know, she was not one. Sophia wasn't buying anything Caleb Stone was selling. Been there, done that.

"Thanks, but I've got it," she said without turning around, just as the door gave way. She stumbled a bit over the threshold due to the long hem of her gown, propelling her forward.

"Easy there," Caleb called out, reaching for her elbow to steady her. Feeling a bit foolish, she shrugged off his hand and walked into the attic, making sure not to shut the door behind her. Her fear of small spaces wouldn't allow her to relax if she was closed in.

He followed behind her, his shoes making a tapping sound against the wood flooring.

"Don't let the door close," Sophia said in a raised voice, whirling around to face him.

"Why not?" he asked with a grin. "Don't worry about being alone with me. I don't bite."

Sophia had to stop herself from rolling her eyes. This man made even an innocent comment seem suggestive.

The door slammed shut with an ominous thud.

"I heard a clicking sound," Sophia said as her heart began to thunder wildly in her chest.

You're okay. You're safe. Nothing's going to happen.

"It was probably just the knob rattling. It's an old door," Caleb said. He sounded so matter-of-fact she wanted to scream at the top of her lungs. She knew what she'd heard.

Sophia walked over and tugged at the door handle. Nothing. She tugged again, feeling frantic. It wasn't budging.

They were locked inside the attic. Panic began to rise up in her throat. How long would it be before they ran out of oxygen? Her throat felt as dry as sandpaper.

Just breathe, she reminded herself. *You're not in any danger.*

"Y-you locked us in," she said in a shaky voice.

Caleb reached past her, his arm brushing against hers as he jiggled the doorknob, to no avail. He let out a grunt as he continued to pull at the door handle without it budging.

"Oh, wow. My bad. You're right," Caleb said, turning around to look at her. "We're stuck."

"Of course I'm right," she seethed. "I don't know why you couldn't just listen to me and accept that I didn't need your help." She wasn't certain about it, but Sophia suspected steam might be coming out of her ears.

"I was trying to be chivalrous."

"That ship sailed a long time ago," she muttered.

Ugh. She really shouldn't have said that. She could only blame it on her fear of small spaces and her annoyance at the situation she had found herself in. But still. Her words were harsh.

His features instantly hardened. Caleb let out a ragged sigh. "You watched *Love Him or Leave Him*, didn't you?"

Sophia shrugged. "I may have watched a few episodes," she sheepishly admitted. "It was mildly entertaining."

Caleb's jaw clenched. Up close he was incredibly handsome. Russet-colored skin. Striking features. Big brown eyes framed by jet-black lashes. And he was sexy in his suit and tie. He looked even better in person than he did on the small screen. How was it possible that he didn't possess a single flaw? His hotness factor was off the charts.

"What's a few?" he asked, arching his brow.

By a few she meant dozens. Reality television was her

secret addiction, and she was hooked. *Born to Wed. 365 Days to Love. Train to Love. Marry Me or Else.* She'd devoured them all like boxes of Godiva chocolates. Caleb's show had been one of the most popular reality shows of all time. He had become a breakout star over the course of the inaugural season. By the conclusion of the series, the audience had turned against him. She herself had loved to hate him. Perhaps it was her own dismal love life that had turned her into a reality show junkie.

"I saw enough to get the gist," she told him, making a face. "You were quite the charmer. Not many people could get two sisters to fall in love with them." She would never admit it to Caleb, but she'd been rooting for a happy ending for him and Gillian. Until he'd blown everything up by romancing her twin sister and turning viewers against him.

He placed a hand over his heart. "All I ask is that you don't judge me by the producer's edit. A lot of things were left on the cutting room floor. I only went on the show to boost my acting career, but I was in way over my head."

"Really?" she asked him. "You seemed to be in the driver's seat the whole time." Could she have been so wrong about what she'd seen on her television screen?

"Not by a long shot," Caleb answered. "Believe it or not, I was the one walking around in the dark with a blindfold on. The audience only saw half of the story."

Oh, he was good. Mr. Hollywood. Smooth. Suave. And somewhat convincing. "Frankly, it's none of my business. Can we use your cell phone to get someone to rescue us?" Being trapped up here was making her jittery.

"Cell phone?" Caleb asked, patting down his suit jacket and throwing up his hands when he came up empty. "I don't have it with me."

"What?" she shouted. "You've got to be kidding me!"

"What about you? Where's *your* cell phone?" Caleb asked, sounding curt.

She supposed he had a point, but she was still annoyed at him for inadvertently closing the door behind them.

She placed her hands on her hips. "Does this dress look like it has pockets?"

Caleb skimmed the length of her in a leisurely fashion, his soulful brown eyes full of male appreciation. Her cheeks warmed at the scrutiny. This was the last thing she needed. Men—especially charmers like Caleb—were off-limits. She was still reeling from her relationship with her ex and not looking for trouble in the form of Caleb Stone.

"You have me at a disadvantage, since you already know my name. And you are?" he asked.

She folded her arms across her chest. "Sophia Brand. A woman who is very eager to get out of here and back to work."

He raised an eyebrow. "Work?"

"Your grandmother hired me to take pictures of tonight's event, and I really don't want to have to give back her check," Sophia explained. She didn't want to tell Caleb, but she needed the money. Badly. Donny's child support payments were sporadic at best. So far her pride had stopped her from taking any legal action against him, but time was running out for him to come correct. The idea of having to hire an attorney to resolve the matter was as appealing as skinny-dipping in Alaska in the dead of winter.

How was this man managing to stay so calm? Caleb didn't seem bothered one bit by their predicament. As the seconds ticked by, she was beginning to feel like the walls were closing in around her. Her throat was beginning to feel tight.

"I'm sure someone is going to come to find us. Maybe we should start yelling at the top of our lungs," he suggested. He let out a series of screams.

"These walls are insulated," Sophia said, looking around at the pink cottony-looking material. "Maybe banging on the door would be better." Surely someone would hear them and come to their rescue.

"Okay, here goes." Caleb banged on the door with his fists. She had to admit, he seemed to be giving it his all. Over and over again he pounded on the door until he seemed spent. She was praying someone would hear the racket and open the door for them.

"I'm not sure this is working. We might just have to ride this thing out." Appearing exhausted, he sank down onto a crate.

"Let me give it a try," Sophia said, standing by the door and copying Caleb's actions. Within a matter of minutes her arms felt heavy from the effort. She made a mental reminder to get back in the gym for her strength training class. This was a pathetic showing.

"I can't be stuck in here with you," she wailed. Seriously, how long would it take before they were out of oxygen? Her head was pounding just thinking about it. Pretty soon she would be gasping for air.

"Well, thank you very much, but you're not exactly winning any Miss Congeniality contests yourself," Caleb cracked.

Sophia sat down on another crate. "That wasn't a dig at you," she explained. "I need to get home."

Their gazes locked. Curiosity radiated from his eyes. "What's waiting for you there?"

"My daughter. And we've never been apart a single night. Not ever." Due to her frazzled state of mind, the words simply slipped out of her mouth. She could barely think straight due to a rising sense of panic.

Sophia then did the unthinkable. She burst into huge, chest-heaving sobs.

CHAPTER TWO

There wasn't anything in the world that Caleb dreaded more than a woman crying. Just seeing Sophia break down made him feel powerless. He knew exactly why tears were his kryptonite. He could trace it directly back to his childhood.

Back when his mother, Daisy, had left Moose Falls and taken him and his brothers with her, she had cried herself to sleep every night for months. Leaving their father and filing for divorce had been brutal. He winced just thinking about the D word. Even as a little kid he'd known that she had continued to love her husband despite her desire to cut him out of her life. He, Landon, and Xavier had taken turns consoling her. She had smiled through her tears, never really managing to convince them that she was all right. She'd just held on for their sakes.

"Your daughter?" Caleb asked, bringing his thoughts back to the present.

"Yes," she answered in a small voice. "Lily. She's four."

Aww. She was little.

"That's a pretty name. Is someone watching her for you?" he asked.

"Yes," she said, sniffling. "My sister, Patience."

"So she's safe?" he asked her.

"Of course," she said, sounding slightly indignant.

"And your sister isn't going to leave her, right?" he pressed.

"She would never," Sophia said staunchly. "She's the world's best auntie, bar none."

Already he could see her calming down.

"So despite the inconvenience of being trapped with yours truly, there isn't really a problem affecting your daughter, right?"

"Right," Sophia said, drawing out the word as if she was pondering the matter. "But I'm a single mother, so I always have to think of her before myself."

"I'm sure the two of you are super close, but remember, this is just a moment in time. Before you know it, you'll be back home with her, and this will be nothing more than a memory."

"I don't like small spaces. They give me a panicky feeling." Her voice sounded really small. Right before his eyes Sophia appeared to have shrunk down inside herself, reminding him of a scared little kid.

Caleb looked around the attic. "It's actually pretty spacious. When we were kids, my brothers and I used to hide up here as part of hide-and-seek."

Sophia shivered. "When I was a kid, my stepfather locked me in our small attic and forgot I was in there. Or so he said."

Caleb didn't react at first. He wasn't sure if she was kidding, although that would be one messed up joke. One look at her face and he knew she spoke the truth.

"Th-that's awful," Caleb said, shocked at her admission. No matter how traumatic his childhood had been due to his parents' divorce, he had never experienced anything like what she'd gone through. He had been well loved and taken care of.

"Sadly, my mother didn't find me for hours." She wrinkled her nose. "It was quite traumatic for an eight-year-old, who became afraid of the dark and small spaces as a result."

Bam! Now his insides were oozing soft, gooey stuff. A few minutes ago he had been certain that this woman was a sharp-tongued ice queen, but now his heart was breaking for the pint-size Sophia. He had the feeling she talked a good game but wasn't half as tough as she pretended.

Caleb swallowed past the huge lump in his throat. "That would do it," he said. "Why don't you try to focus on something other than your past experience? What did you come up here for anyway?"

"An old camera Hattie's been wanting to give me. It's around here somewhere. I think she said by the door," she explained. "I almost forgot about it, what with being locked in and all."

"Why don't we poke around a little bit and see if we can find it?" Caleb figured looking for the camera would be a great distraction from her fear of being locked in the attic.

He stood up and began rummaging through some boxes by the door. After a few minutes Sophia joined him. Thankfully, there wasn't a whole lot of dust up here, and everything seemed to be well organized. He pulled out a few photo albums and tucked them under his arm.

Suddenly, Sophia let out a gasp. "I hit pay dirt. Look at this beauty."

Her face lit up like sunshine as she took the camera out of its case and held it in her hands. She turned it all around, upside down and sideways, her gaze full of admiration. Her movements were almost sensual as she caressed the camera.

"That definitely looks old-school," Caleb said, noticing that it was in pristine condition.

Sophia's eyes were sparkling in a way that made her look even more beautiful than before. He wished he'd been the one to make her glow instead of an old camera in Hattie's attic.

"It's a Leica thirty-five-millimeter rangefinder." She let out a low whistle. "These are hard to find and pretty pricey." She chewed her lip. "She said it belonged to your grandfather."

"She must think a lot of you to part with it." Caleb knew his grandmother had shared a grand love affair with Jack Stone, who had tragically died while mountain climbing. His own father, Red, had witnessed his father's deadly fall. Being back in Moose Falls had revealed a lot of family secrets he'd never known about. So far, Alaska had been eye opening.

"I-I can't believe she would give me something so precious." Sophia ran her hand lovingly over the camera. "And to be honest, I'm not sure I should accept it."

"Have you met my grandmother?" he asked with a snort. "She's not the type who handles hearing the word 'no' very well." It was one of the reasons he and his brothers had relocated to Moose Falls. Hattie had sold them on their inheritance, Yukon Cider, and wanting her dying wishes to be upheld. "When I turned eight, Hattie ordered a snow-making machine for my party. My birthday is in June!"

Sophia began to chuckle. He liked seeing her this way, carefree and light. The graceful slope of her neck made her look even more visually appealing. She was one beautiful and complex woman. He had the feeling that if he scratched her surface, there would be so many more facets to Sophia. But the truth was, he wasn't looking for a relationship, and he didn't even know how long he would last in Moose Falls. Four months down and eight more to go in order to comply with the contract they'd signed with their grandmother.

"You've got that right," Sophia said. "Hattie is no joke."

"If she wants you to have the camera, it's yours," Caleb said. "That's how it works with Hattie. You're going to have a fight on your hands if you resist." Caleb chuckled just thinking about Hattie's feisty nature, and he was grateful she hadn't lost her lively temperament with her terminal diagnosis. Despite being in renal failure from kidney disease, Hattie was a firecracker.

She shrugged. "I just figured that your dad might want it for sentimental reasons."

Caleb scoffed. "Doubtful. Red's not the nostalgic type. Honestly, I wouldn't know. He was pretty much a ghost in our childhoods." He let out a brittle laugh. "Not exactly father of the year if you know what I mean."

"I'm sorry," Sophia murmured.

"At this point it is what it is," Caleb said. He wasn't looking for pity.

Sophia lifted the camera to her lips and placed a kiss on it. "I'm going to treasure it always. I can't wait to test it out."

Caleb's gaze was trained on Sophia's lush, beautiful lips. It had been a long time since he'd been tempted to kiss a woman. Being burned by Abby and Gillian had done a number on him and his desire to get close to anyone, and this was the longest he'd ever gone without female companionship. He wasn't here in Moose Falls to establish a romantic connection. Being here was purely a business move to enable him to truly pursue a career in acting. If they sold Yukon Cider, he could use his share to bankroll his life as an aspiring actor in Los Angeles.

He tried to distract himself with something else other

than Sophia's lips, but there was nothing up here but boxes and boxes of stuff. A light floral aroma rose to his nostrils. His chest tightened at the feminine scent that hovered in the air.

Was it getting hot in here or what? Or was it Sophia's close proximity that was heating up the room? Caleb loosened the top few buttons of his long-sleeved dress shirt, then rolled up the sleeves.

"Wh-what are you doing?" Sophia asked with wide eyes.

Caleb smirked. "Don't worry. I'm not taking my clothes off." He wiped his forehead with the back of his hand. "It's getting a little stuffy in here, isn't it? I figured that I might as well get comfortable." He sat down on one of the sturdy containers.

Sophia nodded. "Of course." She jerked her head in the direction of the photo albums he'd placed next to him. "What do you have there?"

He picked up one of the albums and opened it. "A few old photo books. I'm hoping to find a few pics of me and my brothers. We don't have a whole lot of photos from when we lived here."

It was understandable, he thought. Daisy Stone had picked up and left Moose Falls with her three boys in tow. They had relocated to Arizona, where they'd lived with their maternal grandfather. Clearly, his mother hadn't had time to sort through pictures on her way out of town. Once she had decided to leave her husband and Moose Falls in her rearview mirror, it had all happened fast and furiously. As an adult, Caleb realized that everything had occurred at such lightning speed that his mother hadn't been fully prepared for their new life. For Daisy it must have felt like massive grief. She had been forced to mourn the life she'd left behind, all while raising three spirited children.

There was a reason Daisy Stone was his shero.

The very first picture in the album jumped out at Caleb. Staring back at him were his parents on their wedding day. In his entire life he had never seen any of these photos. Not a single one. And now he was seeing Daisy and Red in all their glory. His mother was wearing a romantic long-sleeved wedding gown that swept all the way down to the ground. His dad was also dressed all in white with a pink bow tie and dark sunglasses. Judging by the lack of snow on the ground, it was spring or summer. They both looked effortlessly cool, as if they had stepped out of the pages of a fashion magazine. They also looked as if they were madly in love with each other. His heart lurched a little bit at the realization.

"What? You look as if you've seen a ghost," Sophia said, leaning forward so she could get a peek at the book.

"That's exactly what I feel like," he said, feeling a bit numb as he turned the pages. "It's like I'm seeing my parents for the first time. They were young...and together. I don't have a lot of memories of them being happy together."

Sophia scooted closer to him, clearly wanting to view the photos. Caleb didn't mind Sophia's close proximity. She smelled nice, and her attitude seemed to have settled down in the last few minutes. She was being way less snarky.

"Is that Hattie?" Sophia asked, pointing to a black-and-white photo of an attractive woman. Caleb did a double take.

"Whoa. It is her." He let out a whistle. "This picture must be more than fifty years old."

"Hattie was a babe," Sophia gushed. "And your father was Alaskan eye candy."

Caleb looked over at her and made a face. "Easy there. Those are my family members you're talking about."

Sophia rolled her eyes and reached out to turn the

page. She let out a tutting sound. "Oh my goodness, this is adorable."

The photo was of him and his brothers with their parents. Landon couldn't have been more than two years old at the time. They were all smiling and happy. For a moment he had the oddest sensation, as if someone had reached into his chest cavity and was squeezing his heart. Because of his parents' divorce, Caleb had somehow pushed a lot of the good times from his memory. But here was proof right in front of him that they'd experienced joy as a family unit.

Raw emotion threatened to swallow him whole. The photo showcased his family before they were fractured by divorce and their rapid exit from Moose Falls. None of them had known what was coming when they posed for the picture. Even to this day he hated saying the D word out loud.

He cleared his throat. "This is proof that I was always good-looking," he said in a teasing voice.

"Indeed," Sophia said, her eyes radiating understanding. Even though he had a habit of making jokes when things got too emotional, he didn't think that he'd fooled Sophia.

"I get it," she said. "My parents split up when I was a kid, so I understand. I would probably think I was hallucinating if I came across a photo like this of my family."

He reached out and ran his hand across the image. "It's kind of mind-blowing to see these pictures and know that this was my life, even though my memories of all of us together are sort of fuzzy."

"Yes, but these photos prove that you came from love, and that's important to know." She shrugged. "Or at least it was for me. My dad used to always tell me that no matter what went down between my mom and him, they'd once loved each other. And that my sister and I came from that love."

"That's nice," Caleb said, wishing that his own parents had given him that reassurance. But his parents' divorce had been ugly, and Red hadn't been present in their lives. There had been a big gaping hole where his father should have been. And it had shaped his life in ways he still was trying to wrap his head around. Being back in Alaska was causing old wounds to reopen.

A grumbling sound emanated from Sophia's direction.

Caleb turned toward her. "Was that you?"

She nodded. "My stomach is rumbling. I'm starving." She let out a groan. "Hattie told me to get something to eat, but I decided to venture up here to find the camera first."

Caleb shook his head. "Never put food on the back burner. That was the motto of the Stone brothers growing up."

She rubbed her stomach. "I bitterly regret not eating, although the camera is pretty epic."

"Not to rub it in, but the lobster tails and crab bites are out of this world. Chef's kiss," he said, making a gesture by pinching his lips with his fingers and then raising them in the air.

"Thanks for not rubbing it in," Sophia said, her stomach rumbling even louder. He imagined visions of lobster tails were now dancing in her head and taunting her. "I've been meaning to lose weight, but not by being stuck in an attic with no food."

Caleb's gaze swung back in her direction. "Lose weight?" His eyes took in her snatched waist and curvy hips. She filled out her dress as if it had been made only for her. The fabric clung to her body in all the right ways. As far as he was concerned, Sophia was flawless.

"You don't need to lose a single inch," he told her. "Trust me on that."

Sophia regarded him with a bewildered expression. She

seemed to be speechless for the first time since they'd been up here.

Didn't she believe him? He would give a million dollars to know what she was thinking at this exact moment. She was choosing to keep her thoughts to herself, which was fine. They'd already shared a few secrets between them. He wondered if Sophia already regretted her candor. There was something about being stuck in this attic that made the space feel like a confessional. He barely knew Sophia, but it didn't feel like that. Strangely, he felt a connection to her, which was baffling and a bit alarming.

"There's an old trick I learned to distract myself from being hungry. Want to know what it is?" Caleb asked.

Sophia eyed him with skepticism. "Sure. Why not?"

He reached over and took her hand and folded her fingers into her palm. "Make a fist," he told her. His hand lay over hers, and although he was only trying to show her a technique, his skin tingled at the contact.

"A fist?" she asked, knitting her brows together. "That's supposed to make me forget about lobster?"

"I know it might sound strange, but it's all about focusing your energy elsewhere," he explained. "If you clench your fist, your mind focuses on that and not on your hunger." He still had his hand over hers. She looked up at him, and for a few moments they were gazing into each other's eyes. All of a sudden, the vibe between them was intimate. He saw the look of recognition pass over Sophia's face. She felt it too.

"Okay, maybe we should try to bang and shout again." She took a quick look at her watch and stood up. "I'm guessing we've been up here for roughly thirty-five minutes with no sign of rescue in sight."

She walked over to the door and tugged at the knob before she began to pound on it while screaming at the top of her lungs. He had to give it to her. She had some serious lung power. Sophia reminded him of one of the scream queens from classic horror films. He stifled the urge to burst out laughing at the sight of her pounding and yelling. Something told him she wouldn't appreciate the fact that he found the situation amusing. He wasn't insensitive to her fears, but all in all, he knew they would be fine. His brothers and Hattie would definitely be looking for him. And since Sophia was the official photographer for the evening, her absence would also be noticed.

"Let me know when you're tired. I can take a turn," he suggested, sitting back on the crate and leaning against the wall. A few seconds later he felt a burning sensation across his chest. He reached down into his shirt and scratched. The feeling spread to his legs, and he began to vigorously scratch. Heat suffused the back of his neck. A fiery sensation was creeping across his body.

What the hell was going on?

"What's wrong with you?" Sophia asked, looking at him with wide eyes. "You're acting like you've got ants in your pants."

He looked down at his chest, quickly noticing red welts on his skin that were spreading by the second. And itchy as hell.

"I have no idea, but I'm itching like never before in my life." Unable to stop himself, he dug his nails into his skin and scratched. The more he thought about not scratching, the fiercer the urge became.

Sophia left her post at the door to rush over to him. "Let me look," she said, scrutinizing his chest.

By this time his body felt like it was on fire. On impulse he ripped his shirt off and threw it to the floor, breaking his earlier promise not to take his clothes off.

"Oh, no," Sophia said, clamping a hand over her mouth.

"What?" he asked, trying not to panic at the situation. "Tell me!"

"I think you're having an allergic reaction to something. You have lots of ... welts all over you. It looks really bad." Sophia's expression was a mix of disgust and pity. He wasn't sure which was worse.

Ugh. Good thing he wasn't trying to impress the most gorgeous woman in Moose Falls. If she was going to see his six-pack abs, Caleb didn't want it to be at a time like this when he was covered with strange red bumps. This could be a sign from the universe to steer clear of Sophia.

Caleb didn't have any known allergies, and he'd never experienced anything quite like this. His mind was racing to figure out what was going on.

Suddenly, Sophia pointed to something behind him. "What are those creepy-crawly things over there?"

Caleb turned to look, immediately spotting the nasty-looking creatures slithering around.

"Those are carpenter ants," he said, leaning over to get a better look. "I think they're coming from the wall I was leaning against."

"Eww, that's so gross," Sophia said in a raised voice.

"Seriously?" Caleb asked. "Where's the compassion? I'm the victim here."

"I'm sorry. I know that's not comforting at a time like this," she said in a meek voice that sounded nothing like her own. "Did they bite you?"

"Well, they certainly weren't blowing kisses," he muttered.

Sophia's lips twitched, and he sensed that she was doing her very best to stop herself from bursting into laughter. Maybe if his body wasn't on fire, he might find the situation humorous as well. He let out a groan. Feeling itchy was the worst sensation in the world.

"I'm sorry, maybe you should turn around. I've got to scratch my legs and I need to take these off." He undid his belt and shucked his pants off. Thankfully, he was wearing a pair of boxers. Sometimes he just went au naturel.

"Oh, for goodness' sake, give me at least a little warning," Sophia said, covering her eyes with her hand.

Just then the door opened with a slight commotion. His brothers were standing on the landing, along with Jacques. All of their mouths were hanging open at the sight of him and Sophia. He was pretty sure that his lack of clothing wasn't helping matters.

A feminine voice rang out from behind them. "Caleb Stone. Why aren't you wearing any clothes?"

His jaw dropped almost to the floor.

"Mom," Caleb said in a surprised voice as Daisy Stone's beautiful face came into view.

CHAPTER THREE

Caleb fought the urge to rub his eyes to make sure he wasn't seeing things. Was Daisy really standing a few feet away from him? She had vowed a long time ago never to return to Moose Falls. Not even if her life depended on it. Yet here she was looking at him with an expression of mortification etched on her delicate features.

"Mom. Wh-what are you doing here?" he asked. As far as he knew, his mother was back home in Arizona teaching art classes and organizing poetry readings. She hadn't set foot in Alaska in twenty years.

"Do you think I would miss my firstborn son's engagement party?" Daisy asked as she made her way past Xavier and Landon. "Not on your life I wouldn't."

She reached out and brushed her palm across Caleb's cheek. "My sweet boy. How I've missed seeing your beautiful face in person."

"I've missed you too. You sure kept this surprise under wraps," Caleb said. He still felt as if he was imagining things. He and his brothers had missed their mother something fierce.

She hadn't given them her blessing to come to Moose Falls for their inheritance, so the situation had been slightly awkward. Having her here in the flesh was a wonderful surprise.

"Hattie arranged it as a surprise for all of us," Landon said. "We started to get worried when we couldn't find you, and you weren't picking up any of our calls, so we combed through the house."

"Then Hattie mentioned that Sophia had disappeared, and we saw her heels on the landing," Jacques said. "That led us straight to you."

"We thought you needed rescuing," Xavier said, wiggling his eyebrows.

"We did," Sophia said, sounding heated. Her cheeks were flushed. His big brother's innuendo hadn't been lost on her.

"I was bit by a bunch of carpenter ants," Caleb explained. "My whole body is itching and on fire, which is why I took off my clothes." He was tripping all over himself to explain.

Xavier and Landon burst out laughing. They didn't even bother to hide the fact that they found the situation highly entertaining, even though it was incredibly stressful for him.

"This could only happen to you," Landon said, clutching his stomach. "Literal ants in your pants."

"Totally," Xavier said, shaking his head and chuckling. "Who knew carpenter ants bit people?"

Caleb glared at them. Neither one had any chill whatsoever. They hadn't even asked him if he needed a doctor. These bites were no laughing matter, and they were embarrassing him in front of Sophia.

"You poor thing," Daisy said, her voice oozing sympathy. "I can whip up a remedy for you. Baking soda and apple cider vinegar." Her gaze swung to Sophia, and her eyes narrowed in on her like laser beams. "Caleb, introduce me to your lovely companion."

His mother was always trying to pair him off with women. Clearly, nothing had changed in that regard. She always told him that "the love of a good woman will change your perspective." He had always thought her outlook was pretty remarkable given her and Red's tangled history. But Mama knew best. She'd never once steered him in the wrong direction.

"This is Sophia Brand, Mom. And we're not together," Caleb explained. "We were just stuck up here at the same time."

"Nice to meet you, Mrs. Stone," Sophia said, sticking out her hand to shake Daisy's.

"Call me Daisy, Sophia. It's a pleasure to meet you, even under these unusual circumstances." She shook her head and chuckled.

"If you'll excuse me, I really have to get back to my post. I'm the photographer tonight," Sophia explained. "I don't want to disappoint Hattie."

"Hattie knew something was off when you disappeared," Jacques said. "We were hoping there wasn't an emergency at home."

Sophia placed her hand against her chest. "No, there wasn't. Thank goodness for that."

For the first time Caleb noticed that his dad was standing at the bottom of the steps. Red was pacing back and forth as if he didn't quite know what to do with himself. Caleb imagined that seeing his ex-wife after all this time was intense. From what he knew, Red and Daisy hadn't spoken to or seen each other in a very long time. With Red traveling out of town a lot on Yukon Cider business, he didn't get to see him much.

"Thanks for the rescue," Sophia said. She turned toward Caleb. "Take care of those bites, okay?" They locked eyes, and for a moment, it seemed as if it was once again just the two of them in the attic.

"Will do," Caleb said, wishing they weren't surrounded by so many people. Everyone had their eyes glued to them, going back and forth between them as if they were watching a tennis match. He wanted to shout, "Nothing to see here, people. Nothing to see." Normally he didn't mind being the center of attention. Some might even say he craved it, but at this moment he wished that he'd had more one-on-one time with Sophia. With every moment that went by, he'd felt as if he was peeling back her layers. Something about being trapped in the attic had allowed them to open up to each other.

"Let me assist you," Jacques said, holding out his arm so Sophia could lean on him as she navigated the stairs.

Sophia was still one of the most beautiful women he'd ever seen, and they'd bonded a bit in the attic. Once she'd confessed about being claustrophobic, he had glimpsed a softer side of her. Maybe they could meet up for coffee or a night out at Northern Exposure. His soon-to-be sister-in-law had just purchased the establishment from Red, which made True the official owner.

Before he could think of a suave way to ask her to hang out with him, she was walking down the stairs and away from the attic. And he didn't fail to notice that she looked just as good walking away as she did coming. *Have mercy!*

"I see you," Xavier said as soon as Sophia was out of earshot. A smug smile was plastered on his face.

"What are you babbling about?" Caleb asked, annoyed at himself for showing such an obvious interest in Sophia. He should have known that his brothers would be all over it like white on rice. First rule of being a Stone brother: Never show the cards you're holding.

"We all see you," Landon said. "You're practically drooling."

He gritted his teeth, from both pain and annoyance. "I am not drooling. I might be foaming at the mouth due to these ant bites, but I am not drooling."

"Could have fooled me," Xavier said, smirking.

"Enough of this nonsense, all of you. Caleb needs my salve and cold compresses," Daisy said, sounding annoyed. She made a shooing motion with her hands. "Xavier, go back to the party and True. Landon, come help your brother out. We need to get him to his room."

"Yes, ma'am," Landon said, immediately following her instructions and heading over toward Caleb.

Red came up the steps. "Let me help," he said, darting a glance in Daisy's direction.

Oh, this should be fun, Caleb thought, with his father tiptoeing around his mother like an awkward teenager. Not that he blamed him. Daisy Stone was a badass who didn't hold back on telling it like it was. Over the years she had gotten even tougher, most likely due to having to raise three boys on her own. Caleb wished life had been easier for their mother, but things hadn't worked out that way. She'd carried the weight of the world on her shoulders for so many years. He still hadn't forgiven his father for dropping the ball so disastrously. So far he'd put on a smile around Red, never letting him see how deeply his absence had affected him. At some point, Caleb knew his feelings would bubble over and explode. All this time his emotions had been simmering, but being in his father's orbit changed everything.

"Guys, my body is on fire, but my legs are still working. I can walk out of here under my own steam," Caleb said, shrugging off Landon's arm.

"Aren't we testy," Landon said, rolling his eyes. "You didn't even thank us for coming to your rescue."

"You would be annoyed too if you had insect bites in your nether regions," Caleb muttered. "It's uncomfortable."

Xavier and Landon looked at each other and burst into another round of laughter.

Daisy shook her head. "And here I thought that the two of you were slightly mature. I see that you've reverted back to your middle school years." She rolled her eyes.

Caleb let out a snort. "You're giving them way too much credit. I'd say they were still in elementary school."

He bent down to pick up his shirt and spotted the Leica camera on the floor next to the crate where Sophia had been sitting. In all the commotion, she had forgotten her precious possession. Caleb reached for it and tucked it under his arm. He planned to hold on to the camera for a little bit.

This way he would have a reason to see Sophia again, if only to reunite her with her vintage camera. They had shared a few bonding moments in the attic that made him want to learn more about Sophia. She intrigued him. And maybe, just maybe, he could convince her that he was way more than the man she'd gotten a glimpse of on reality television.

Sophia nestled into her comfy knitted blanket and burrowed her head under her pillows. Contentment oozed from every pore in her body. Her alarm kept going off, but each and every time she reached for it and set it back on snooze. Sleeping in on the weekend was hard to resist.

"Mama, wake up." Lily's voice washed over her like a bucket of cold water. She slowly pulled off her eye mask as streaks of sunlight streamed through her blinds. What time was it? Clearly, judging by Lily's appearance bedside, she'd overslept. She had been having such a wonderful, relaxing dream, the type you didn't want to wake up from.

Although the details were a bit hazy, she knew Caleb had featured prominently in her dream. Her cheeks flushed at the realization that she couldn't even escape him when her mind and body were the most relaxed. There was simply no denying reality. She was wildly attracted to the middle Stone brother. He might be the Love Rat, but he was also the hottest man who had ever stepped foot in Moose Falls. Maybe in all of Alaska if she was being honest.

And maybe, just maybe, there was more to him than the reality show had revealed. Or perhaps she was just fooling herself. In her experience, men who looked like Caleb had massive egos. Or was she simply putting up barriers to protect herself against Caleb's charms?

"Good morning, sunshine," she said to her daughter, patting the space next to her so Lily could join her. Without hesitation, Lily jumped up on the bed and snuggled up against her. "I'm sorry that I overslept."

"It's okay, Mommy. You were up late last night at the party." Lily sounded so matter-of-fact and way more mature than her years. Sophia wanted to keep her as little as possible for as long as she could. As it was, she was growing up way too fast.

"What do you want for breakfast? I can whip up some pumpkin pancakes if you want," Sophia suggested. Those were Lily's favorite, especially on a lazy Saturday morning.

"Can you make them into Minnie Mouse ears?" Lily asked, crossing her hands in front of her in a prayerful pose. "Pretty please."

"You got it," Sophia said, sitting up and swinging her legs over the side of the bed. "I'm just going to grab my robe and slippers. Okay?"

"You didn't say anything about my outfit," Lily said, sticking out her lip. "I got dressed all by myself." She jumped down from the bed and did a few twirls.

"You sure did," Sophia said, her lips twitching as she checked out the plaid leggings, pink dress, and red button-down sweater decorated with hearts. As mismatched as the outfit was, Lily still looked adorable. And Sophia was a big believer in not stifling her child's creativity.

"You look fabulous!" she said, bending at the waist to place a kiss on Lily's temple. With her mocha-colored skin and big brown eyes, she was Sophia's mini me. She couldn't love this child more than she already did. Donny may have been a bust, but he'd given her the greatest blessing in Lily.

"Thank you, Mommy. I can't wait till G-pop sees this fit," she said, grinning from ear to ear. "Maybe we can bring him some pancakes."

"Oh, I think he'll already have eaten breakfast by the time we get there. He invited us for lunch, and you know how he likes to cook." Her father was self-taught, and now that he was semiretired, he enjoyed cooking up a storm in his newly renovated kitchen. Sophia couldn't bring her dad anything that he couldn't whip up on his own ten times better.

Sophia headed to the kitchen with Lily at her heels. Her daughter was such a morning person, full of sunshine and smiles. Try as she might, Sophia couldn't make herself enjoy mornings.

"Can I watch *Bluey* while you make the pancakes?" Lily asked.

"Sure thing," Sophia said, heading toward the playroom and turning on her daughter's favorite show. Lily didn't watch a lot of television, but she was a *Bluey* fanatic at the moment.

Once she'd set Lily up, Sophia headed toward the kitchen

and began to assemble her ingredients for pancake making. Despite her best efforts to focus on the here and now, thoughts of last night wouldn't leave her alone. Caleb's gorgeous face kept popping into her mind. Dimples. Check. Russet-colored skin. Check. Six feet tall. Check. This man literally checked off all the boxes.

As much as Sophia had been ecstatic about being rescued from the confines of Hattie's attic, she hated the fact that his brothers seemed to think she and Caleb were involved in some hanky-panky. Yes, Caleb was half dressed when they were discovered, but he'd also been covered in red, angry bug bites. Sophia didn't want any assumptions being made about her due to Caleb's past indiscretions. She supposed the Stone brothers' suspicions made sense considering Caleb's history of being a player, but it was still annoying to be dragged into the situation. She remembered Caleb acknowledging having a messy past in his video diary on *Love Him or Leave Him*. With his killer smile and gorgeous dimples, he'd looked straight into the camera and said, "Don't hold my past against me. I'm a player by nature, but willing to be reformed by the love of a good woman."

Sophia let out a snort. Caleb had been full of crap. It had been a tagline to gain the public's attention, as well as Gillian's, the star of the show. His shtick had worked perfectly for him, as well as his good looks, earning him a place in the finals.

Now that she had been up close and personal with Caleb, she could see how he used his charisma to win people over. If she had been trapped with him in the attic any longer, she might be singing his praises right now. He had that type of over-the-top magnetism! No wonder he'd sought out the limelight. It totally made sense.

Sophia hadn't been interested in anyone in almost four

years. What were the odds that Caleb Stone would come along and make her pulse race? He had a certain swagger that money couldn't buy. He was the sort of man who walked through life effortlessly. Caleb led with confidence.

Stop thinking about him. Focus on something else, like feeding Lily.

Once she'd finished making breakfast, Sophia sat across from Lily at the butcher-block kitchen table, eating pumpkin pancakes in the shape of Minnie Mouse ears, scrambled eggs, and sausage. Afterward, she placed their dirty plates and utensils in the dishwasher, then headed upstairs to take a quick shower and get dressed. Forty minutes later they were in the car and on their way to her dad's place.

While she was in the shower, she had been hit with the realization that she'd left the Leica camera in Hattie's attic. With all the commotion related to their rescue, Sophia had completely forgotten to grab it. She would have to head over to Hattie's place at some point to reclaim it. After all she'd gone through to get it, she didn't want to let it slip through her fingers. And as Caleb had pointed out, Hattie wanted to pass the camera on to her. Knowing that such a dynamic woman as Hattie Stone valued her meant the world to Sophia.

Sophia loved antiques, especially cameras. It brought her back to her childhood and discovering her love of photography through her father's eyes. He had been the owner of a vintage shop called Remember When here in Moose Falls. Sophia had loved to putter around the shop while her dad was working. Right before her freshman year in college he'd sold the place. Sophia had always wondered if he'd done so to pay her tuition bills. She had once asked him, years later, and his response had been cryptic. There wasn't a single doubt in her mind that she would also make huge sacrifices for her own daughter.

Lily ran ahead of her once they had arrived at her dad's home and parked. Her daughter didn't bother knocking or ringing the doorbell. She simply turned the knob and pushed her way in, beckoning to Sophia to hurry up.

"Hey there, Daddio. What's cooking?" Sophia asked as she followed the aroma emanating from Skip Brand's kitchen. As usual, her father was standing by the stove stirring a pot of something that smelled heavenly. She sniffed the air, immediately recognizing his world-famous chili.

"G-pop," Lily cried out as soon as she spotted her grandfather.

Skip opened up his arms and bent down to embrace his granddaughter. Sophia loved the joyful expression etched on her father's face as he rained kisses down on Lily. As close as she had always been to her father, his relationship with Lily was like no other. Her daughter needed a strong man in her life, since Donny wasn't much of a father. He barely saw his daughter and couldn't be bothered to even remember her birthday. Sophia had swallowed her bitterness against her ex in an effort to make the relationship between father and daughter easier, but so far it hadn't worked. Ever since Caleb had talked about the absence of his own father during his formative years, Sophia hadn't been able to stop thinking about the damage the situation was inflicting on Lily.

Just the thought of Lily bearing the weight of Donny's neglect caused a hitch in the region of her heart. With her lovely brown complexion and light brown eyes, Lily was a beautiful child, inside and out. According to most people, she was Sophia's mini me, which served as a blessed relief. She knew it was a petty feeling, but she was thankful Lily didn't resemble Donny.

"The two of you are a sight for sore eyes," Skip said, turning toward Sophia and pulling her in for one of his famous hugs. Just being held in his arms made Sophia feel like a little girl again.

"Right back atcha," Sophia said. Being able to see her dad on a regular basis was good for the soul. It was also important for Lily to spend time with a male role model who adored her. Skip thought the sun rose and set on his granddaughter.

"How was the shindig at Hattie's house?" her father asked as he handed a juice box to Lily, who scampered off toward the playroom and the three-story dollhouse G-pop had handcrafted for her.

"It was . . . interesting," Sophia said, making a face.

"Well, that's a loaded comment. How so?" he asked. Sophia loved how her father soaked up all the details of her life. He wasn't just asking either. Skip truly wanted to know all the goings-on in her world. And she enjoyed having a father she could confide in. When the storms of life came, he was always there in her corner.

She quickly filled him in on getting stuck in the attic with Caleb.

Her father winced when she got to the part about the insect bites. "Carpenter ants? Oh, those can be painful. I've endured quite a few over the years."

"He was a good sport about it, especially since his brothers thought it was hilarious." She made a tutting sound. "I felt bad for him."

His eyes widened. "I can't believe you're feeling sorry for him. Wasn't he the one on your favorite reality show? The guy you loved to hate?"

She folded her arms across her chest. "Hate is a very strong word. Let's just say I disliked him intensely. He was pretty awful."

He frowned. "Really? I kind of felt bad for the guy. He

was caught between a rock and a hard place. I only watched a few episodes with you, but he seemed genuine."

Sophia let out a groan. "You're such a softie. He was a walking red flag."

Pop stirred his chili. "And now? Is he growing on you?"

"I wouldn't go that far, but he's not on my awful human list." She was reluctant to admit it out loud, but Caleb wasn't anything like she'd imagined him to be. He had been a reassuring and comforting presence in the attic. She knew that her own experiences with Donny had left her jaded, so a part of her wondered if she had been biased against him.

"Well, Hattie seems to be over the moon about those boys being back home, so that's a good thing. She deserves some happiness after everything she's done for Moose Falls." He took a spoonful of chili and blew on it before turning toward Sophia and offering her a taste.

"Don't mind if I do," Sophia said, taking the spoon from her father and putting it in her mouth. She closed her eyes and let out a satisfied sound as the spicy flavors hit her tongue.

"What do you think?" Skip asked, his gaze narrowed as he carefully watched her reaction.

"I think it's amazing," Sophia gushed. She handed the spoon back to him. "I can't wait for lunch, and that's saying something, since we had a big breakfast."

Her father grinned. "That's what I like to hear." A timer rang out from the direction of the stove. "There goes my cornbread. I need to check it real quick." As always, he became a whirlwind in the kitchen, turning down the heat on the chili before opening up the stove and peering in to check on the cornbread. "Perfect," he said, reaching for oven mitts and pulling out a beautifully cooked sheet of cornbread. Sophia's stomach grumbled at the delightful aroma circulating around the kitchen.

Her cell phone began to ring with the ringtone of her favorite Beyoncé song, "Halo." Although she wasn't inclined to answer her phone during family time, a quick glance at the screen showed that Hattie was on the other end of the line. She only called Sophia for important matters such as last night's gig. She wasn't about to ignore the call.

"I've got to take this," she told her father before reaching for her phone and answering the call.

"Good afternoon, Sophia. It's Hattie." The older woman's voice sounded a lot less robust these days, although she would know Hattie's voice anywhere. It still rang out with distinction.

"Hey, Hattie. How's it going?" Sophia asked. "You threw a wonderful party last night. I so appreciate you hiring me to capture the event."

"Thank you. I'm very regretful about you getting trapped in my attic. Those hinges must be a little rusty."

"No worries. I made it through in one piece," Sophia reassured her. At this point in Hattie's life she didn't need to feel guilty about a single thing.

"I hope my grandson kept you entertained." Sophia wasn't certain, but she thought Hattie's tone sounded a bit mischievous. "Caleb is quite the rascal."

"Well, he was calm and cool under pressure while we were stuck up there. I'll give him that," Sophia said, as memories of him talking her through the panicky feelings washed over her. He had really grounded her so that she wasn't freaking out about being confined in a small space.

"Sophia, the reason I'm calling you is because I'd like to offer you a full-time position at Yukon Cider. We have a lot of new campaigns starting, and I really enjoy your photography work. I would love to have you on board to help us capture the essence of the brand and boost our social media reach. Perhaps we can meet up this week and discuss the particulars if you're interested."

Was she interested? Sophia felt like doing a cartwheel in celebration of Hattie's offer. Honestly, it couldn't have come at a better time. Her financial situation was dicey at the moment due to limited work hours, paying a mortgage, and a lack of child support from Donny. Working for an established company like Yukon Cider would be a dream come true.

"That would be fantastic," she replied, practically sputtering out the words. Pure adrenaline was racing through her veins. Her head was spinning at the possibilities. If this worked out, being employed by Hattie could help her out financially and creatively. There was so much she could learn by working at Yukon Cider.

"How does Wednesday sound? We can meet in my office," Hattie suggested.

"Wednesday is perfect. I so appreciate the opportunity," Sophia said, her stomach doing flip-flops. She certainly didn't want to get ahead of herself, but this sounded promising.

"Your work is impeccable, so it's well deserved, Sophia. See you soon," Hattie answered.

"Thanks again, Hattie." Sophia ended the call and clutched her phone against her midsection. She turned back toward her father, feeling a bit breathless. If everything went smoothly, she would be working for Hattie Stone, the grande dame of Moose Falls. Sophia had always held Hattie in high esteem. Even as a little girl she had looked at her as if she was the queen of a kingdom.

Her father was regarding her with a quizzical expression. "What was that about? It sounded important."

She could feel her smile stretching from ear to ear and threatening to crack her face wide open. "That was Hattie," she said, sounding as breathless as she felt. "She's offered me a position at Yukon Cider. I'm going to meet with her this week to go over things."

Skip let out a loud whooping noise. "Way to go, Sophia. You must have really impressed her last night. This is great news. I know you've been waiting for something to change with your career, and this could be it."

Lily came running into the kitchen. Her eyes were as wide as saucers in her little face. "What happened? I heard you shout."

Sophia went over and scooped Lily up in her arms. "Oh, it's nothing to worry about, sweetheart. Mommy just got some good news and G-pop was excited." She pressed a kiss on Lily's cheek.

"Did you win the lottery?" Lily asked, her expression serious.

Skip and Sophia chuckled.

"I guess so, in a way," Sophia answered. "Mommy has a wonderful opportunity to work with a great lady she really admires."

"Oooh," Lily said. "I like that."

"I like it too," Sophia said, pulling Lily close to her chest for a hug.

This job working for Yukon Cider could be life-changing. She didn't want to assume that she had the position until she met with Hattie, but it sounded like she was being offered the job. At Yukon Cider, one of the most prestigious companies in Alaska.

Things were definitely looking up.

CHAPTER FOUR

Caleb walked around the following day with thoughts of Sophia on his mind. He was wracking his brain trying to come up with a perfect way to get the Leica camera back to her. He couldn't stop thinking about the expression on her face as she had held the camera. It had brought her such joy, and he wanted to see that beautiful look on her face again.

In the meanwhile, he, along with his brothers, was going to be spending some quality time with their mother. She would be in town for a few more days, which would give them all time to catch up on things before she headed back to Arizona.

Daisy looked around the dining room, her gaze intense as it swept across the room. "It's so interesting how nothing has really changed, yet at the same time everything feels different."

"You've been gone a long time," Hattie said with a nod. Caleb wasn't sure as to Hattie's feelings about Daisy being back, even though she had engineered her surprise return. Back in the day they had been great friends, bonded by their shared love of Red. By all accounts, Daisy had gotten along well with her mother-in-law, but things had changed after Daisy's departure from Moose Falls. He suspected that his grandmother felt some kind of way about their mother never bringing them back to Alaska.

As they sat down over breakfast, none of them could ignore the strange dynamic humming and pulsing in the air around them. Daisy and Red Stone hadn't been together in the same space for decades. Once upon a time they had been deliriously in love, yet their fractured marriage had resulted in Daisy's rapid departure from Moose Falls and a divorce.

"I still can't believe you're here," Landon said, sounding emotional.

For once Caleb couldn't blame him. As the youngest brother, Landon was the one who always wore his heart on his sleeve. Caleb and Xavier harbored the same emotions, but they weren't as effusive in expressing themselves. It was all the more impressive that Xavier had been able to open himself up to finding love with True. As much as he wanted to believe it was possible for him as well, his romantic past hung over him like a dark shadow. Not only had he been betrayed, but he had been put on blast by the media and mislabeled as a cheat and a liar. Being kicked when he had been at the lowest point in his life still stung.

It was no small wonder he felt disillusioned by the notion of love. He wasn't going to let it stop him from doing what he did best—attracting women. Love was just off the table now. Caleb wasn't ever going to be played for a fool again. He would settle for a fling, something light and flirty.

Sophia's face flitted through his mind. There was nothing about this particular woman that fit that particular bill. She was the type of woman who would seep into his bloodstream. No, it was best to steer clear of her.

His mother grinned at him from across the table, yanking him out of his thoughts. "I had to come. I was having withdrawal symptoms from not seeing my boys."

He exchanged a look with his brothers. Forever and always, they would continue to be boys in Daisy's eyes. It was a running joke among them. For quite some time now they had all been men.

"Anything you want to do or see while you're here?" Xavier asked.

"To be honest, I'd love to see True's tavern," Daisy said. "After all, it's where you met the love of your life."

"And nearly had my lips burned off by ghost pepper wings," Xavier muttered.

"Ouch," Red said, wincing. "Sounds like a painful meet cute."

"A small price to pay for meeting True," Caleb said, giving Xavier a nod of approval. Although it was hard for him to accept that his big brother was getting married and settling down in Moose Falls, he knew True was Xavier's other half. She was a good woman who loved and cherished his brother. After all Xavier had been through with his ex-fiancée, Heather, he deserved a happily-ever-after. Caleb knew that a part of him worried that the closeness he'd always shared with his brothers would evaporate. He fretted that Xavier's priorities would shift away from him and Landon.

Maybe, if he was being honest, he was a little envious as well. He had dreamed of a blissful happy ending with Abby, but it had blown up in his face. He had put himself out there and been vulnerable, only to be met with betrayal and disillusionment. No one had really understood his heartbreak other than his brothers and mother. Everyone else had believed that he was playing a role on the reality show and that he had been unable to keep his pants zipped up. The truth was he'd fallen in love with Abby. Yet he'd been given the moniker the Love Rat. Ugh. If he lived to be a hundred, folks would still be calling him by that awful nickname. No wonder he couldn't land an acting gig to save his life.

Xavier grinned at him. "I would eat a bucket of those wings just to meet her for the first time all over again." Everyone at the table reacted to his comment by letting out a chorus of *awws*.

"Nice," Landon said. "Look at you showing a mushy side. I knew it was in there somewhere."

"That's my sweet X man," Daisy said, tearing up as she looked at her son. "What a blessing to see you so in love and on the cusp of settling down." She bit back a sob. "True is such a lovely young woman. I can see how much she loves and adores you."

"Aww. Don't cry," Xavier pleaded. "I've found my soulmate."

"I always told the three of you that you would find your other half," Daisy wailed.

"No tears, Mom," Caleb cautioned. "We only want to see smiles while you're visiting."

"Okay, okay," Daisy said. "I'd like to make the most of this short visit, so bring it on."

"A hike by the mountains would be nice," Xavier said. "I'm sure Jaylen would love to come with us." True had been raising her brother for the last eight years after the death of their parents. He'd just turned ten, and he loved outdoor adventures way more than video games. Xavier had stepped into a parental role with Jaylen.

"Why don't we go to Northern Exposure tomorrow?" Caleb asked. "Aren't they having a line dancing night?" In addition to line dancing the establishment also had karaoke nights, open mic events, and comedy nights. As the new owner of the tavern, True was always fine-tuning the place to increase business.

"I think so," Xavier said. "Let me text True and ask her to make sure."

Daisy clapped her hands together. "Oh, I love line dancing. Let's go!"

Xavier's cell phone pinged. "Yep. You were right, Caleb. Line dancing is tomorrow night."

"How about it, Red? Are you game?" Hattie asked her son.

Red, who had been unusually quiet up to this point, said, "Sure. I may not dance, but the people watching is always entertaining." Caleb had the impression that Red was dumbstruck in the presence of his ex-wife. According to Landon and Xavier, he had nearly passed out when she had shown up at the engagement party. Of course Caleb had missed out on that scene while being locked away in the attic. He would have paid good money to see their first meeting after such a long time apart.

"I'm with you, Red," Landon said, wrinkling his nose. "I've got two left feet."

Hattie leaned over and grasped his hand in hers. "Don't worry. Granny will teach you."

Landon's eyes widened. "Are you coming too?"

"Of course I am," Hattie said, cackling. "You know my motto."

"'I may be dying but I'm still living,'" Caleb said, along with Landon, Xavier, and Red.

"Exactly! YOLO. I've taught you well," Hattie said, smiling, as she looked around the table at her loved ones.

"So why don't we take a hike by the falls?" Daisy suggested, pushing her plate away from her. "It used to be one of my favorite places here in town." The falls was one of the

most picturesque places in Moose Falls—now that temperatures had risen to thirty to forty degrees and sunlight was in
effect for at least eleven hours of the day, it was the perfect
spot to explore.

"We used to have family picnics there in the summer,"
Red said, his gaze focused on Daisy. Caleb didn't think he
was imagining the look of tenderness etched on his father's
face.

Uh-oh. Was Red still harboring feelings for his ex-wife?
Caleb didn't think Red was indifferent to Daisy. Despite
the fact that they hadn't been together in more than twenty
years, there were still feelings. Caleb didn't know all the ins
and outs of their breakup, but it was Daisy who had ended
things.

"Yes, we did," Daisy acknowledged, locking gazes with
Red. "It was always such a tranquil spot."

"Caleb, can I speak with you for a moment? There's
something I would like to discuss with you," Hattie said as
breakfast ended.

"Sure thing," Caleb said, watching as everyone else left
the room.

Hattie patted the seat next to her, inviting Caleb to sit
beside her. Once he rounded the table and joined her, Hattie
gifted him with a beatific smile.

"I have a business proposition for you," Hattie said,
affectionately patting his hand. Over the past four months
he had been working alongside Hattie and his brothers at her
hard cider company. Despite the fact that Hattie had been
out of his and his brothers' lives for decades, they had grown
close ever since his return to town. Hattie held a special
place in his heart. Knowing her time on Earth was nearing
an end served as a daily reminder to cherish their moments
together.

"That sounds intriguing," Caleb said, curious to hear more. Working at Yukon Cider was interesting, but it wasn't his life's passion. He respected the company, but he'd never imagined himself sitting at a desk all day.

"I want you to be featured in the next campaign for our newest flavors. We need to shore up our younger buying base, which is why we are jazzing up the packaging with brighter colors, creating commercials with popular musical artists and bringing you into the mix."

Caleb was taken aback by the fact that his grandmother wanted him to be part of the marketing plan. "What does that mean exactly?"

"Well, it means that I want you to be in all of the advertising for our new collection, including the print ads and our upcoming commercials. We haven't done a great job of advertising Yukon Cider, but all of that is going to change. I think you would be a great spokesperson for the company."

"Me? I-I'm flattered, but are you sure?" he asked, stunned by the offer. This almost sounded too good to be true. Being the face of Yukon Cider could do amazing things for his future in the entertainment industry. Instead of being notorious for a reality show, he would be aligned with an amazing product created by his grandmother.

"Of course I'm sure, Caleb. Look at you. You're handsome as all get-out, you've got an athletic physique, and you'll increase our sales simply based on your looks and charisma. Trust me, it's a no-brainer. Plus, from what I hear, you have some acting chops. Why not put those to use to help the family business?"

He bit his lip. "You're not worried that my stint on the reality show will harm the brand?" he asked, holding his breath as he awaited her answer. Caleb was so sick of his past hanging over him like a dark cloud.

Hattie let out a hoot of laughter. "Caleb, I'm a woman living on borrowed time. I'm not afraid of anything. You're part of my vision for bringing Yukon Cider into the future." She winked at him. "So far I haven't been wrong about a single thing."

Feeling relieved, Caleb placed his elbows on the table and leaned toward Hattie. "I'm all ears, Hattie."

The more they talked, the more Caleb was drawn to her idea. If he was being honest with himself, he had missed the spotlight. There was nothing he loved more than the glare of the lights and all eyes focused on him. Back in high school when he'd been cast in a lead role in *Othello*, he had been transformed by the applause and the accolades. Finally, he had felt that he was good at something. He'd shined on that stage.

Caleb had decided then and there that he wanted to be an actor more than anything else in the world. To this day there wasn't anything else he truly wanted to pursue as a career more than acting. He enjoyed taking on different personas and creating new characters.

"So I'll be doing commercials? With lines?" he asked, blown away by the sudden turn of events. It was almost more than he'd ever dared to dream. Maybe being back in the spotlight could put him in a perfect position to relaunch his acting career.

"That's the plan," Hattie said. "I want you to be on the team brainstorming our advertising and social media campaigns. I think this will be a great way for us to increase our reach, especially to a younger demographic." She winked at him. "From what I hear, you're quite a hunk."

Caleb chuckled. "You don't say." His grandmother was a trip. She had the best personality of anyone he'd ever known. She made him laugh like no other. Even though they had only been reunited for a few months now, they shared a tight bond. He wondered what might have been if they hadn't been estranged. But there was no use in thinking about things he couldn't change. All it led to was turmoil.

"So I would like for you to start attending meetings this week pertaining to the ad campaigns we're going to launch. That is, if you're on board with this plan. You haven't really given me an answer." She eyed him sharply. He could almost see the wheels turning in her head.

Caleb rubbed his hands together. "It's a yes. Of course I want to do this. It's right in my wheelhouse." He hadn't wanted to complain about being an executive at Yukon Cider, but it wasn't his passion. Caleb knew he was privileged to be able to walk into the position as Hattie's grandson and one of her heirs, so he hadn't balked at the assignment. He had been working hard alongside Xavier and Landon, attending meetings and learning the ropes of Hattie's operations. But this opportunity to star in ad campaigns and commercials would be extraordinary. Not only would it bring him joy, but he would be able to use his acting skills and show the world that he was way more than a punch line.

Hattie raised her fist in the air in a triumphant gesture. He couldn't help but notice her arm seemed thinner and she appeared more frail. "Yes! We're going to have so much fun and you're going to be a smash hit." She reached out and tweaked his cheek. "With that gorgeous face, you're going to make our ciders a household name."

"No pressure," he said, throwing his head back in laughter. Hattie had made it clear that she wanted to focus on living and not dying, so he was going to match her vibrant tone measure for measure.

Hattie leaned over toward him. "Have I told you how happy I am that you and your brothers are back home?"

Home. He didn't quite think of Moose Falls as home, even though he had been born here and had spent the first eight years of his life here.

"You have indeed," Caleb said, raising Hattie's hand to his mouth before placing a kiss on it. "But I'm not sure that I've told you how grateful I am that you invited the three of us back to Moose Falls. And that you're entrusting us with your empire. It's quite extraordinary."

Hattie's eyes gleamed. "I know you haven't made any decisions about whether to stay and run the company, but I want you to absorb everything about Moose Falls. The people. The beautiful Alaskan landscape. Your childhood memories. And, if your heart allows you to, your father." Before he could respond, Hattie said, "I know he hasn't done a whole lot to earn your forgiveness, but like my mama used to tell me, it's good for the heart and soul."

Caleb knew Hattie was right. He was carrying around a lot of extra weight on his shoulders, remnants from a childhood fractured by divorce and his father's absence. Coming back to Alaska provided him with an opportunity to heal, not just from his disastrous stint on reality television, but from so many things he'd bottled up inside himself.

A few hours after his discussion with Hattie, Caleb was behind the wheel of a Range Rover driving toward the mountains at his mother's request. Daisy was riding shotgun while Landon, Xavier, and Jaylen were seated in the back. He cranked up the tunes and played some old-school Prince, his mother's favorite. As they jammed to "When Doves Cry," it almost seemed as if he'd been waiting for this moment since he'd returned.

Being in Moose Falls with Daisy was surreal. Caleb was still trying to wrap his head around her being here with them, especially since she had been so adamant about not returning.

"I remember this area so vividly," Daisy said as they drove past a heavily forested area. "The natural beauty of Alaska is truly magnificent. I once thought I would live out the rest of my days here." She sounded emotional, and he wondered if the past had more of a hold on her than she had ever been able to acknowledge. This was way more than she had ever disclosed to them about her feelings for Alaska. He shouldn't be surprised. This visit was complicated, since she'd left under somber circumstances.

"Well," Landon piped up from the back seat, "Alaska has the highest mountains, the biggest glaciers, and the longest days of any state, so it's not surprising that it's the most beautiful."

"Excellent points, Landon," Daisy said, turning in her seat to send a smile in her baby boy's direction. Her tone sounded more upbeat.

For once Caleb was grateful for Landon's scientific musings and the fun facts he loved to spit out. His comment had lightened their mother's mood.

"Are we almost there?" Jaylen asked for what seemed like the tenth time.

Xavier chuckled. "Almost. Why don't you focus on something else like all the birds we've been seeing?"

"I guess," Jaylen mumbled. Caleb wasn't sure that birds were of much interest to Jaylen. He seemed to prefer football to robins.

Ten minutes later Jaylen let out a whoop of excitement as they reached their destination.

Hiking with his mother, Jaylen, and his brothers on the

mountain trails was a nostalgic experience—a true blast
from the past. It took Caleb all the way back to when he'd
been a little kid. Daisy had always been an athletic and
outdoorsy person. Seeing his mother so happy and relaxed
made him smile. It was almost as if the years melted away
and Daisy was a young woman again. He knew there had
been hard times in Moose Falls, especially the dissolution
of his parents' marriage, but there had been happy memories
too. Some he remembered, but others he saw imprinted on
his mother's face. It hadn't all been bad.

Having lived in California and Arizona, Caleb had seen
some beautiful vistas. The Grand Canyon. Yosemite. Alaska
rivaled them all. There was still a light coating of snow on
the ground, but signs of spring were everywhere. The snowcapped mountains of winter had melted a bit, revealing majestic, craggy rock surfaces. The towering peaks were impressive.

The air was crisp and chilly, but not bone-chillingly cold
as he had experienced in the winter months. The sun was
out, shining down on them with a brilliance that set the tone
for the day. As their wonderful outing came to an end, Caleb
was pulled to the side by his mother.

"This really filled the well," Daisy said, patting the place
over her heart. "I've missed this togetherness we've always
shared. You boys are my life."

Caleb could see a hint of fragility in her. Emotions were
riding high with Daisy during this visit. "Aww, Mom. I know
this hasn't been easy for you. I'm so glad you came."

"I waited a long time to come back to Alaska, but
I wouldn't have missed celebrating Xavier and True's
happiness."

"Why didn't we ever come back?" he asked. It was a
topic she'd always dodged, but being back here made him
want the truth. "I've always wondered," he admitted.

"Oh, Caleb, it's complicated. I won't be in town much longer. I would rather not focus on the past, if that's all right with you."

His heart sank. "Okay," he said, nodding. "I want you to enjoy your time here, so I'll let it go."

Actually, it wasn't all right. He sensed that Daisy didn't want to revisit the issues that had kept her and her kids away from Moose Falls. All these years later, and he still was dealing with unanswered questions.

Leaving the house for a night out twice in the span of a few days wasn't just unusual for Sophia. It was extraordinary. The only reason she had agreed to go line dancing with Patience was because Donny had popped up to exercise his limited custodial rights. Usually he canceled at the last minute or totally blew off his time with Lily. Bless her little heart, Lily had been so excited to sleep over at her dad's house and spend time with her "bonus mom," as Donny called his new wife, Zora. From what Sophia had gleaned, Zora seemed to be a kind, caring person, but Donny had always been inconsistent as a parent.

It had taken all of her wherewithal not to drive over to Donny's house and demand her daughter back. But Patience had talked her down, reminding her that Lily deserved to cultivate a decent relationship with her father. If Sophia stood in her way, Lily might resent her. She couldn't allow her own relationship with her ex to impact Lily. Sophia let out a sigh. It wasn't easy taking the high road.

Even though she had major reservations about Donny's ability to go the distance and remain in his daughter's life, she had to allow him the opportunity. They had a custody agreement that she had to abide by, even if he cherry-picked the times he devoted to Lily.

She had just arrived at Northern Exposure, where she was meeting up with her sister and a few other friends. She loved line dancing, even though she usually did it in the comfort of her own home while watching it on YouTube. Once she walked through the tavern doors, the smell of cedar wood wafted in the air, along with the aroma of barbecue sauce. Her hunger was piqued by the savory aromas floating around. She hadn't had time to grab dinner, so she definitely planned to order some appetizers. Chicken wings. Potato skins. Her mouth was watering at the prospect of indulging in some comfort food. On a night like tonight she needed the comfort.

The interior was rustic and full of Alaskan charm. The flooring was hardwood and slightly scuffed, as if many a patron had trod all over it. Large flat-screen televisions hung from various vantage points around the bar and dining area. Retro Alaska signs hung on the walls, emitting an old-fashioned vibe.

This place was True's baby, and with the backing of Hattie Stone, she had put in a lot of work to renovate the place over the years. Now that True had bought the place from Red, Hattie's son and the father of the three gorgeous Stone brothers, her friend was over the moon about owning her own business. Sophia didn't blame her. After all the hard work she'd put in over the years, it was the only thing that made sense, especially with Hattie's health failing and the sobering news of her terminal illness. According to True, the Stone brothers were working their butts off at Yukon Cider and learning the ropes at the business they were set to inherit.

"Sophia!" Her sister's voice rang out seconds before

she enveloped Sophia in the tightest of hugs. "You made it. I wasn't sure if I'd have to drag you here kicking and screaming."

"I'm not in that bad shape," Sophia said. "I took a deep breath and didn't make a scene when he picked Lily up." She flashed an oversize grin. "I deserve a prize for that."

"Let's order some drinks at the bar," Patience said, tugging on Sophia's arm. "My treat."

"I'm down for hard cider and some apps." Hattie had really done something amazing with the creation of the hard cider company, which was why Sophia seized every opportunity to support the local brand. Hattie had put Moose Falls on the map with her hard cider.

"Say less," Patience said. "I haven't eaten since lunch."

When they reached the bar, True was standing there, along with Bonnie Walker, one of her waitresses. They were playing rock, paper, scissors and laughing uproariously. Sophia loved the friendship between the two women. It was a true sisterhood. Although Bonnie was True's employee and a good eleven years older than True was, they had formed a tight bond. With vibrant red hair and a bubbly personality, Bonnie was beloved in Moose Falls. A recent engagement to her boyfriend, Tucker Jennings, had surprised them all due to Bonnie's reluctance to settle down after a past abusive relationship. Tucker, however, was the real deal, and he adored his fiancée.

"Hey, ladies," Bonnie said in a bubbly tone. "What's your poison tonight?"

"And by poison she means your drink of choice. First round's on me," True said with an easygoing smile. As of late, True had seemed happier than ever, now that she'd found love with Xavier and purchased the tavern.

"I'll have a martini," Patience said. "On the rocks."

"Cranberry and apple Yukon Cider for me," Sophia said. "And can we see a menu? Apps are calling my name."

"Here's the menu," Bonnie said, "but we have some new lobster spring rolls that are to die for."

"You don't have to tell me twice," Patience said. "We'll take an order of the spring rolls and some chicken wings." She winked at True. "Just not the ghost pepper variety."

True covered her face with her hands and shook her head. "I'm never going to live that down, am I?" she asked, chuckling.

"Nope," Sophia said, laughing along with her. "It's now firmly engrained in Moose Falls town lore."

Hattie walked in a short time later with an entourage. Although she was surrounded by her three grandsons, Red, Daisy, and Jacques, all Sophia could focus on was Caleb. Smoking hot, witty Caleb. She hadn't wanted to like him, hadn't expected to find him so appealing. And it wasn't just his good looks, she realized. It was the man himself. The way he walked and talked. The sound of his laughter. Most of all, it was the way he made her stomach do somersaults. As a child she had adored the thrill of the roller coaster, and Caleb was that ride in human form.

She hadn't expected to be drawn to him like a magnet.

She hadn't expected to believe that he had been misunderstood on reality television.

She hadn't expected someone like Caleb to enter her orbit. He was almost like a comet blazing through the sky. If she blinked, he might be gone from Moose Falls in an instant.

Sophia hadn't imagined he would be here tonight. No, that wasn't true. She'd known that there was a distinct possibility he might show up. Wasn't that one of the reasons she'd come tonight? In the hope of seeing him again?

He was walking straight toward her, and she couldn't take her eyes off him.

Look away! Look away! she urged herself. *DO NOT STARE!* Being around Caleb made her feel as if she was being treated to a banquet after not eating for months. She needed to be calm, cool, and collected. Completely unbothered by his presence.

Patience jabbed her subtly in the side. "Look who's coming over here. And he's staring straight at you, little sis. I guess being stuck in the attic with you made an impression on him."

"Shush before he hears you," Sophia muttered. Thankfully, the chatter in the tavern was noisy enough to prevent Patience's voice from carrying. Her sister was the type of person who didn't stop and think before she spoke.

Even from ten feet away Caleb was already showcasing a dazzling smile. And those perfectly shaped lips! *Stop looking at his lips.* Thoughts of kissing him flitted through her mind. *Don't go there!* she told herself. With his track record, he was the last man she should be interested in. After her disastrous relationship with Donny, she had vowed not to ignore red flags. Caleb's past on the reality show was a glaring crimson warning.

Butterflies were fluttering in her stomach, and her mouth felt as dry as cotton. She wasn't the type of person to be tongue-tied, but she had no idea what to say to Caleb as he sauntered toward her.

"Hey, Sophia," he said, disarming her with his dimples. He was dressed in jeans, a flannel shirt, and a pair of Timberland boots. Caleb was giving off a rugged Alaskan vibe, even though he normally radiated pure California sunshine.

"Hey, Hollywood," she said, trying to sound unbothered

by his presence. She wasn't sure, but she thought she might be breaking out in a sweat. He looked that good!

If she could just make it through this evening without making an utter fool of herself over the hottest man who had ever landed in Moose Falls, Sophia would consider that a huge success.

CHAPTER FIVE

As soon as he spotted Sophia at the bar, Caleb made a bee-line in her direction. In the process he left his mother and Hattie with his brothers, Red, and Jacques. He felt a tad guilty, but he knew they were in good hands. Hattie was like royalty in Moose Falls, and she could work a room better than anyone he'd ever known, including Hollywood movers and shakers.

Sophia, dressed in casual clothes, looked just as amazing as she had the other night decked out in formal wear. She was the type of woman who would look good no matter what she was wearing. And she wasn't wearing much makeup other than a little shine on her lips.

Oh, those lips. What he wouldn't give to taste those plump, sensual lips.

He wasn't sure if Sophia even liked him, so the likelihood of locking lips with her seemed negligible. A guy could still dream, though, right? And he could put his best foot forward and try to flirt his way into her good graces. It was worth a shot. Maybe he could get her out on the dance floor.

Sophia was with another woman, and they were sipping drinks, nibbling on appetizers, and looking as if they were having a grand time.

"Hey, Sophia. Nice to see you again," he drawled, trying his best to sound smooth, even though he was slightly rattled by the sight of her.

"I'm Patience," the woman standing next to Sophia said, grinning wildly at Caleb.

"I'm Caleb Stone. Sisters, right?" he asked, looking back and forth between the two women. The resemblance was striking. He was shocked that he could focus on anything other than Sophia. She had occupied a great deal of his time lately, with thoughts of her running rampant in his head.

"We sure are," Patience said, leaning in to put her head on Sophia's shoulder.

"My better half," Sophia said, patting her sister on the head.

"Lies," Patience said, swatting Sophia. "No one's better than you."

"Aww," Sophia gushed. "Right back atcha."

Their banter reminded him of him and his brothers, although they didn't gush over one another. They tended to use humor to downplay the way they felt about one another while still always having each other's backs and staying close. The truth was, they were one another's best friends. Nothing and no one could ever get in the way of their bond.

"I want to go say hi to Peggy," Patience said. "Nice meeting you, Caleb." She let out a loud squeal as she headed in the direction of a tall blond woman.

"Are you both dancing tonight? Or just watching?" Caleb asked. He looked around the place. It was pretty jam-packed. He spotted a few of his co-workers from Yukon Cider and waved in their direction. With each and every day he was becoming more enmeshed with in the fabric of Moose Falls. Establishing those relationships made being in Alaska more palatable. As someone who'd always enjoyed a strong social network, he savored the camaraderie.

"Absolutely," Sophia said. "I'm wearing my dancing shoes." She pointed toward her cowgirl boots. "And Patience loves to dance."

He let out a low whistle. "Those are nice. I'm fully expecting you to tear up the dance floor and show off your moves." He could imagine her strutting her stuff on the makeshift dance floor, drawing all eyes in the room in her direction.

Sophia made a face. "Don't get too excited. I'm more of a low-key dancer. I'm not MJ."

Caleb let out a low chuckle. "Well, who is?" he asked.

"How are the bites?" she asked. "They were pretty bad the other night. They sure made a meal out of you."

"They're much better. My mother gave me some salve for them. Apple cider vinegar and baking soda, along with a few other things. She's a bit of a natural healer. She's been patching us up since we were kids."

"I love that," Sophia said, her eyes lighting up. "She seems like a really cool lady."

"She is, although when we were growing up she was no joke. Whether it was trying to sneak in after curfew or not keeping up with our grades, she didn't hesitate to put Xavier and me in our places. Of course Landon was never in any trouble," he said with a shake of his head. "The only crime he ever committed was reading under the covers with a flashlight after bedtime or turning in library books late and incurring steep fines."

"I love how the three of you were so different, even as children." Sophia let out a hearty laugh. He loved the crinkles that formed around her eyes when she laughed, as well as her carefree expression. This was the side of Sophia that her daughter saw each and every day, he imagined. Joyful and lighthearted.

"So how's Lily?" he asked. He knew that going out on the town was a big deal for Sophia based on her comments from the other night.

"She's great," Sophia said, smiling. "I can't believe you remembered her name."

"It's a beautiful name," he said. "So is she with a sitter?"

A ragged sigh slipped past her lips. "No, she's actually with her dad tonight." Something about the way she said it let him know that it wasn't an easy situation.

"And are you okay with that?" He wasn't trying to pry, but at the same time he wanted to know how she was feeling. Maybe it was frustration, but she was giving off an unsettled vibe.

"I am. Sort of. Ish," she said, scrunching up her nose. "I figured coming here tonight would be a great distraction from my reality."

He leaned in close, immediately getting a whiff of her sweet floral perfume. If he wasn't mistaken, it was jasmine. "I can be your distraction." Turnabout was fair play. She had been distracting him ever since the night of Xavier and True's engagement party.

Her eyes widened in response to his comment. He had her full attention now.

Before Sophia had a chance to respond, the DJ announced the start of the line dancing, as well as asking for any musical requests.

"Let's go dance," Sophia said, jumping up and grabbing his hand before pulling him toward the dance floor. Caleb followed along after her as a throng of people headed in the same direction. He ended up standing with Sophia on one side and True on the other. A quick glance around the area showed no sign of Landon. As usual, he was probably hiding out somewhere away from the crowd. Sooner or later, his little brother was going to have to stop avoiding social situations so he could get started on living life to the fullest.

An instructor stood at the front of the formation, demonstrating the specific steps for the first line dance, the Cupid Shuffle. Caleb already knew this one by heart, since he'd had to learn it for a dance sequence in a commercial he had been featured in. As the music filled the tavern, everyone began moving to the beat.

Instead of going left, Sophia went right, banging into him. She covered her face with her hands. "I'm so sorry."

"Keep going," Caleb said. "No worries. You'll get in the groove. Just keep moving."

In the next instant, he felt another crash against him. Sophia was looking at him and mouthing another apology. He had placed his hands on her arms as she fell onto him. Man, this was pretty nice having Sophia in such close proximity. She didn't need to apologize for a single thing. Line dancing wasn't as easy as people assumed.

A quick look at Sophia showed him she was still struggling a bit to get it right. She darted a glance around at the other folks dancing, a confused expression etched on her face.

"Let me help," Caleb said. "Just stand behind me and follow my moves."

"Okay," Sophia said as he got in front of her and began dancing along with everyone else.

Her movements were a bit hesitant, but she was moving in the right direction and going with the flow. By the time the song ended, she was crushing it.

As the song concluded, Caleb noticed Hattie and Landon sitting at one of the nearby tables.

"I'm going to check on Hattie," he told Sophia, raising his voice over the din.

"Let me come say hello," Sophia said, walking alongside him. "I don't get to see her nearly enough."

As soon as they reached Hattie's table, she gave them the thumbs-up sign. "You two look good out there," she said.

"Caleb does for sure," Sophia said. "I got confused with my left and right feet."

"It's not how you start, it's how you finish. And you turned things around. I had my eye on you," Hattie said with a wink.

"Why are the two of you sitting?" Caleb asked. He lightly kicked Landon with his shoe. "It's a lot of fun out there."

Landon wrinkled his nose. "Too many steps to learn. I'm content just to watch."

"I'm not," Hattie said. "I've been waiting for the perfect song to join in on the action. Jacques just went over to request my favorite line dancing song." Hattie had a huge grin on her face, which made Caleb happy. She deserved every ounce of joy the world had to offer. He had a feeling it was Jacques bringing her the smiles. Clearly, she was a woman in love. Seeing their love story play out was a wonderful gift for him. Each and every day he was learning more and more about life and love. Between Hattie, Jacques, True, and Xavier, he was getting a master class in how to find a soulmate. Maybe there was hope for him yet.

He'd never thought about love at Hattie's stage in life, but Hattie and Jacques were the real deal. Their devotion to each other was touching.

Suddenly, Jacques was standing there with an identical grin on his face. "Done, milady," he announced as the music for the Electric Boogie filled the tavern. "Let me escort you out there."

Hattie let out a squeal of excitement as Jacques pulled her gently to a standing position before dipping his head down and planting a kiss on her lips. She looped her arm through his before turning toward the group. "I expect to see all of you out there on the dance floor," Hattie said in a no-nonsense tone as she took off.

"I can do this one with my eyes closed," Sophia said, following after Hattie.

Caleb turned to Landon. "You can't disappoint Hattie. Come on!" He beckoned him to join in. When Landon stubbornly shook his head and folded his arms across his chest, Caleb reached out and pulled him to his feet by his shirt.

"I don't want to dance," Landon protested. "How many times do I have to tell you? I'm not a dancer."

"Do it for Hattie," Caleb insisted. "It means a lot to her to have us all out there doing the Electric Slide. That might seem silly to you. All I know is that we have to make sure she's surrounded by love for every moment that she has left."

Suddenly, all the fight went out of Landon. "Okay, I'll do it. I understand. Even if I make a colossal fool of myself, I want to make our grandmother happy."

"That's what I'm talking about," Caleb said as he put his arm around Landon and pulled him into his side as they joined the dancers. Once they got in step with everyone else, Caleb could see that Landon was way better than he'd let on. That was the thing about his baby brother. He kept things close to the vest. If he asked him, he knew Landon would say that simply because he didn't want to dance didn't mean he couldn't dance. He was that kind of frustrating.

The floor was packed, and Hattie was right in the thick of it, beaming as she perfectly executed the moves. All eyes were on his grandmother. The crowd parted, and Hattie was in the center. Everyone stopped dancing and began to cheer Hattie on.

"Hattie! Hattie!" The crowd chanted and clapped as Hattie danced the Electric Slide. She loved the attention, preening and posing as everyone looked on.

Jacques was standing nearby, watching his lady like a hawk. Despite her illness, Hattie was killing the dance moves. Her vivacity was deceiving. Because of her kidney disease, she'd been doing dialysis treatments for decades. At this point, her condition was terminal.

All of a sudden Hattie wobbled as if she'd lost her balance.

"I think that's enough for tonight," Jacques said, moving quickly toward Hattie's side and clutching her by the arm. His brow was furrowed, and his features were tightly drawn.

"But I'm not tired," Hattie protested. "I could cut a rug all night long."

"I bet you could, sweetheart, but I think you should quit while you're ahead," Jacques suggested. He wasn't easily swayed by Hattie, despite the pleading tone in her voice.

A mutinous expression was etched on her face. "I don't want to be treated like an invalid. I'm feeling terrific."

Uh-oh. She was being feisty with Jacques. Caleb knew that Hattie was struggling to maintain her independence while dealing with the realities of her terminal illness. His heart went out to her. If he were in her shoes, he might not get out of bed in the morning. His grandmother continued to walk around with a smile on her face and an iron will, as well as continuing her leadership role at Yukon Cider. Her fortitude was spectacular.

"I bet you're feeling on top of the world," Jacques said to Hattie in a low voice that was barely audible to Caleb. "You love being the center of attention."

"It's not my fault I'm fabulous," Hattie said as she stopped dancing and leaned on Jacques. For all her protestations, she looked winded.

"I would never dispute that in a million years," Jacques said, leaning down and kissing Hattie on the lips. Once again, the crowd roared. Everyone enjoyed seeing a love story up close and personal.

Caleb could see the signs of wear and tear on his grandmother's face, as well as noticing her labored breathing. Jacques, who knew her better than anyone, had made a good call. Everyone knew that he cared deeply for Hattie and always watched out for her best interests.

"Come on, Grandmother," Caleb said, lending her his arm. "Give other people a chance to shine. With you on the dance floor, no one else stands a chance of being a breakout star."

Hattie patted his cheek. "Oh, you silver-tongued flatterer."

He winked at her. "You know I'm simply speaking the truth."

"Okay, okay. I'll go sit down and take a break." She looked around the tavern. "This is quite a crowd. True really has done wonders with the place. I'm so glad Northern Exposure will be in good hands."

Caleb didn't miss the wistful tone that laced her voice. Hattie knew she wouldn't be around much longer. She wasn't the sort of woman to sugarcoat things.

"You laid the foundation for all of this," Caleb said, bending over and placing a kiss on her temple. "That won't ever be forgotten."

And neither will you.

Watching Caleb handle Hattie with such finesse caused a warm feeling to flow through Sophia. She could tell from the expressions on both of their faces that they were sharing a tender moment.

Hattie's grandson was turning out to be way different than she had imagined. Reality television hadn't done him any favors, and she had to wonder if production had created a false narrative about him. This version of Caleb couldn't be a cheater and a liar. He was way too sweet.

Hmm. Or was she simply ignoring her own tendency to focus on the positive. People could be a mix of a bunch of different things. Just because she wanted to believe Caleb was a stand-up guy didn't mean he was like that in relationships. Everyone had pegged Donny as a nice guy, until he had proven them wrong.

"If you stare any harder, you might end up cross-eyed." Patience was standing next to her, smirking.

"Shh. Someone might hear you." The last thing she needed was for people to think she was crushing on Caleb. It was ridiculous feeling this way, since without a doubt she was crushing on Caleb.

"And so what? With the way you're eyeballing him, I'm sure other folks have noticed by now."

"I was simply watching him with Hattie. It's really sweet," Sophia said, downplaying the way she'd been staring at him. It had been a long time since someone had come along who drew her in like a moth to a flame.

"Mm-hmm," Patience murmured. "I totally believe you. Not!" Patience stuck out her tongue.

Sophia rolled her eyes. "Why don't you focus on your own love life?" She jutted her chin toward the bar. "Jason is staring at you. When are you going to put him out of his misery? He's been chasing you for years now."

Patience glanced over at Jason and waved. "I'm thinking about going out with him the next time he asks. At least one of us has to put ourselves out there." She made a face at Sophia.

"If you remember, I did put myself out there," Sophia responded. "It was a train wreck. Other than the part where I ended up with Lily."

"You can't let one bad experience take you out of the game," Patience said. "I've had a few heartbreaks myself, and they haven't stopped me from hoping and dreaming. You should try it sometime. It'll do you a world of good." With a cheeky wave, she took off, walking toward the bar and straight toward Jason. Sophia barely had a moment to check out the interaction between Patience and Jason when Caleb walked over.

"Hey, I have something that belongs to you." His tone was light and flirty. But maybe she was reading into it. Perhaps she was hoping he was trying to flirt with her. She had the feeling she wasn't the only one either, considering all the stares he was getting.

"Really? What would that be?" she asked, trying to focus on his words and not his striking features or the way his shirt accentuated his taut chest.

"The Leica. I guess you were so overjoyed to be rescued that you forgot all about it when you made your mad dash out of the attic."

She slapped her hand to her forehead. "I keep meaning to pop over to the house to collect it, although I have no intention of ever going back in that attic again."

"Seriously? I thought being trapped with me was a little slice of paradise."

Sophia placed her hand over her heart. "It was actual heaven on Earth, particularly the part where the ants invaded your pants." Her lips twitched at the memory of Caleb discovering that he'd been swarmed by the insects.

"Ouch. Making fun of my pain. Not cool, Sophia," he said, his eyes twinkling.

She reached out and touched his arm. "Sorry about that. Just a little carpenter ant humor. I appreciate you holding on to the Leica for me."

"No worries. The camera is safely out of the attic. It's only fitting that you have it in your possession, since it's the reason we got trapped up there."

"Well, actually it was because you closed the door behind us. Lest we forget," she quipped.

"Tomato, tomahto," Caleb said, showcasing a pearly toothed smile. "Let's meet up for coffee or tea or baked Alaska so I can give it to you."

Sophia burst out laughing. "Baked Alaska? That's kind of random."

Caleb laughed along with her. "Guilty as charged. But I made you laugh, didn't I? And you have a terrific laugh."

She basked in the compliment for a moment, realizing it had been a long time since a man had given her one.

"Let's exchange numbers," Sophia said, still chuckling while taking out her cell phone and handing it over to Caleb. He quickly put his information into her phone and handed it back.

His hand lingered on hers as she took the phone back. "Soft hands, warm heart," he murmured. Their gazes locked and held. For the life of her, Sophia couldn't look away from him.

Even though Caleb's comment bordered on being corny, she felt her cheeks getting flushed. This man was making her feel flustered.

"I'm going to make sure Hattie is all settled," he said. "Hope to see you soon, Sophia."

"Night, Caleb." Her eyes trailed after him, lingering on his rugged physique and the huge amount of swagger he exuded.

Caleb Stone was turning out to be someone who intrigued her way more than she had ever imagined. There seemed to be a lot more to him than met the eye, and she was eager to find out more about this mysterious man.

CHAPTER SIX

Caleb was more excited than he'd been in a very long time. On his way to work he drove leisurely along the lake area, enjoying the stunning view of the mountains and the last remnants of thawing snow. He couldn't ignore the raw beauty of his surroundings. Sometimes he felt as if he was living in a postcard or a vivid painting. Being back in Moose Falls was full of discoveries, mostly good ones. His favorite thing about Alaska was the abundance of trees—spruce, evergreen, hemlock, and birch dominated the area. The other day during their hike his mother had identified several species of eagles, which excited her to no end.

He could tell that she had been a bit emotional about revisiting the places in Moose Falls that had once meant the world to her. Despite being a tough cookie, Daisy had a marshmallow at her center. She was sentimental like Landon. Caleb was going to miss her a lot, but he was happy she'd been in Moose Falls to celebrate True and Xavier.

Feeling upbeat, he turned on the radio and let it blast. Driving on Alaskan roads was so much easier, now that the roads weren't covered in snow and ice.

This morning's meeting with Hattie was full of so many possibilities. Coming to Alaska to explore an inheritance had been a no-brainer, but doing so had delayed him from trying out for acting roles in Hollywood. If he could be the face of Yukon Cider, it would fill a void in his life and allow him to pursue his creativity in front of the camera. He didn't want to assume anything, but if the campaign was even a modest success, he would be grateful.

As he headed into the corporate building, Caleb was greeted warmly by various employees. He loved the social atmosphere here more than anything. Everyone treated him and his brothers like they were old friends. That was a true benefit of living in a small Alaskan town. People weren't strangers for very long. He had come across so many folks who remembered him from when he was little. They always had a story about his parents or memories of Caleb with his brothers. It served to remind him that he was part of the fabric of Moose Falls. He hadn't expected to be so accepted by the townsfolk after being MIA for two decades. All of a sudden he was being inundated with a lot of sensory memories from childhood. Moose Falls had been his happy place.

He made his way quickly to the conference room after dropping his leather work bag in his office. The last thing he intended to do was make Hattie wait for him. She wasn't the type of person who responded well to tardiness. It didn't matter if they were blood relations. She wouldn't hesitate to dress him down in public.

When he crossed the threshold of the conference room, Caleb stopped short. Sophia was standing by the table, sipping a cup of coffee. She was dressed professionally in a beige-colored suit and black heels. He sucked in a deep breath. Sophia should come with a warning sign like the ones he saw in Arizona. *Dangerous Curves Ahead*.

"What are you doing here?" Caleb asked, his tone radiating surprise.

"Hattie invited me. I'm going to be one of Yukon Cider's employees," she explained. "I'm super excited to be working for such an amazing company."

He hadn't been prepared to see Sophia this morning at a meeting Hattie had set up for him to attend. As far as he'd known, the meeting was just for the two of them. Wasn't it classic Hattie to throw him a curveball?

"As a photographer?" he asked, taken aback by this turn of events.

"No, as a taste tester," she said with a smirk. "Of course as a photographer. It is my profession. Sadly, I don't have many other skills."

"I find that very hard to believe." He locked gazes with her, tumbling headfirst into her beautiful brown eyes. They were like a vortex, pulling him in.

Something hummed and pulsed in the air between them. He wondered if she felt the sparks. Honestly, how could she not? There always seemed to be a layer of tension between them that had everything to do with attraction. Although he was still wary of getting involved with anyone, it was going to be impossible for him to ignore his feelings for this woman.

Just then Hattie walked into the conference room dressed all in green, leaning heavily on her cane. Caleb wasn't sure if it was her pride or stubbornness, but she rarely used her electric scooter at work. Everyone respected Hattie, but he sensed she was worried about being perceived as a weakened leader. His wish for his grandmother was that she could spend the rest of the time she had left doing all the things she couldn't from within the confines of her office. Yukon Cider was a magnificent accomplishment, but he wasn't sure Hattie should spend her remaining time consumed by work. It wasn't his decision to make, but he wondered if she would rather be playing blackjack in Vegas or canoodling with Jacques.

"Good morning, beautiful people. It's a wonderful day to have a wonderful day." Hattie was grinning from ear to ear.

"Morning, Hattie. That color looks gorgeous on you," Sophia said, warmth radiating from her voice.

Hattie patted her on the hand. "Thank you, Sophia. I love colors. Ever since I was a little girl, I've chosen to wear vivid hues." She let out a throaty chuckle. "It used to frustrate my mother something fierce trying to find yellows and oranges and lilacs. Talk about a challenge."

"I can imagine," Sophia said, her eyes widening. "I guess that I should be jumping for joy that Lily isn't a fashionista."

"Yet," Hattie said. "That could change in the blink of an eye."

Caleb pulled a chair out for his grandmother and said, "Here you go, Grandmother."

Hattie looked over at Sophia as she sank down into the leather seat. "Isn't he a gorgeous boy?"

Sophia's lips twitched. "He sure is," she said in a chirpy voice. He sensed she was holding back a fit of laughter.

Her response flowed over him like warm honey. It didn't matter that Hattie had put Sophia on the spot. For Caleb it was a win. Sophia thought he was good-looking! Since when had he needed affirmation about his looks? He couldn't recall a single instance.

"Let's get down to business," Hattie said in a crisp tone as both Caleb and Sophia sat down. "I figured the two of you should meet in a professional capacity since you'll be working together."

Caleb hadn't seen this one coming. Not at all. He and Sophia?

Hattie must have seen his confusion. "Sophia will be working on the ad campaign we discussed." She turned her gaze to Sophia. "What I didn't mention is that Caleb will be the star of the new campaign. He'll be featured in the print ads and some commercials. I know it's going to be difficult, but it'll be your job to make him look like the most desirable man on the planet." Hattie's tone was full of mirth. Her lips were twitching. She was cracking herself up with her own jokes.

Sophia looked over at Caleb. "I'll try to make you look decent, Hollywood," she teased.

"I would appreciate that," he quipped. He turned his head. "This is my good side."

"Who are you trying to fool?" Hattie asked, rolling her eyes. "You have no bad side. Am I right, Sophia?"

"Yeah, your grandson is pretty easy on the eyes," Sophia acknowledged.

"And you're a bona fide bombshell," Hattie said to Sophia. She turned toward Caleb. "Isn't she stunning?"

"Flawless," Caleb said. And he meant it. Sophia was the most surprising thing yet about Moose Falls. Her ex was beyond foolish to allow a woman like her to slip through his fingers.

He wasn't sure if he was imagining things, but his grandmother seemed to be trying to establish something between him and Sophia. She was coaxing compliments from both of them at an alarming rate.

Hattie wiggled her eyebrows. "By the way, I have no rules about employees dating."

Sophia's cheeks flushed and she said, "I-I'm good, Hattie. I have my hands full raising my daughter. I'm not looking for any romantic entanglements."

I'm good? He tried to shake off her comment, but he felt insulted. Was he beneath her high standards that she wouldn't consider the possibility of dating him? It wasn't as if having a child excluded a person from romantic entanglements, as she'd called them. Hmm. In his mind he was replaying the events at the tavern. She'd given him her number, hadn't she? Now he was confused, but unwilling to look like an idiot. If she wasn't interested, then neither was he.

"I'm good too," he answered in a clipped tone. "I'm on a relationship-free diet."

Sophia's lips twitched until she couldn't hold her laughter in any longer. There was no doubt in his mind that she was laughing at *him*.

It didn't sit well with him that she considered him a punch line. He'd believed that coming to Alaska would allow him to get away from all the ridicule and fallout from *Love Him or Leave Him*. "Seriously? You find that funny?"

Sophia cracked up. "Sorry, it's just the way you said it."

Caleb sat back in his chair and folded his arms around his chest. "I'm still traumatized by being on reality television, in case you were wondering."

"What is all this business about the reality show? Tell me exactly what happened," Hattie requested. "It's never made a bit of sense to me. All I know is that you were on this show and the star picked you out of all the other men to be her forever. Is that right?"

"Pretty much," Caleb muttered. He'd gone this far without Hattie hearing the nitty-gritty details. Thank goodness she didn't watch television or comb the internet. It was humiliating to have to spill the beans with Sophia listening.

"Then something went disastrously wrong, as life sometimes does." Hattie made a tutting sound. "From what I heard they did a number on you."

"You've got the major points, Grandmother," Caleb said. He just wanted this conversation to end. Although he knew the experience had made him a stronger man, Caleb wasn't particularly proud of his time on the show. He cringed at the thought of his grandmother thinking poorly of him based on an editor's cut.

"Well, you're skipping the best part," Sophia said, correcting him. "Just as Gillian picked Caleb as the man of her dreams, it came out that Caleb was having sexy times with her twin sister, Abby, who was supposed to be there providing support for her sister." She paused to take a breath. "Then Caleb confesses his love to Abby and tells Gillian he doesn't love her. Pandemonium ensues. Gillian is devastated. Twin sisters are torn apart by a man." Sophia made a face. "Your grandson."

Hattie appeared to be horror-stricken. Her mouth hung open, and her eyes went wide. She raised a hand to her chest. "Did you do all of that?" Hattie let out a distressed sound. "Oh, my goodness. Good thing I wasn't tuning in."

Caleb let out a groan. He glared at Sophia. "I thought you said you were only casually watching. Sounds like you were the show's number one fan."

Sophia shrugged. "What can I say? It was highly entertaining. I was hooked."

He arched an eyebrow in Sophia's direction and clenched his teeth and glared at her. Was she seriously saying all this in front of Hattie? At his expense? "I'm glad I could entertain you, even though you really don't know what went down." He couldn't hide the note of anger in his voice. It had been almost two years of this crap, with everyone painting him as the bad guy. A mixture of fury and hurt caused his eyes to moisten. He was seeing things through a red haze.

"Okay, you two. Back to business," Hattie said with a clap of her hands. "We're going to have meetings all this week with the marketing and PR departments. I would like to hit the ground running on this campaign so we can have everything lined up for the launch of the new ciders in the fall."

"I'm all in, Hattie," Sophia said. "I'm really excited about working for Yukon Cider. I think Caleb is going to make a great lead for the campaign."

The words coming from Sophia's mouth surprised him. Was she actually giving him a genuine compliment? So far he hadn't exactly been feeling the love from her, especially when she gave Hattie the recap of his time on *Love Him or Leave Him*. Although he had kept his mouth shut, he'd really wanted to set her straight. Sophia didn't have a clue as to what had actually gone down behind the scenes. And based on her armchair analysis, he was the bad boy of reality television. A two-timer.

That wasn't him at all. Never had been. Never would be.

Caleb wasn't prepared to revisit the past and bare all to Sophia about what had really transpired. Nope, he barely knew her, and if she was going to judge him unfairly, then Caleb wasn't really interested in getting to know her any better.

He was better off alone anyway. The fewer complications, the better.

Hattie clapped her hands together. "Well, I'm glad we're all on the same page. This campaign is going to be wonderful. Stay tuned."

Caleb stood up and pulled out his grandmother's chair for her, then handed the cane to her for support. He resisted the urge to help her to her feet, knowing she would frown on the gesture. She stood up under her own steam, let out a ragged breath, then made her way to the door. With a little wave, she disappeared down the hall.

And then it was just Caleb and Sophia with another kind of tension crackling in the air between them. He felt some kind of way about her dragging him through the mud with Hattie. It wasn't cool at all. He couldn't even look in her direction at the moment.

The sound of Sophia clearing her throat drew his attention. "Caleb, is something wrong? You seem a bit withdrawn all of a sudden."

He glanced over at her. Caleb wanted to choose his words carefully instead of lashing out at her. "You really went on a tear during the meeting. The way you portrayed me was in a very unflattering light. I've had a lot of negativity like that, but I didn't expect to be blindsided by you." His voice shook a little as he spoke. He wasn't good at hiding his emotions.

"I'm sorry if I hurt your feelings when I was talking about the show. I didn't mean to insult you or put you in a bad light in front of Hattie."

He studied her expression. Sophia's face was a mask of contrition. From what he could tell she was being sincere. But, honestly, what did he know about Sophia? She was proving to be a mass of contradictions. And he wasn't an expert in the female department. Not by a long shot. In his past he'd been made a fool of by someone he'd cared about. His feelings had been completely overlooked. He was sensitive to being an object of ridicule. That probably hadn't been Sophia's intention.

"Forgive me for going too far," she said. "We're just getting acquainted and trying to feel each other out, so I learned something today about you. I promise it won't happen again."

Her tone was way softer than he'd ever heard before and a little bit shaky like his own.

Before Caleb could say anything, Sophia had sailed out the door, leaving him feeling a bit thunderstruck. Just when he thought that Sophia couldn't throw him any more off-kilter, she did or said something to surprise him. Sophia had reeled him back in, reaching into his chest cavity and tugging with all her might.

Sophia left the meeting at Yukon Cider feeling like a complete jerk. This wasn't the first time she'd opened up her mouth in an attempt to be witty and funny, only to have it backfire on her. But blabbing about Caleb's stint on *Love Him or Leave Him* to Hattie without considering his feelings on the matter was a new low. If only she had stopped for a moment to consider the fact that he might not have wanted his grandmother to know all the details.

So far, she had mostly seen the jovial, always laughing Caleb. Even after being bitten by angry ants he hadn't lost his ability to joke around. She'd never imagined that his experiences on the show were so painful.

Clearly, there was a lot more to Caleb's stint on reality TV than she had ever considered. The wounded expression stamped on his face had spoken volumes. Something bad had gone down, and it wasn't anything viewers had seen.

"Big mouth," she said out loud as she stepped into her vehicle. She had been too embarrassed to stick around and see his response to her apology. She let out a sigh. Why had she been so eager to believe that Caleb had been deceptive in his on-air relationship? Her relationship with Donny had messed her up. It was difficult for her to believe the best of people. She needed to let those feelings go. They were clearly holding her back.

How in the world was she going to work with Caleb after this? Tears of frustration pricked her eyes. This job was a wonderful opportunity that could legitimately change her life. A nice salary. Health. Dental. Ample vacation time. All Caleb would have to do was tell his grandmother that he didn't want to work alongside her. As lovely as Hattie was, Sophia knew who she would pick if pressed. All Hattie had wanted for many years was to be reunited with her three boys, her grandsons. Being terminally ill meant her time with her family was more precious than ever. Sophia may have just killed her chances at the job of her dreams, and she had only herself to blame.

Sophia pulled up to her sister's house and honked her horn to announce her arrival. As a journalist, Patience worked at home and normally didn't allow for interruptions during her work hours. She knew that Patience would make an exception for her.

Before she had even made it to the door, Patience flung it open. With her cinnamon-colored skin and light brown eyes, she looked like a mixture of Sophia and their mom. She was dressed in a flannel robe and pajamas, her shoulder-length dark hair swept up in a high ponytail. Her sister always said that working in her pajamas was a great perk that came with being a writer. "What are you doing here? I thought you had a meeting with Hattie?"

Sophia let out a groan as she walked over the threshold and headed straight to the kitchen. Patience trailed after her. "Hello. Aren't you going to say good morning and tell me what brings you here?"

She sat down at Patience's kitchen table, put her head down in her arms, and let out a wail. "I am an absolute fool."

"Uh-oh. Do I need to break out the Oreos?" Patience asked. She began rummaging in her pantry.

"It's way too early for Oreos, but I will not say no to a mimosa."

"Coming right up," Patience said. "While I'm making them, tell me what's going on. And don't dramatize. Just give me the cold, hard facts."

Sophia dragged her head up. Patience was uncorking a bottle of champagne. "I don't dramatize, Patience."

Patience didn't have to say a word. She just sent Sophia a look that spoke volumes.

"At least not much," Sophia acknowledged. "Just a smidgen."

"Okay, talk. I'm almost done."

"I went to Yukon Cider for my meeting with Hattie."

Patience began pouring champagne into the flutes, holding the glasses at an angle until they were filled halfway. She then slowly poured orange juice into the flutes until they were filled to the rim. "Well that's good news. Working for Hattie could be a game changer."

Sophia let out another groan. "Unless a person flaps their gums and ends up insulting the CEO's grandson."

"You didn't." Patience placed a filled champagne flute in front of Sophia.

Sophia reached for the glass and guzzled down the contents. "I sure did," she admitted. "And it wasn't until I saw his expression that I realized what I'd done. I talked about his appearance on the reality show and the sordid details. I said way too much about things Hattie didn't know about." She covered her face with her hands. "He was mortified. And angry."

"What in the world!" Patience exclaimed. "I hate to say I told you so, but I knew that your love of reality TV was going to come back to bite you."

Sophia pushed her glass toward Patience. "Hit me up again. I can't believe you're lecturing me when I'm so down."

"You know I like to keep it real, sis. Tough love, baby." Patience refilled her flute with another mimosa.

"What if Caleb isn't comfortable working with me now? Or what if he tells Hattie to give me the boot? As you said, working for Hattie could change my life . . . and Lily's." She let out a sob. "What if I blocked this blessing by running my mouth?"

Within seconds Patience was wrapping her arms around Sophia and murmuring words of comfort in her ear. "Don't assume the worst, Soph. It sounds bad but not earth-shattering bad. I mean it's kind of cringey that you brought up the reality show, but I don't think it's a deal-breaker."

"Hattie asked, but I should have kept my mouth shut," Sophia muttered.

"So tell Caleb that. Do a mea culpa and make sure he doesn't cut you off at the knees. And, honestly, you have no indication that he would do something like that."

"I already apologized, but he didn't seem like he accepted it." His silence had spoken volumes. She'd left the conference room out of sheer embarrassment.

"Well, Soph, it might be time to level up and grovel," Patience suggested, taking a sip of her mimosa. "Look at it this way. At least you'll get some more face time with a gorgeous Stone brother." She wiggled her eyebrows. "You wouldn't have to tell me twice."

Ugh. Sophia hated the thought of chasing Caleb down to beg for forgiveness. Maybe it wasn't that deep, after all. She flashed back to the angry look on Caleb's face. Nope, this was pretty bad. She needed to smooth things over before it all exploded in her face. Unless of course it already had. She'd beaten a fast path out of the conference room due to extreme embarrassment, but maybe she should've stuck around to talk to Caleb.

She wouldn't forgive herself if she'd ruined her chances of a once-in-a-lifetime position. She truly needed this job.

Her dwindling bank balance depended on it.

CHAPTER SEVEN

For the rest of the morning Caleb couldn't focus on anything other than the meeting with Sophia and Hattie. Of course he'd been stewing about all the things he should have said in the moment but hadn't thought of until afterward. His mother had taught him and his brothers to be gentlemen, but Sophia had been pushing it. She had stuck a knife in a raw wound and twisted it all around. And to make matters worse, they would be working together on the new hard cider campaign. Up until this morning he had been excited about his new role and the possibility of making a connection with Sophia. Now, he was sitting in his office with his brothers, who'd met up with him for lunch. He could barely think straight, thanks to Sophia.

"What's your problem?" Landon asked Caleb. "You look like you lost your best friends in the world."

"And that can't be true since we're sitting right here," Xavier said, grinning.

"I got blindsided," Caleb said, his mind still whirling.

"How so?" Landon asked, taking a bite of his tuna fish sandwich.

Caleb put his fork down on the table and pushed his salad away. He didn't have an appetite, which was unusual for him. "Well, when I walked into the conference room, Sophia was there," Caleb said, remembering how thrilled he'd been at the sight of her.

"And wasn't that a good thing?" Xavier asked. "I couldn't help but notice the two of you dancing around each other at Northern Exposure. No pun intended."

"Yeah," Landon said. "I noticed it too. She's pretty stunning."

Caleb let out a snort. "Well, that's over and done with. She made a big point to let Hattie know the details about the reality show. Of course it made me look like an idiot, but since when does the truth matter?" Bitterness infused his tone, and he didn't bother to hide his emotions. He was tired of his good name and image being smeared.

"That's not cool," Xavier said, frowning. "You've been through it, little bro. And that's all in the past. Part of being in Alaska means a new beginning."

"That's what I thought too, but it appears I'm destined to be remembered as the Love Rat." Caleb clenched his teeth. He detested being linked to a ridiculous reality show. He'd auditioned on the advice of his now former agent, but instead of a stepping stone into the acting world, Caleb had earned himself a reputation as a Z-list reality star.

"At least they could have given you a better moniker," Landon said, shaking his head. "Being compared to a rodent is such an insult."

"Thanks, Landon. You always know how to cheer me up," Caleb snapped.

"What? I'm on your side," Landon protested, throwing up his hands.

Xavier wiped his mouth with a napkin and tossed his

trash in the bin. "We realize that you got a raw deal, but as all three of us know from our recent experiences, life isn't fair. And one of the football-isms that has stayed with me over the years is that when you get knocked down, you've got to get up."

Caleb nodded. He did believe that he was moving past one of the worst times in his life, but every now and again something happened to remind him of the past. And his own foolishness. He hadn't expected Sophia to be the one to drag him down.

"You're right. I just need to focus on inheriting Yukon Cider and making the decision whether to stay and run the company," Caleb said.

"I'm going to say it again for the record," Xavier said, looking back and forth between Landon and Caleb. "Regardless of what my future holds with True, I intend to make a unanimous decision with both of you. We came into this as the Three Musketeers and that's how we'll finish it."

"I hear that," Caleb said, his soul feeling lighter just knowing that he and his brothers were going to tackle this inheritance issue as a threesome. Nothing else made sense.

"That's a relief," Landon said, letting out a deep breath.

Xavier's engagement to True had made things a bit more complicated, but, thankfully, the Brothers Stone would make a final decision as a unit. Stay and run Yukon Cider or sell the company to the highest bidder. By the time the decision was made, Hattie would most likely be gone. It was a sobering thought. A quick look at his brothers' faces revealed that they were thinking the same.

A knock on his office door dragged all three of them out of their thoughts.

"Come in," Caleb said, half expecting to see Hattie standing at his door. She had a sweet habit of coming to check on her grandsons and bounce ideas off them. Sometimes he couldn't help but wonder what might have been if they hadn't left Alaska all those years ago. Would his parents have reconciled? Would he and his brothers have pursued different career paths? Maybe Red would have been a solid part of their lives.

When the door opened, Sophia was standing there, looking every bit as stunning as always. His pulse still raced at the sight of her. His tongue felt thick inside his mouth, as if he might not be able to get actual words out. He had no idea what she was doing here, since her job hadn't actually started yet.

She fumbled with her fingers, moving them around in jerky movements.

"Caleb. Can I talk to you for a moment?" She darted a glance at Xavier and Landon. "Alone?"

She had to give it to the Stone brothers. As soon as she made her request, they scrambled to pack up their things and exited the room after saying a quick hello to her in passing. Once they were gone, she found herself wishing that she had asked them to stay for moral support. Not that they would be on her side, but she might need a buffer against Caleb. He was staring daggers at her.

She shifted from one foot to the other. He wasn't going to make this easy for her, was he?

"I'm sorry to crash your lunch, but I wanted to clear the air. I didn't like how we left things earlier."

Crickets. All he did was give her a slight nod.

She let out a ragged sigh. "Caleb, I know you're ticked off at me. And I don't blame you."

He folded his arms across his chest. It was the ultimate defensive gesture. Ugh. She had a battle on her hands.

"I got a little carried away this morning, so I came back to sincerely apologize. What you said earlier made me think about the fact that I wasn't considering how your time on the show affected you. Judging by the look on your face, that experience hurt you." Her chin quivered. "I know what it feels like to be hurt."

"Hurt people hurt people?" he asked, quirking his mouth.

"Umm, I guess so. I want our working relationship to be a good one, so we need to clear the air. I need to set things right."

"Go for it," he said, leaning back in his chair.

"I talk too much when I get nervous. Hattie makes me nervous. Not that she's not amazing and delightful, but she's also a strong and successful businesswoman who has accomplished way more in her lifetime than I ever will. This opportunity to work for Yukon Cider is life-changing for me and my daughter. And that reality stressed me out." She crossed her hands in front of her and began to twist her thumbs around. Was she rambling? Nerves had taken over; she hoped that she was getting her point across without sounding pathetic.

She inhaled a deep breath. "And somehow all this time before I met you, I thought of you as a character and not a living, breathing human being. I know how wrong that was of me, because now that I know you just a little bit, I can see that you're nothing like the way you were portrayed. I sense that you're a good person and I should have kept my lips zipped."

Sophia noticed the instant his features softened. He was way less intimidating now.

"I like you," she blurted out. Oh, now that the words had slipped out of her mouth, she felt a little squirrelly. Their gazes were locked, and she noticed a slight twinkle in his eyes.

A slow grin began to spread across his face. "You like me?"

Heat suffused her cheeks. "Don't get all cocky about it, but I do. You're kind and funny. You were supportive when we were trapped in the attic. I watched you with Hattie at the tavern, and you were so sweet with her. And you remembered my daughter's name."

"You're definitely going to give me a swelled head." He was more relaxed now, reverting back to the warmhearted version of himself.

She moved closer toward him, closing the gap between them in a few easy strides.

"So, you forgive me?" she asked, her heart thumping wildly in her chest.

"Tell me again how amazing I am and I'll consider it," he said in a playful tone. Something had shifted between them in the last few moments, letting Sophia know that Caleb was softening up toward her. Her chest loosened up a bit, and her pulse slowed down. Maybe she wasn't toast after all.

"I think I've said enough for one day," she answered.

Caleb stood up so that he was facing her, their bodies mere inches away from each other. He was standing so close to her that she could hear the sound of his light breathing. Her gaze found his mouth, and for what felt like the millionth time, she wondered what it might feel like to kiss those amazing lips. She suspected it would be some kind of wonderful.

"I forgive you, Sophia Brand. Everyone makes mistakes." He leaned in closer. "And now that I know you like me..."

Her stomach was fluttering, and she almost felt like a

teenager in the presence of her first crush. "You're not going to let that one go, are you?" she asked.

"Nope," he said, showcasing his dimples as he smiled. "I'm having way too much fun with it. I might just have a T-shirt made."

Sophia giggled. She was so relieved that things were back on track with them. "I'd pay actual money to see you sporting a shirt like that."

His lips twitched. "Don't tempt me."

"I should let you get back to work." Although she could stand here all day and talk to him, they both had things to do. Today was Lily's early day at preschool, and she didn't want to be late picking her up. She had memories of being the last kid picked up at school, and she never wanted Lily to feel that way.

He reached out for her hand, taking it in his. "Thanks for stopping by. It means a lot to me that you cared enough to seek me out."

"I owed you an apology," she said, meeting his gaze head-on. He had the most beautiful eyes. They were the deepest shade of brown with gold flecks. Her insides were rejoicing at the way he was looking at her. Not with anger, but with admiration.

"And by the way, Sophia, I like you too. But I'm guessing you already knew that."

Bam! His words were like a jump start to the heart. If she was being completely honest with herself, Caleb was a clear and present danger to her carefully curated world.

Ever since having Lily, she had constructed a life for herself based simply on the two of them. Men need not apply! She was good on her own. But that was then and this was now. Caleb intrigued her, and she wanted to peel back his layers. She wanted to see what was possible!

What was it about this man that caused her to get tongue-tied in his presence? She thought of a dozen snappy come-backs, but not a single word emerged from her mouth. So instead Sophia gave him a little smile and beat a fast path out of the room.

Even though she could feel his eyes trained on her as she walked down the corridor, Sophia reminded herself not to turn around. DO NOT TURN AROUND.

Play it cool.

Just as she reached the stairs, Sophia gave in to tempta-tion and glanced over her shoulder.

Caleb was leaning against the doorjamb with his arms folded. She could see his grin from all the way down the hall.

No matter what she'd thought before about possibly get-ting involved with Caleb, Sophia now knew with a deep cer-tainty that she wanted to explore things with him, no matter where they led.

CHAPTER EIGHT

Clearly, winter weather wasn't quite done with Moose Falls. The fluffy white stuff had left a snowy covering all over town. Caleb wasn't used to driving over snow-covered Alaskan roads, but nothing was going to get in the way of his coffee date with Sophia at the Charmed café. Maybe "date" was the wrong word to use. Meetup? Caleb wanted it to be a date, but he was still testing the waters with Sophia. Ever since their face-to-face last week when she'd apologized to him, thoughts of Sophia hadn't been far from his mind.

The café was located in the heart of the main downtown area. He pulled up in front of a pink gingerbread-style house that looked as if it had come straight out of a storybook. Even the windows had colorful shutters that brought to mind Hansel and Gretel.

Once he walked inside, the smell of baked goods and coffee assailed his senses. The aromas were tantalizing, making him observe that he was hungrier than he'd realized. Or maybe it was just the heavenly aromas swirling around the establishment. A brick hearth boasted a roaring fire.

Caleb quickly realized that Sophia had beat him to the café. She was sitting at a table waving at him. She couldn't have looked any more vibrant in a poppy-colored peacoat and a jaunty black beret. She stood up when he reached the table, and they shared a quick hug. He inhaled the light fragrance that clung to Sophia.

"This is a nice spot," Caleb said, looking around after they both sat down. The interior was cozy with pictures of fairy-tale stories hanging on the walls. The colors were bright and warm.

"It's new," Sophia told him. "Owned and operated by my good friend Vincent Loupin. He's so creative." She gestured toward the menu. "What do you want? It's my treat as part of the apology tour."

"That's not necessary," Caleb said. "I invited you."

Sophia winked at him. "Vincent gives me a pretty good discount, so just go with it."

Caleb held up his hands. "Okay, it's your treat. Now I just have to decide what to order." He picked up the menu and began looking it over. "I love these fancy names for the drinks. Merry Matcha. Lover's Latte. Ever After Espresso." He let out a chuckle. "Someone has a great imagination."

"Well, thank you very much," a thickly accented voice said. "I'm the owner, Vincent." A tall, balding man in his mid-thirties stood next to their table, smiling broadly.

"I'm Caleb. Caleb Stone," he said, introducing himself.

Vincent's eyes lit up. "Hattie's grandson? It's a pleasure to meet any relation of Hattie. I'm a huge fan of hers."

"If I had a dollar for every time I've heard that since I arrived in Moose Falls, I'd be a rich man," Caleb said. "Is that a French accent I hear?"

"Oui," Vincent said with an amiable smile. "I'm from a small town in the south of France. La Gaude. I came to

Alaska about five years ago, and only some months ago opened up this café. My life's dream."

"It's a wonderful place, Vincent," Sophia gushed. "Wait till you try les patisseries, Caleb. The croissants are to die for." She closed her eyes and let out a moan of appreciation.

"Merci, Sophia," Vincent said. "I'm grateful for your patronage."

He knew from his high school French that *patisseries* meant baked goods. Other than that he was lost with the language. He did believe that everything sounded better when spoken in French.

"You don't have to tell me twice. The moment I walked in, the aroma nearly brought me to my knees." Caleb sniffed the air. "If you could bottle this scent, people would line up to buy it."

Vincent nodded at Caleb. "I like your style. Let me know if I can help you with the menu. Sophia here is an expert, so you're in good hands."

"He's nice," Caleb said once Vincent had walked away. "Loads of personality. And creativity. It takes a lot of courage to open a new business, especially these days."

"He's the best," Sophia said. "I hope this place takes off with the locals. He'll be crushed if it doesn't."

"I've got a good feeling about it. I'll spread the word at Yukon Cider to my colleagues. They'll fill this place up fast."

"That would be wonderful," Sophia said. "I'm going to slip Hattie his card so she can use his services for any upcoming events she might be hosting. He has a full-service catering menu."

Caleb chuckled. "Are you sure you're not his business partner? You're really hustling for him." He liked seeing Sophia stepping out and doing a good deed to help someone else. It told him a lot about the woman he was just getting acquainted with. Vincent was a small-business owner who could use the boost to his business.

"So, what looks good to you?" Sophia asked. "I'm eyeing the gingerbread swirl latte and the chocolate croissant."

"This is a tough choice," Caleb said, frowning as he studied the menu. "I'm just going to bite the bullet. I could stare at this menu all day." He stroked his jaw. "How about I try the cinnamon mocha cappuccino and the sourdough doughnut?"

She gave him an approving nod. "Great choices." She turned to wave at the waitress, who quickly came over and took their order.

"I've got something for you," Caleb said, leaning over and reaching into the bag he'd brought with him. He had wrapped the Leica in tissue paper and a soft blanket with an abundance of caution. A little research had shown him that the camera was a rare piece that sold for a great deal of money. He wanted to make sure he handed it over to Sophia in one piece.

She let out a gasp of surprise mixed with joy as he handed the camera over. "Here's your baby. Why don't you take the bag as well? For safekeeping."

Sophia reached for the camera, her movements gentle as she ran her hand over the Leica. She looked through the lens as a huge smile broke out on her face. It was evident to him that she was handling the camera with love and care. She still seemed in awe that Hattie had given her such a precious gift. It was apparent that she would treat it with reverence. Hattie must have known Sophia would deeply appreciate the gift, because as much as Hattie treasured the memory of her precious husband, she had gifted Sophia with his camera. Once she'd lovingly inspected the Leica, Sophia wrapped it back up and gently placed it back in the bag.

"Thanks for reuniting me with this," she said. "If you can't tell, I'm over the moon about it. Some girls love Louis Vuitton purses, but I'm all about vintage cameras."

"So, what led you into photography?" he asked. As someone who had a creative side himself, he was always fascinated with origin stories. He wanted to know everything he possibly could about Sophia. Her likes. Dislikes. What made her tick.

"It was the only thing I was ever any good at," she said.

Caleb rolled his eyes. "That's doubtful."

"No, seriously, my dad was the one who stumbled upon an amazing camera, a Nikon. He owned a vintage store, and cameras were always big sellers. This particular one was a beauty." She let out a low whistle. "I fell in love with it, and rather than selling it, my dad gifted it to me for Christmas." Her face lit up at the memory. "If you had seen me open that box up on Christmas morning, you would have known that at that moment I was the happiest little girl in the world. Ten years old and I had my own Nikon. It still gives me goose bumps."

Just then their order was delivered to their table. Steaming mugs of coffee were placed in front of them, filling their space with heady aromas. They both dug into their baked goods. Caleb had never had a sourdough doughnut before, but this was delicious. He was discovering that sourdough was a thing in Alaska. Sourdough bread in particular was a regular staple here.

"Mmm. Good, huh?" Sophia asked after taking a bite of her croissant.

"Delicious," he agreed, blowing on his coffee before taking a sip. "So when do you start at Yukon Cider? I'm looking forward to being in front of the camera."

"I start on Monday, and from what Hattie told me, she

wants us to get started right away. I would love your input on some brainstorming I've been doing. I want to do a lot of outdoor shots to take advantage of the gorgeous Alaskan landscape."

"I like the idea of a natural setting. Maybe by the mountains or the falls," he suggested. "We took my mom on a hike near the mountains, and all I can say is it was pretty incredible."

"That's what I was thinking as well," Sophia said, excitement laced through her voice. "Hattie gave me some information about the new campaign. This cider is going to be like nothing on the market. All natural."

Caleb was excited about the idea of the campaign being successful. "I'm hoping to help knock this one out of the park. I really want to make a contribution at Yukon Cider." He didn't want to take anything for granted. This was an amazing opportunity for him to prove his worth.

"Are you enjoying working at the company? Is it in your wheelhouse?" Sophia asked.

"I'm actually surprised by how much I'm enjoying it. I've never done anything like this before. I never felt particularly good at anything growing up. Xavier had sports. Landon had the laboratory. And I didn't really have anything until I tried out for *Romeo and Juliet* in middle school."

"Let me guess. You won the part of Romeo."

"Oh, no. That went to my best friend, Hal. I got the part of Tybalt, and if I may say so, I ate that role up. The acting bug bit me, and ever since then it's been my passion."

She knitted her brows together. "So how did you end up on reality television?"

A sigh slipped past his lips. "Rodney, my agent, thought it would be a great stepping stone. He believed that America would fall in love with me, and I could write my ticket in

Hollywood." He let out a snort. "Here I was imagining myself as the next Michael B. Jordan, when in reality that show sank my credibility and made me a laughingstock."

"That's tough," Sophia said, her eyes radiating compassion. "Is it still a passion of yours?"

"Yes," Caleb admitted. "I tried for a long time to get acting gigs, but it never went my way. Now, after being on *Love Him or Leave Him*, nobody wants to even give me a shot at auditioning. But, honestly, I still harbor the dream of being a working actor." He ran a hand over his jaw. "I can't seem to let it go."

"Maybe being the focus of this campaign will change things for you. Repping Yukon Cider will put you out there in a new light." Sophia was nodding at him from across the table as if it weren't a fantastical thing for him to aspire to.

That was Caleb's hope. If the campaign and product took off, Caleb might gain a little traction in the entertainment world. If he did a good job, who knew where this could lead? He tried not to dream too big or allow his mind to wander to a life in California as an actor. Caleb knew it was a long shot, but stranger things had happened. Who would have thought that Xavier would become an NFL player and win the Super Bowl with his teammates?

Dreams, as his mother often said, were hopes wrapped up in ambitions.

Why shouldn't he continue to hope for all of his Hollywood dreams to come true? Honestly, it was all he had ever truly wanted. Sometimes it seemed as if he'd been born with this particular dream etched on his heart.

"And you…what do you dream about, Sophia?" he asked, hoping for another glimpse into her heart and mind.

"Well, I love what I do. This chance to work for Yukon Cider is beyond my wildest dreams. Being able to make a wonderful life for my daughter is pretty high on my list."

The tenderness laced in her voice was telling. A mother's love for their child was like no other.

"Something tells me you've already created an amazing world for Lily." He reached across the table and squeezed her hand. Caleb sensed that Sophia worried a lot about Lily. His mind flashed back to the moment in the attic when she'd burst into tears at the idea of not making it back home to her daughter. Caleb just knew that Sophia was an incredible, caring mother.

Sophia ducked her head and focused on the table. When she finally drew her head up, he spotted a sheen of moisture in her eyes. "Thanks for saying that. As a single mother I'm always questioning if I'm doing right by her."

"Is she a happy kid?"

"Yes, I think so." Sophia crinkled her nose. "She likes to laugh a lot. And she's super funny and smart."

"If she's happy, then you're doing loads of things right," Caleb said. "And I was raised by a single mom. And look at how I turned out," he said, playfully puffing out his chest.

Sophia giggled. "Daisy did a great job with her three sons. She's an inspiration to me."

"I come from a long line of outstanding women," Caleb acknowledged. He considered himself privileged to share blood ties with them.

Forty minutes later he and Sophia were saying their goodbyes outside on the sidewalk. Sophia stood up to give him a hug goodbye and the soft tendrils of her hair brushed across his face. His stomach started doing flips and bounces. He very much wanted to kiss her, wanted to pull her against him and press his lips against hers. But they were in broad daylight with town residents rushing by all around them. Life was all about timing.

He took a step toward her so that there was very little

space between them. Caleb was feeling so good about Sophia at this moment. He wanted to stretch out their time together as much as possible. She was looking up at him with a certain brightness in her eyes that made him think she wanted to be kissed. One step closer and their bodies would be touching. He reached out and brushed his palm across her cheek. Caleb was within a hair's breadth of placing his lips on hers. It was becoming harder and harder for him to remember his vow to not become embroiled in a romantic relationship.

At the moment the urge to lock lips with Sophia was more potent than anything else.

No, he would wait until the time was right. When he didn't have a single doubt in his mind that kissing Sophia was something they both wanted and needed. And when that moment came, he had the feeling it just might be like fireworks in December.

The moment had quickly passed during which Sophia had believed that Caleb was mere seconds away from kissing her. Her face heated at the memory of how she'd turned her face upward in anticipation of the kiss. She had been ready, willing, and able to lock lips with him. Rather than lay one on her, Caleb had stepped back and told her that he would see her on Monday.

Talk about feeling deflated. She didn't think she had ever been as disappointed in her life! It had been ages since she had enjoyed a wonderful kiss, and every instinct told her that Caleb was an amazing kisser. Those lips of his didn't lie. Sophia burst out laughing at the direction of her thoughts. This is what happened to a person when they went too long without romance in their life.

Over coffee and treats at Charmed, Sophia had found out a lot about Caleb. Being on the reality show had clearly been a misstep, one that continued to affect him. And it wasn't fair that Caleb had been made to feel as if his dreams couldn't come to fruition simply because of a reality show that had presented a slanted view of him.

"That's okay, Caleb. You're going to be a rock star by the time I'm through with you," Sophia said. She felt such a burst of confidence about shooting Caleb and him being the star of the ad campaign. She knew from having watched him on television that the camera loved him.

There was nothing she loved more than a challenge when she was doing photo shoots. Bringing people out of their shells, making a plain person pop on film, creating magic out of the ordinary. But Caleb was extraordinary, and with the right setting and wardrobe, he could really take off as a brand ambassador. With his looks and personality, he would do well in commercials and interviews. It had been a burst of genius from Hattie to pick Caleb as the spokesman. For a woman who was counting down her days, Hattie Stone wasn't resting on her laurels. She was continuing to make an impact.

Just getting her grandsons to come back to Moose Falls after a twenty-year absence had been miraculous. And everyone in town wanted to give her a standing ovation for bringing three of the hottest men in creation to Alaska. Sophia tried to keep her sadness at bay at the reality that their return wouldn't completely be a happily-ever-after. Hattie was slipping away from them, more and more with every passing day.

I'm dying, but I'm still living. Hattie's motto came to mind, serving as a reminder that Hattie still had a lot of living to do. Sophia totally wanted to be a badass like Hattie when she grew up. She wished that she could be more like her—fearless and bold.

When she pulled up in front of her house, she was surprised to find Donny standing by his parked car. She had no idea what he was doing here, unannounced and unwanted. Sophia groaned as she stepped out of her vehicle. This day had started out so well, but now it had taken an unpleasant turn. Nothing good ever came from Donny's surprise visits.

"Donny. What are you doing here?" she asked as she walked toward him.

"Aren't you going to invite me in? It's cold out here." Donny flashed her a dazzling smile, the same one that had caused Sophia to fall head over heels in love with him. Lily had the same stunning smile on a heart-shaped face.

"You can come in, but I need to pick up Lily soon at her playdate."

"Well, that's what I want to talk to you about. Lily."

Something about his expression told Sophia he was serious about whatever had brought him here. She turned toward her house and walked down the snow-covered path until she reached her front porch. Donny trailed behind her, his feet making a shuffling sound in the snow. Once she was inside, Sophia ushered Donny in and led him toward the den.

She looked at her watch. "I would offer to make you some tea, but I've barely got ten minutes before I need to get on the road."

Donny sank down into a leather chair while Sophia sat in the matching love seat next to him. "What's going on? You mentioned Lily," she said, waiting with bated breath for him to speak.

He fiddled with his hands and let out a nervous cough. "I-I want to set up a formal custody agreement with you."

"We already have one, Donny," she said with a sigh.

"And the majority of the time you don't honor it. I had to stop even telling Lily you were coming to get her so her little heart wouldn't get broken when you didn't show up."

Donny winced. "I hate that I did that to her, but that's all in the past now. Lily and I had a great time together, and I want more moments like that with my daughter."

"Well, start showing up when you're supposed to," she snapped. "That would be a good start."

"I want joint custody, Sophia."

BAM! His words exploded like fireworks.

"What?" she shouted, thinking she must have misheard him. "You've got to be kidding me!"

He clenched his teeth. "I'm serious. I want to make a commitment to our daughter."

"Wh-where is this coming from?" she sputtered. "You've barely spent any time with her at all, and now all of a sudden you want joint custody."

"I don't want to miss out on any more of her life. It may seem hard to believe, but I'm being sincere."

Sophia shook her head, filled with disbelief. "This isn't a game, Donny."

"I've retained an attorney, Sophia. If nothing else, that should show you that I'm serious."

She couldn't believe his nerve. All this time and she had never once resorted to retaining an attorney. Not when he'd missed child support payments or bailed on visitation. Yet now, out of the blue, he was making demands and throwing down the gauntlet.

"I-I think you should leave my house," she said, gritting her teeth.

"Sophia, let's not make this adversarial—" he began.

"Stop trying to gaslight me!" She jumped up from her seat, clenching her hands into fists at her side. "That sailed out the door when you went to consult an attorney before having the decency to talk to me first."

"I had every right to talk to an attorney," Donny said.

"All the times I've shown you grace, and this is how you repay me? By making demands and threatening me with legal action?"

Sophia stormed toward the front door and wrenched it open. "Go, Donny. Leave. Right now. I don't want to talk to you. I mean it." The tone of her voice brooked no argument. He knew she wasn't playing around.

Donny walked over the threshold and out of the house. After walking a few feet away, he turned around and said, "This isn't over, Sophia. Lily's my daughter, and I have rights that I fully intend to exercise."

She went back into the house and slammed the door, dissolving into tears as soon as she was alone. Donny had sounded serious about seeking joint custody. She had never imagined this day would come. And she couldn't imagine sharing custody with Donny. He was irresponsible and completely undependable. He knew nothing about Lily's daily routine, the names of her best friends, or her favorite stuffed animals. Donny had been breezing in and out of her life ever since the day she was born.

What was behind this sudden desire to be more present in Lily's life? Shared custody? If it wasn't such a serious situation, she might laugh at his audacity. She didn't even know where to go from here. Should she retain legal counsel to advise her? Not that she could afford it, at least until she started her new position with Yukon Cider. Maybe this was just a passing fancy with Donny. All she could do was hope that in a few days he would reverse course and drop this nonsensical plan.

Leave it to her ex to ruin a perfectly nice day.

CHAPTER NINE

Monday morning dawned bright and beautiful. Streams of light trickled through Caleb's bedroom window, gently waking him up so he could greet the day head-on. He wasn't sure that he would ever get used to the sight of the majestic mountain peaks looming in the distance. He had to hand it to Alaska. The views were spectacular. After a quick shower and getting dressed, he headed down to breakfast. Sitting down for a meal with his brothers and Hattie was always a highlight of the day.

"What do you look so chipper for?" Xavier asked as Caleb sailed into the dining room in a burst of energy and excitement for what lay ahead.

"It's going to be a wonderful day," Caleb announced. "I'm going to be Yukon Cider famous." He grinned at his brothers as he ran a hand along his jaw.

"Don't get ahead of yourself," Xavier said, shaking his head. "That's when things go wrong. Trust me on that."

"I was joking," Caleb said. "Where's your sense of humor? Lighten up a little."

"I'm good," Xavier said. "Just be careful not to get an inflated ego over being in the spotlight."

He knew exactly what Xavier meant. Caleb was aware that he'd gotten a little too gassed up about himself after being cast on *Love Him or Leave Him*. He had been of the belief that his star was on the rise and nothing could stop him. It had all come to a grinding halt when the show aired and he was vilified by the public. His reputation had been in tatters. And he had never quite recovered and restored what he'd lost.

"I'm curious. Did you get enough beauty rest last night?" Landon asked, unable to hide his smirk.

"Actually, I did. I used one of those face masks before bed and then I put on a gel eye mask. I'm also trying out this hydrating moisturizer. I think it's going to become my new routine," Caleb said, filling his plate with fruit and protein. He didn't want to feel stuffed to the gills for the photo shoot. If he'd had a few more weeks to prepare, he would have hit the gym a few times a week. They were just test shots, but still, he wanted to make a good impression.

"Look at you," Xavier said, "Caleb Stone. Alaska's next top model."

Landon chuckled along with Xavier.

"Laugh all you want, but this is exciting for me," Caleb admitted. "It's a chance to get back to doing what I love. I can't tell you guys how much I've missed it."

"We're happy for you, Caleb," Landon said. "It's nice to see you smiling the way you used to before you were on the show."

Xavier grinned at him. "That's right. We won't ever stop rooting for you, Caleb. We always want to see you shine. You're going to rock this campaign."

"I hope to make all of you proud, including Mom," Caleb said. "I already miss her."

"She's been proud of you since the day you were born, Caleb," Xavier said. "She would be proud of you if you ran butt naked through Moose Falls."

"Don't give me any ideas," Caleb said, causing his brothers to burst into a fit of laughter. Within seconds they were all letting out belly laughs and clutching their sides. Caleb wiped his eyes with his sleeve as his laughter subsided.

"So, I hate to get heavy, but I think we should all check in. Any thoughts on what to do with our inheritance?" Xavier asked, his gaze narrowed as he looked back and forth between them. "I'm good with both scenarios since I'll be permanently living here with True."

"I'm on the fence. It's too soon for me to make an ethical decision," Landon told them. "It hasn't been lost on me that Yukon Cider is our legacy." He shrugged. "But I'm a scientist."

Caleb was taking it all in. Being in Moose Falls was complicated. So far he was enjoying the experience and soaking in the wonderful aspects of Alaska. But he had no clue as to what they should do. "I need more time," he admitted. "My natural inclination is to sell, but like Landon said, it's so tied up with Hattie. I can't imagine letting go of all that."

"Hey, where is Hattie?" Landon asked, looking toward the door. "She's never late for breakfast."

"You're right. Maybe she's just sleeping in," Xavier said.

"Hattie? Not likely," Caleb said, reaching for his orange juice and swigging the last of it down.

Soft footsteps heralded the arrival of Jacques, who quickly made his way over to them.

"Good morning, gentlemen. Hattie isn't feeling that well this morning, so she wanted the three of you to head off without her," Jacques announced.

"Oh, no," Landon said. "What's wrong? Should we call her doctor?"

Xavier jumped up from his seat. "Should we go see her?"

Jacques waved his hand at them. "Let's not get ahead of ourselves. Your grandmother is terminally ill, and she's going to have ups and downs. She won't want any of you to make a fuss." He made a face. "You know Hattie."

Caleb sighed. "Yes, we do. She probably told you to minimize whatever's going on. Am I right?" Hattie was the type of person who had probably denied being in labor when she was ten centimeters dilated. She didn't like a fuss being made over her. Celebrating her birthday was the one exception. On that occasion they had been allowed to throw her a party with gifts and cupcakes.

"If I thought she needed medical attention, I wouldn't hesitate to tell you," Jacques said, convincing them in a matter of seconds that he wasn't withholding crucial information. All three of them knew that he was an honorable man. He was motivated by his love for their grandmother and a deep sense of integrity. Caleb thought that his brothers, much like himself, couldn't rid their minds of the image of Hattie passing out a couple months ago during a reception at the mayor's mansion. It had been their first rude awakening about the unpredictability of her illness. Despite her putting on a good act, they all realized she was rapidly declining.

"I'm going to bring her some tea and try to get her to eat some scrambled eggs and toast," Jacques said as he turned on his heel and headed straight toward the kitchen.

Once Jacques left the dining room, a hushed silence descended over them.

"I don't know why I always forget what brought us here," Caleb said, pushing his plate way from him. His appetite was gone, decimated by the news about Hattie.

"I know what you mean," Landon said. "Obviously we

came due to the inheritance and Hattie's situation, but it seems impossible that she won't be around a year from now."

Xavier frowned. "A year? It could be six months or less. We don't know what the future holds with regard to her health. I think that's what Jacques was getting at." He ran a hand over his face and let out a deep breath. "It's time we started having more discussions about Yukon Cider and where we see things going. We can't wait until the year's up to decide."

"But what if we aren't sure?" Landon asked. "This could change the entire course of our lives."

"I think it already has," Caleb said, thinking about Xavier's engagement to True, their bond with their long-lost grandmother, and having their father back in their lives.

At the moment it felt as if things were moving quickly in Moose Falls. Their contract with Hattie stipulated that they must stay in Moose Falls for a period of one year and learn the ropes at Yukon Cider. More than five months had passed, leaving them with less than seven months to make an earth-shattering decision.

If he voted to stay and run the company, all of his Hollywood dreams would evaporate. He couldn't pursue an acting career from Moose Falls. But he would be with his brothers, which was the best part of returning to Alaska. And there was Sophia. Sweet, gorgeous Sophia. She was a definite inducement for sticking around. On the other hand, selling Yukon Cider would provide financial independence and give him a pathway to a life in California.

Frankly, he was just as confused as he'd been on the first day he arrived in Alaska. And he still had no idea how he was going to come to a decision.

As Monday rolled around, Sophia couldn't be more excited for her first test shoot for Yukon Cider's new campaign. Lily was staying with her grandfather today, as she did twice a week, so after dropping her off with G-pop, Sophia headed straight to work, doing her best to decompress by absorbing the beautiful landscape that she drove past. She would never get used to the jaw-dropping sights Alaska provided. Sophia cranked up the radio and mellowed out to Adele ballads.

Just breathe in and out. Relax. Rid your mind of the yucky stuff. Today is going to be a wonderful day. She repeated these mantras over and over again until they sank in.

Today was going to be a wonderful day, and she was going to greet it with positivity and clarity. She was going to be spending time with Caleb, which was a win-win for her. She had never imagined that she would like this man so much after hating his guts on television. There was a disconnect between the man he'd been portrayed as and the man he was in actuality. She knew it with every fiber of her being. Caleb Stone was a good man. And she hoped with all her might that this campaign took off and Caleb got some of his good name back. If she could do anything to help him soar, she would do it in a heartbeat.

As she was discovering, Caleb was a special man, and she hadn't had much special in a long time. If ever. Lily was the magic fairy dust in her life, but she yearned for something romantic, something real. It wouldn't be enough for her to venture into a relationship that was purely physical. She'd done that in her younger years and come to deeply regret it. Her relationship with Donny had leaned on the physical as well, which had resulted in Lily. Although she hadn't been planned and Donny hadn't stuck around, Lily was the absolute love of her life.

Once she arrived at Yukon Cider, Sophia discovered that she had her own office on the second floor, complete with her name on the door and a fresh bouquet of flowers sitting on her desk. Her pulse raced as she read the card. *Looking forward to working with you. Don't forget to make me look good. Caleb.*

At this point she couldn't wait to make her way downstairs to the space they had set up as a studio for today's test shoot. Although she was accustomed to working solo, she'd been surprised to be given a team to work with. Sophia had told Hattie she didn't need a producer since that was a job she wanted to perform herself. Video production was in her skill set, and she was confident about her abilities. Having a team was an added bonus that she hadn't been expecting.

When she walked in the studio, her eyes went straight to Caleb. *Good golly, Miss Molly.* He was looking like the sweetest Alaskan eye candy. He was wearing a nicely fitting pair of charcoal-colored slacks and an oatmeal-colored sweater that accentuated his rugged physique. Caleb was fine! No wonder he'd been the final man standing on *Love Him or Leave Him.* Could she really blame the twins for falling for him?

She immediately walked over to Caleb and greeted him. "Hey, Hollywood. Looks like you got your beauty rest last night. Thanks for the flowers," she added. "It was a nice way to welcome me to Yukon Cider."

"You're very welcome. It's a great place to work, and everyone is excited you're coming on board. Hattie has been shouting it from the rooftops."

Hearing that made Sophia feel good. Especially since she held Hattie in such high esteem. It was like getting the golden stamp of approval from the head honcho.

"So, are you ready to go viral?" Sophia asked. She had

a gut feeling that Caleb would blow up as the spokesman for Yukon Cider. The product was gaining in popularity, and with Caleb's looks and personality, he was destined to take the company to greater heights. And along the way, Caleb would find himself getting tons of publicity and shine.

Caleb crinkled his nose. "As long as it's in a good way this time. I definitely don't want to go viral for being in a love triangle. Been there, done that," he said, rolling his eyes.

Although Caleb was trying to make a joke of his past, he had already let her see how deeply affected he had been by his appearance on the reality show. She suspected his wounds ran deep. His coping mechanism was to act self-deprecating about it at times.

"I think natural colors would work with your complexion and the setting. Why don't we go for the taupe and the cream? We're just doing some test shots today so we can play around with a few concepts."

While Caleb changed into his first outfit for the indoor shots, Sophia checked and rechecked her camera to make sure she had everything perfectly lined up.

Her mood was a bit muted due to the issues with Donny. She had thought about his visit all weekend, asking herself what had prompted his unexpected decision. On some level she knew he loved Lily, but he had never expressed a single desire to actively raise her. This sudden reversal was mind-boggling. And concerning. It made her stomach clench up just thinking about being separated from Lily. For the last four years it had been the two of them against the world. Honestly, it wouldn't be easy to be accommodating to a man who wasn't even paying child support, but she would do so if it was in the best interest of her child.

Shake it off! She needed to strut her stuff today and showcase her skills so Hattie would see she had made the right choice in hiring her. When Caleb returned from the changing room, Sophia gave him a nod of approval. Although she couldn't imagine him not appearing attractive, at the moment he looked amazing. The clothing fit him like a glove. Taupe cords, a V-neck cardigan, and a pair of Timberland boots. He had the requisite swagger to totally pull off this photo shoot and elevate the Yukon Cider brand.

"Looking good, Hollywood," she said, giving him a thumbs-up sign.

"Thanks. You've got a good eye for clothes," Caleb said. "This is an outfit I want to own."

"Ready to rock and roll?" she asked.

"I was born ready," he quipped, winking at Sophia.

She let out a groan. "Come on. You can do better than that."

"Let's go," Caleb said. "I'll put my money where my mouth is."

"Save some of this energy for the shoot," Sophia said, getting into photographer mode as she told Caleb where to stand for the first batch of pictures.

"That's it," Sophia said as she took photo after photo. "Put your chin down, eyes looking up. Awesome," she said, excited at what she was seeing. Caleb was a natural. He exuded raw sex appeal while at the same time projecting a laid-back, natural vibe.

She had to give it to Caleb. A lot of her subjects, even professional models, got tired of the repetitive nature of photo shoots. Caleb was a pro. His hundredth photo was as sharp as the first one.

Toward the end of the shoot, Hattie crept into the room, clearly trying to make a discreet entrance. She stood on the sidelines, proudly watching her grandson's every move. Her face lit up like sunshine, even though her complexion seemed a bit pale. Sophia thought it might just be the sweetest thing she had ever seen. She knew her dad looked at Lily in the exact same manner.

"Okay, I think that's a wrap for this session," Sophia said. "Time for a break, Caleb. Why don't you get some water in the break room?"

Hattie appeared at her side, shaking her head as if in amazement.

"Imagine being that good looking. God took extra time with that one," Hattie said, gazing adoringly in Caleb's direction.

"Hard to imagine," Sophia quipped. She knew better than to argue the point with Hattie. As it was, the older woman wasn't wrong.

Hattie locked eyes with her. "Did I tell you there's no policy against employees dating?"

Sophia chuckled. Leave it to Hattie to brighten her mood and make her laugh out loud. "Yes, Hattie. You sure did."

"Caleb is as single as a dollar bill," Hattie added, a gleam twinkling in her eye.

"Is he?" Sophia asked, trying to keep a straight face. Hattie was all kinds of adorable when she wore her matchmaker hat.

"Just like you, in case I missed something." Hattie's gaze was steely and unwavering.

"Nope. You haven't missed a thing." As if Hattie didn't know everything there was to know about every single resident of Moose Falls. She was always privy to all the goings-on in Moose Falls. She suspected it was because Hattie was old-school Moose Falls, having been born and bred here. The older woman was trustworthy and solid. She'd also put their small town on the map with Yukon Cider.

She tapped a finger to her chin. "If I didn't know any

better, I would think you're trying to play matchmaker. Or maybe you just want all of your grandsons to fall for locals and stay permanently in Moose Falls."

"Who, me?" Hattie asked, pressing her hand to her chest. "I would never."

"Wouldn't you, though?" Sophia asked, shaking her head. She wasn't certain, but she recalled hearing that Hattie had done a little matchmaking between Xavier and True. She was probably gloating on the inside about their engagement.

"What's cooking over here?" Caleb asked as he walked up to them. "The two of you look as if you're hatching some sort of plot."

"Never ask two ladies what they're discussing in private. Didn't Daisy teach you that? You might get your feelings hurt." With a smirk Hattie walked off, leaning heavily on her cane.

Caleb's gaze trailed after her. "I should have known better than to ask. Sometimes I feel like a fly walking right into the spider's web."

Sophia chuckled at the image of Caleb as a fly and Hattie as a spider.

"You need to bring your A game to deal with Hattie."

"I know that's right." Caleb shrugged. "And she wasn't even feeling well this morning. Imagine if she was in tip-top shape?" Caleb winced.

Sophia frowned. Although she had been noticing signs of wear and tear on Hattie, it was par for the course for someone in her condition. It was a bit sobering to hear she wasn't feeling well. Most of the time Sophia thought Hattie sucked it up and put on a front for her family and friends. Being sick meant weakness to a woman like Hattie.

"I'm sorry to hear that," Sophia said. "And a bit surprised she came to the test shoot."

"I think she's making a point to show my brothers and me how much she cares about us while she can." She heard a little hitch of emotion in Caleb's voice. Sophia sensed he was grappling with Hattie's illness and coming to terms with the fact that the clock was ticking. Time wasn't on their side. "I really don't want to do a single thing to disappoint her as a spokesmodel."

"I don't think you have anything to worry about in that regard."

"Thanks for the vote of confidence," Caleb said.

"You've gotten close these last few months," she told him. She had noticed their tight bond at True and Xavier's engagement party. They seemed to get along like a house on fire. Objectively, she surmised that out of the three Stone brothers, Caleb was most like Hattie. They were both energetic extroverts who were at ease in social settings. Both had charismatic personalities. She found it interesting, since they'd been separated for the better part of two decades.

Caleb made a face. "We have. It seems unfair that for so long we were separated. I know it was hard for Hattie to come to us due to her dialysis and being ill, but I wonder why my mother wouldn't take us back home for short visits."

Home. He was now referring to Moose Falls as home, a development she found interesting. From what she had gleaned from True, the Stone brothers hadn't thought of Moose Falls as home in decades.

"Have you ever asked Daisy that question?" Sophia asked. From her brief encounter with Daisy Stone, Sophia sensed she was a loving yet resolute woman. Raising three boys on her own couldn't have been easy, and Daisy projected a little bit of Hattie's iron will. She wasn't a woman who would bend easily. "And not to pry, but maybe your parents' divorce was a bitter one."

"I used to ask questions all the time when we were kids," Caleb explained. "But now, as an adult, I know it's futile. She shuts down whenever we bring it up." He made a face. "Matter of fact, it just happened while she was here."

"You deserve answers. All of you do. I mean, it changed the course of your lives." She didn't want to overstep, but clearly Caleb was still affected by choices that had been made on his behalf.

"You're right about that."

There was a look in Caleb's eyes that let her know that this issue wasn't even close to being squashed. Caleb was struggling to get answers from his mother. And she had the feeling that he would be in limbo until he could get to the bottom of it.

"You did a great job today, Caleb. I'm really stoked about this campaign," Sophia told him. Her words lifted him to the stratosphere, giving him a feeling of confidence about his new role. Normally he didn't need a boost to feel good about himself, but ever since his reality show debacle, Caleb had allowed negative thoughts to creep into his head.

"Thanks, Sophia. It felt good to be in front of the camera again. I'm not sure why, but it always feels really natural." Every single time it felt as if a light bulb had been turned on inside him whenever cameras were around. He never felt shy or uncomfortable.

"Well, you come across as if you were born to do this. Come take a look." She waved him over to her side. "I know this isn't your first rodeo, but you really took to my instructions well. These test photos are pure gold."

Caleb moved closer to her and looked at the pictures she

brought up on her camera. As she flipped from one photo to the next, Caleb felt goose bumps pop up on his arms and neck.

"You're an amazing photographer," he said, awestruck. He knew that he was a good-looking guy, but Sophia had managed to capture him in the best light possible. And he didn't mean the actual light. She had pulled something out of him that really popped in the photos. He had taken many head shots in his time, but none had looked this professional.

"I'm only as good as my subjects," Sophia said. "Let's just say we make a great pair. I think Hattie is going to love these test photos and where the campaign is headed." Despite the positive words coming out of her mouth, her brow was furrowed, and there was a look of tension etched on her face.

"Hey, anything wrong?" Caleb asked. "Maybe it's not any of my business, but I don't like those little crinkles on your forehead."

"Just some personal stuff," she said curtly. Her mouth was set in a grim line that he wasn't sure he should try to cross.

Was this her way of telling him to stay in his lane? He was going to press on anyway. If there was any way he could help her, Caleb was committed to doing so.

Some of her team members, including her married assistants, Max and Laura Abbott, were still in the room, so he knew she might be reluctant to discuss anything personal. But he was going to ask anyway and let her know he cared.

"Anything you want to discuss? I'm a good listener." And he wasn't exaggerating. Since he had two brothers, Caleb was used to having his ear bent with their troubles. Between cheating fiancées and underhanded colleagues at work, Caleb had heard it all.

"I'm just frustrated. Lily's dad has been MIA for four-plus years." She began packing up her camera equipment, her movements jerky. "Trust me, he would never be a candidate for father of the year. He has a history of canceling his allotted weekends with Lily." She let out a snort. "And don't get me started on child support payments. If he ever cuts me a check, I'm going to pass out from shock."

"Sounds like a winner," Caleb spat out. Men like Sophia's ex made him angry. It wasn't fair that she had to shoulder the child raising all on her own with no support.

This issue was a little bit of a trigger to him due to his own father's parental neglect. At least Red had made regular child support payments. Money had never been the issue with Red's absence. Three boys going without a father was a recipe for disaster.

"On Saturday when I returned home from having coffee with you, Donny was in my driveway waiting for me." He could see a look of escalating tension on her face. "He informed me that he's retained an attorney in the hope of getting joint custody." She let out a strangled sound. "This from a man who barely sees his child and doesn't know the first thing about her likes and dislikes." Tears pooled in her eyes, and she tried to blink them away.

"Yet he wants joint custody!" she said, her voice raised. Several of her team members were still in the room and within earshot. They quickly packed up their belongings and made a fast path out of the room.

"And now I'm being unprofessional," she said, wiping tears from her cheeks and breathing heavily. It made his soul ache to see her so broken up about the situation. She had every right to be upset.

He placed his arm around her and pulled her close. Now, it was just the two of them in the space. He ached to do what he'd been wanting to do since the first time they'd met. Caleb wanted to kiss her as she'd never been kissed before.

"It's not unprofessional to be emotional," he told her. "Plus, the shoot is over. You're on a break."

"You're a sweetheart, Caleb. Has anyone ever told you that?" she asked, making a sniffling noise. Her eyes were a little red, but she couldn't have looked more beautiful in this moment. He gave her a lot of credit for showing her vulnerability.

"My mom says it several times a week," he said, smirking. He got just the reaction he wanted from Sophia. Her lips began to twitch, and a smile stretched across her face.

She placed her hands on his chest and threw her head back in laughter. "I walked right into that one, didn't I?" Suddenly, she was so close to him, tantalizingly close. She smelled like something sweet, a mix of flowers and vanilla. Maybe some sort of soap. Whatever it was, he just wanted to be near her, to immerse himself in this alluring scent.

"I don't know if this is the time or place, but—" he began, before being interrupted by Sophia.

"Kiss me, Caleb," she said, grabbing hold of his sweater and pulling him toward her so that he had easy access to her lips. Caleb dipped his head down and placed his lips over hers in a kiss that went from tender to fiery in an instant. Her lips were soft and supple. This kiss had been months in the making. He'd wanted to kiss Sophia ever since he first spotted her across the room in True's tavern.

It had been well worth the agonizing wait. He wasn't sure if his feet were still on the ground. He was soaring. Flying.

Sophia kissed him back fiercely, as if she too was feeling a sense of urgency. Want pulsed in the air between them. He felt a little bit frantic, as if they needed to make this connection in the here and now before anyone interrupted them. There had been so many moments that had passed through his fingers when he had wanted nothing more than to kiss her. Caleb encircled Sophia's waist with his hands and pulled her against him so that no space lay between them.

It wasn't until after the kiss ended that Caleb remembered that he'd promised himself not to allow his heart to overrule his head.

CHAPTER TEN

Kissing Caleb during work hours probably hadn't been the smartest move she had ever made, Sophia realized. On the other hand, she didn't regret doing so for a single second. She reached up and touched her lips. They still felt scorched by Caleb's kisses. Their moment of intimacy had been inevitable since they had begun circling around each other since the night of the engagement party. She found herself attracted to him in a way she'd never experienced before, and she didn't quite know what to do with herself.

Was something real brewing between them? Or was this just random stolen kisses spurred on by mutual attraction? What were Caleb's feelings on the matter? Was a kiss simply a kiss? Only this make-out session hadn't been ordinary in any way, shape, or form.

Relationships had always disappointed her. Not that she and Caleb were in a relationship or anything. They were simply feeling things out with each other. There was no sense in getting in over her head since she didn't even know if he was sticking around Moose Falls. By this time next year, he might be back in California chasing moonbeams and stardust.

I hope he stays. The thought came out of nowhere, surprising her with its intensity. She didn't want to get too attached to this man. He was a walking, talking embodiment of potential heartbreak.

Her mind was racing, and she couldn't seem to slow it down.

When it was time to head home, Sophia thought about stopping by Caleb's office to say goodbye, but nixed the idea. She already had Caleb on a nonstop rotation in her head. Why add to it? He might even start thinking she was assuming they were an item, and that could be embarrassing.

She knew that she was overthinking things, but being so out of practice with men was hampering her quite a bit.

When she pulled up to her house, she saw her father's car in the driveway, along with Patience's truck. It was thoughtful of her dad to finish the day at her home so she didn't have to go to his house, pack Lily up, drive home, and then start dinner. He truly was the sweetest man in the world. She didn't know what she had ever done to deserve such a loving father. Sometimes she wondered why her mother had been so eager to divorce such a wonderful man. According to Skip, she'd been looking for a more exciting romantic partner, which had always seemed like a choice one made in high school.

As soon as she opened the door to her house and stepped inside, the aroma of barbecue sauce made her weak in the knees. Her stomach grumbled noisily. Barbecued ribs. She would know the scent anywhere. Her father was literally an angel walking the Earth.

The sound of laughter led her straight to the playroom, where her father was playing the role of horsey while Lily rode on his back.

Sophia cleared her throat to announce her arrival. Her father looked up at her with a pained expression on his face. "Oh, thank God, you're here. One more round of this and I might end up in the ER."

"Horsey! Horsey!" Lily cried out as she held on to an invisible pair of reins.

"Lily, I think horsey needs a break, okay?" Sophia asked, bending down to scoop her up in her arms. "Where's Patience?" she asked, looking around the room for her sister.

"She's in the kitchen," Lily announced. "Do you smell the food she's making?"

"Okay, I'm going to go say hello to the chef," Sophia said. "Lily, do you want to come with me?"

"Yes, Mama," Lily said, vigorously nodding her head.

Sophia held out a hand and helped her father to a standing position. He winced as he stood up, then placed a hand on his lower back.

"Dad, next time she asks, just say no," Sophia instructed. At this rate her poor father was going to have spinal issues. "She's going to love you whether or not you play horsey."

"Okay, okay," he said, sounding annoyed. "This is the last time."

Sophia knew full well it wasn't going to be the last time. Lily had G-pop wrapped tightly around her finger. He would go to the moon and back for his special girl. Lily needed this type of devotion in the absence of a present and attentive father. Despite his newfound interest in his daughter, Donny hadn't shown a bit of devotion over the past four years.

When she walked into the kitchen, Patience was pulling open the stove and peering inside. "Almost ready," she crooned. She closed the oven door and turned toward Sophia. "Hey, lady. How was the first day at Yukon Cider?"

Sophia greeted her with a warm hug. "It was really good.

And coming home to ribs makes this an outstanding day. You had me thinking dad was cooking. It smells fabulous."

"Glad to hear your day went well," Patience said with a warm smile. "I wanted to treat you to a good meal since I know it must have been tough working with Caleb all day." Patience playfully stuck out her tongue.

Sophia dramatically wiped her brow with her arm. "It's tough work, but someone's got to do it," she said, letting out a wild laugh. Patience wiggled her brows and laughed along with her. Her sister had such an expressive face. On many occasions she'd thought Patience would have been a great actress.

"Who's Caleb?" Lily asked, her little brow furrowed.

Patience looked as if she was going to bust a gut laughing while Sophia struggled with being an adult and answering in a grown-up manner.

"He's someone Mommy works with," Sophia explained. "Miss Hattie's grandson."

"Tell her the truth," Patience whispered. "He's somebody that Mommy has the hots for."

"Mommy says it's rude to whisper," Lily said, sticking out her lip.

"I'm so sorry, bitsy," Patience said, bending down and tickling her. Lily burst into giggles, instantly forgetting her aunt's infraction.

"How soon is dinner?" Sophia asked. "I can set the table," she offered.

"It's about fifteen minutes to sheer perfection," Patience said. "I'm hovering by the oven so it doesn't overcook."

"Let me go upstairs and change out of my work clothes," Sophia said. She let out a groan. "I need to get comfy." Five minutes later she was back downstairs. Lily had her nose in a picture book while her father and Patience were sitting at the table drinking wine.

"Oh, a glass of wine would be wonderful right about now," Sophia said, sinking down into a chair. Just then the doorbell rang, causing all of them to stop what they were doing.

"Are you expecting anyone?" her dad asked, placing his wineglass down on the kitchen table.

"Not that I know of," she said, standing up to answer the door. "Let me go find out."

"Do you want me to answer it?" her dad asked, poised to get up from his chair.

"Just enjoy your wine, Daddio. I don't think it's a serial killer or anything," Sophia said, sharing a glance with Patience. They both knew their father was overprotective of them. He made a habit of supplying them with mace and signing them up for self-defense lessons.

Moose Falls had a very low crime rate, and she was more worried about an annoying neighbor than a criminal.

Without bothering to look out the window first, Sophia yanked the door open.

"Caleb!" she said, her voice coming out a little louder than she'd intended. He was standing at her doorstep wearing light washed jeans and a black peacoat and looking way more fine than any man had a right to look.

"Sophia," he said, saying her name like it was a caress. He smiled, showcasing his captivating dimples.

"What are you doing here? And how did you know where I live?" she asked, practically sputtering. She smoothed back her hair, suddenly wishing she hadn't scrubbed her face clean of every inch of foundation, mascara, and eyeliner.

"You left something at work," Caleb said, holding up her crimson-colored purse.

Her jaw dropped. She had left Yukon Cider so fast, only managing to grab her keys, her coat, and her saddlebag. "Oh my goodness. Thank you, Caleb. I can't believe I did that."

She let out an uneasy chuckle. "I was on autopilot when I left work, and I guess leaving my purse was the end result."

"One of the janitorial staff discovered it while cleaning your office. The staff at Yukon Cider are pretty incredible." He handed the purse over to her. "I didn't mean to intrude on your night, but have a good one."

"Wait," she said as he turned around to leave. "Are you hungry? Patience made ribs. The least I could do is feed you since you brought me back my purse. A woman's purse is pure gold." She waved him into her home.

Caleb grinned. "You had me at ribs," he said as he stepped inside.

Sophia's house was just as charming on the inside as it looked from the outside. What it lacked in size it made up for in coziness. From her yard one could catch a stunning glimpse of the lake area that was just beginning to thaw for spring. Heat embraced him as soon as he walked into Sophia's house. Lights were gleaming in every room. The corridor had family pictures hanging on the wall.

The smell of the ribs was enticing. He couldn't think of the last time he'd eaten some good down-home cooking. He hadn't known that ribs were a thing in Alaska, but from the aroma floating around Sophia's house, Patience knew how to throw down in the kitchen.

"Come in the kitchen and meet everyone," Sophia said, beckoning him as she walked toward the back of the house.

Everyone? He had no idea who everyone was, but he was hoping to meet her daughter. Caleb wanted to know every-thing about Sophia's world, and he knew Lily was at the center.

When they reached the kitchen, Caleb quickly scanned the room, noticing a little girl sitting in a breakfast nook playing with a doll. He spotted an older man at the stove while Patience was sitting at the table sipping from a goblet.

"Everyone, I'd like you to meet Caleb Stone," Sophia said by way of introduction. "Patience, the two of you have already met. Caleb, this is my dad, Skip Brand." Her father wiped his hands on his apron and stuck out his hand.

"Nice to meet any kin of Hattie's," Skip said.

"It's a pleasure to meet you, sir," Caleb said, enthusiastically gripping his hand.

"Call me Skip. 'Sir' make me feel old," Skip said.

"And this is Lily," Sophia said, taking Lily by the hand and bringing her over toward Caleb. "Lily, this is my friend Caleb."

Lily buried her face behind Sophia's legs. "Hi, Lily. You have such a beautiful name. My mom is named after a flower too. Daisy."

Lily inched away from her hiding spot until he could see her entire face. Looking at her was like gazing upon a pint-size Sophia. The same gorgeous mocha complexion. Big brown eyes that radiated pure innocence. Her hair was a mane of curls, while Sophia's was straight. Other than that, they were doppelgängers.

Caleb stooped down so he was at her eye level. Lily took a few steps toward him.

"I like flowers," she said, tugging at the hem of her sweater and looking down instead of gazing directly at him.

"So do I," Caleb said. "Do you like forget-me-nots?"

Lily nodded, finally looking at him. She gifted him with a beautiful smile. "They're my favorite ones."

"I just found out they're the state flower of Alaska," Caleb said. "I think I might've known ages ago, but I've been gone from Alaska for a long time."

"Mommy likes them a lot. Don't you, Mommy?" Lily asked, turning toward Sophia for confirmation.

"I sure do, but I'm partial to all types of flowers," Sophia said. "They make the world a better place."

"So, Caleb, are you joining us for supper?" Patience asked. "Far be it from me to brag, but my ribs are to die for. Some have said they've actually brought tears to their eyes."

Skip rolled his eyes. "Modest, isn't she? Her ribs are amazing, but she learned everything from me." He puffed out his chest. "I'm the original barbecue king."

Sophia shook her head. "This isn't a contest, Dad. I already invited Caleb to eat with us, so why don't we get settled. I'm going to set the table."

"Let me help," Caleb offered.

"You don't have to do that," Sophia said.

"It's a small contribution toward this amazing meal."

"I want to help too," Lily piped up.

"Okay, you two. Here are the plates," Sophia said, handing them over to Caleb. "Why don't you put out the napkins? Lily, show Caleb to the dining room, please."

"Follow me," Lily said, looking pleased at her task.

Caleb followed behind her, and after he placed each plate down, Lily put a napkin beside it. Sophia came behind them and added glasses, along with utensils. Within minutes they gathered at the table and sat down. Much to his surprise, Lily insisted on sitting next to him. During dinner she kept stealing glances at him. He wasn't really used to being in the presence of small kids, but she was making him feel like a welcomed guest. A few times he looked back at her, which caused her to giggle.

As promised, the ribs were finger-licking delicious. During the meal they engaged in lively conversation, which he was actively involved in. He loved being in the presence of people, even those he didn't know very well. The Brands made him feel like he was part of their crew. He couldn't have felt more at home if he'd known them all for years.

"The meal was delicious," Caleb said, placing his napkin down on his empty plate. There wasn't a single morsel left on his plate. Just bones. "Thanks for including me."

"It was our pleasure," Patience said. "We hear you're going to be the face of Yukon Cider."

"That's the plan," Caleb said. "We'll see how it goes." He didn't want to get too carried away as Xavier had warned him about this morning. Sometimes it all came down to everything working out just right. Serendipity. Although he didn't want to let Hattie down, he had decided not to stress over failure or success. After what he'd been through in the last few years, he had a healthier attitude toward what it meant to be successful. It wasn't all roses and moonlight. There were plenty of thorns and storms along the way.

"I think Caleb is going to be a smash hit," Sophia said, a knowing look on her face. Her belief in him made Caleb feel ten feet tall.

"You're the real star," he raved. He looked over at Skip. "Your daughter is immensely talented. If I make any impression at all, it'll be due to her talent."

"Sounds like the two of you make an amazing team," Patience said from across the table. He wasn't sure, but he thought she was smirking at them.

Sophia gave her sister a look, and it appeared as if the two of them had a silent conversation. He easily recognized the behavior since he and his brothers had been engaging in the same sort of communication since they were kids.

As dinner ended and they all pitched in to clear off the table, Caleb found himself stacking dishes in the dishwasher with Sophia.

"You really don't have to do this," she protested.

"I know. But it gives me an excuse to hang out with you a little bit longer," Caleb said.

"Is that so?" she asked, looking up at him with her big brown eyes. They were the type a person could get lost in. And little by little he was forgetting all about his true goals for being here in Moose Falls. Falling for a stunning single mother hadn't been on his bingo card.

"Sophia, I haven't met anyone who draws me in the way you do in a very long time. I want to get to know you better."

Patience walked into the kitchen. "Sorry to interrupt, but there's a little lady upstairs who's requesting a bedtime story."

"I can finish this up," Caleb said, taking several plates from Sophia's grip. "Go see to Lily."

"Umm, no. It's not Sophia who's being requested. It's you, Caleb," Patience explained with a snicker. "Clearly, you've made a huge impression."

Sophia let out a sound of outrage. "She's a fickle girl, dropping the rest of us like hot potatoes when a handsome man comes to dinner."

Caleb smiled extra wide. He knew Sophia thought he was handsome, but he never tired of hearing her say it. He loved the way she didn't hesitate to lift him up.

"Wow. I won't be able to walk out of here, now that Lily's given me a swelled head," Caleb said with a chuckle. "Point me in the right direction," he said, rubbing his hands together. "I can't wait to read to her. If it's all right with you." Caleb looked over at Sophia to make sure it was okay.

"Of course it is. It's rare that I get a night off from reading to her before bedtime," she said. "On the other hand, it's shocking that I'm so easily replaceable."

"I'll tell you what," Patience said. "Why don't the two of

you head upstairs and I'll finish up. Then I'll head into the TV room to make sure Dad hasn't dozed off."

"You're the best, Patience. Follow me, Caleb," Sophia said, heading out of the kitchen and toward the staircase. He followed after her, glancing at the framed photographs on the landing. A few were portraits, but the majority were photos of the Alaskan landscape. He recognized local spots in Moose Falls, Kachemak Bay, Denali, and Homer Spit. Sophia's talent was limitless. Caleb was in absolute awe that he had the privilege of working with her. Hattie had scored a major coup by hiring Sophia to work at Yukon Cider. He had the feeling that in a few years she would have made quite a name for herself in the industry.

At the top of the stairs Sophia turned left then entered the first door. A soft light glowed from inside.

Lily was sitting up in a little pink bed with a frilly comforter and heart-shaped pillows. She was wearing purple fuzzy pajamas and a stuffed lamb sat beside her. A pink canopy hung over her bed. Pictures of castles and fairy-tale princesses hung on the walls.

"Caleb!" Lily cried out. "I was waiting for you."

"Hey. What about me?" Sophia asked. Caleb could tell by the smile twitching at her lips that she wasn't at all offended.

"Caleb, sit," Lily said, patting the spot beside her. Once he sat down next to her, Lily handed him a book with a brown-skinned princess on the cover. "This one, please."

"Oh, I'm sensing a theme here," Caleb said. "*Princess of Hearts*," he said, reading the title out loud. Lily let out a squeal of approval, which went straight to Caleb's heart. She was so excited and endearing.

"She's in her princess era," Sophia said in a loud whisper.

"Shh, Mommy. He's about to start the story," Lily said, frowning.

"Once upon a time," Caleb began, using his most dramatic, princely voice, "there was a beautiful little princess named...Lily." Lily's eyes went wide. Caleb had changed the name, just to see her smile. Mission accomplished.

By the time he was finished reading, Lily was fast asleep. Caleb gently stood up and closed the book. Sophia tiptoed over to Lily's bed and placed the cover on top of her until only her face was showing. She leaned down and pressed a kiss on Lily's forehead. "Good night, sweetheart," she whispered. A soft night-light glowed next to her bed.

"Good night, Princess Lily," Caleb said, before taking Sophia's hand and heading out of the bedroom. They stepped outside into the hallway, with Sophia softly closing the door behind them.

"Thanks for reading her a bedtime story," Sophia said. "That was awfully sweet of you."

"My pleasure," Caleb said. "That used to be me as a kid. Always clamoring for a story before bedtime."

"Just like Lily," Sophia said. "You two are birds of a feather."

"I should head home, since we've both got work in the morning," Caleb said, "but I'm so glad I stopped by."

"I am too," Sophia said. "And thanks again for bringing my purse over. I'm sure panic would have set in once I realized that it was missing."

"Happy to oblige," Caleb said. "Meeting your family, especially Lily, was incredibly special. She's one amazing kid."

"I'm so lucky," she said, letting out a contented sigh. He was happy to see her in such a good place after her frustration earlier over her ex. Being with family and Lily had to feel reassuring, he imagined.

"I hope to see you tomorrow," he said, knowing he

wouldn't be working with her again for a few days. She'd told him earlier that they were going to do an outdoors shoot by the mountains. He rubbed his hands together and shifted from one foot to the other.

"Me too," she said in a soft voice. He knew she was probably talking in a low voice so she didn't wake Lily up.

Caleb leaned down and brushed a kiss over her lips. Sophia reached up and placed her arms around his neck and kissed him back with an abundance of tenderness. In its own way this kiss was just as spectacular as their earlier one. After it ended, he was buzzing with endorphins.

A few minutes later he was in his vehicle driving back to Hattie's house. The moon was brilliant in a pitch-black sky. The back roads were dark, save for the moon and a smattering of twinkling stars. The soft rhythms of an R & B station filled the air. He began to hum along to the music, experiencing a peace of mind he hadn't enjoyed in quite some time. Never in a million years had he imagined finding such peace here in Alaska. It was strange how one's life could turn on a dime. Coming to Moose Falls had been a risk, but at the moment he felt like it had been one of the best decisions he'd ever made in his life.

CHAPTER ELEVEN

The rest of the work week passed by in a blur with Sophia's workload centered around the new campaign featuring Caleb. Although they took more pictures, she was so busy trying to get the project off the ground that there was no time to really connect with him. He had invited her to dinner, but she had asked for a rain check for another time. Between work and spending time with Lily, she was totally swamped.

It was a shame, since she enjoyed every moment she spent in his presence.

Sophia had an important meeting with Hattie, who weighed in on the initial batch of photos. Although she didn't usually get nervous about her work, Sophia knew there was a lot riding on this campaign. Like Caleb, she didn't want to let Hattie down.

"I'm thrilled with what you've done so far," Hattie told her. "These photos are all winners. Not a bad one in the bunch. You're good, Sophia."

"Thank you," she said. "It's pretty incredible to be able to do what I love. And thanks for hiring me. Working for you is a privilege."

Hattie had reached over and patted her hand. "The privilege is all mine. Working with so many young people is giving me life." She cackled.

"Hattie, I've never met anyone who has a bigger zest for life than you do." And she meant it. Hattie was such an inspiration for all those in her circle and in the Moose Falls community. She was still pushing and striving despite a diagnosis that would have kept most folks confined to their beds. Sophia was going to soak up everything she could from Hattie in the weeks and months ahead.

"Have you shown these to Caleb?" Hattie asked, tapping the photos with her finger.

"Not all of them. The first day we were shooting I gave him a peek at some of the initial shots. He was pretty excited." Just the thought of Hattie's grandson made her smile. It had been a pleasure to work with him. He had a good attitude and a strong work ethic. He also had a great sense of humor.

"I think that I'd like to see how it goes if we bring in a female model to shoot with Caleb. We're going to show these photos to some test audiences, and I'm curious as to how they'll respond to a romantic angle. What do you think?"

"Honestly, I can't imagine the photos turning out better than these, but it's a good idea. Caleb has lots of masculine appeal, so he could generate some real chemistry."

"Sounds like a plan. Let me know when you book a model and plan the shoot. I love being on set to watch it all unfold," Hattie said, sounding gleeful.

"Will do," Sophia had said, making a mental note to contact a modeling agency ASAP. This campaign was proceeding at a lightning-fast speed. She wondered if Hattie was fast-tracking it due to her illness. Maybe she wanted to see this new line—and Caleb—take off into orbit.

And now, after an intense week, Patience was treating her to a pedicure at Nailed It, their favorite nail salon spot. Her sister wouldn't take no for an answer, which was par for the course for Patience.

She felt a little guilty being away from Lily, but doing something relaxing for herself would benefit her daughter. Or so everyone always told her. While she was away, G-pop was going to take Lily to a playdate and then out to lunch. She was planning to bring Lily to a toy shop this afternoon so she could pick a plush toy to stuff. Her little girl would be fine.

At the moment she and Patience were seated side by side at the nail salon, getting luxurious pedicures. She had to give it to Patience. She had suggested getting deluxe leg and foot massages, and all Sophia's worries evaporated as her muscles were kneaded and manipulated.

"This was a brilliant idea," Sophia said, closing her eyes as the nail tech continued her soothing treatment.

"So, what's happening between you and Alaska's Next Top Model?" Patience asked.

"Would you believe me if I said that I didn't know?" Sophia answered.

"Not really. That night at Northern Exposure the two of you were vibing, and it was even more obvious during dinner at your house."

"I don't know how to pace this thing between us. Should I take things slowly? Back off because we're working together? Kiss his face off the next time I see him?" She shrugged. "It's been four years since I even looked at a guy. I didn't think I'd want this...whatever this is brewing between us."

"Donny sure did a number on you." Patience frowned. "Remind me to kick him in the shins the next time I see him."

"Please don't. I already have enough to worry about with him. He might file charges against you," she mumbled.

"What now?" Patience asked, clenching her teeth.

Sophia lowered her voice to a whisper. "I didn't want to say it in front of Dad the other night, but he's going after joint custody of Lily." Just saying the words out loud made her body tremble. As ridiculous as his claim might be, all it took was one judge to side with him and uproot Lily's life.

"Joint custody?" Patience asked in a raised tone. Sophia made a motion for her to lower her voice. She didn't want her business spread all over the salon.

A few moments later they were moved to a more private station for drying their nails. Cups of tea were placed in front of them, adding another layer of comfort to the experience.

"You've got to be kidding me about Donny," Patience continued, now that they were alone. "He doesn't even see his daughter on a regular basis as it is."

"I know," she said, burying her face in her mug of tea. "All I can do is hope he gets tired of this ridiculous idea and drops it."

"I can't believe that I ever liked the guy," Patience groused. "I thought he was a good dude until he started acting like a punk. I'm so sorry this is happening to you. You're such a great mom to Lily. You don't deserve this hassle. Especially from someone who's been MIA for years."

"Donny was a good guy, Patience, back when we met. I don't even recognize who he's become, but I just need to remind myself that Lily is what's important." Sophia hated that the man she had fallen in love with had transformed into someone she no longer recognized. He'd been selfish and verbally abusive. That's what scared her about getting into another relationship. People changed right before your eyes into someone you no longer knew or loved.

"You're important too. You need to remember that. You deserve good things," Patience said, putting her arm around her.

"I lost so much confidence when he bailed on our relationship. I kept thinking it was my fault, that I did something to change the way he felt about me."

"He didn't deserve you, if you want to know how I truly feel. I know raising Lily on your own hasn't been easy, but it's a lot better than making a life with someone who wasn't committed to the type of life you deserve."

"That's all true," Sophia said, "but I just wish my experience with him hadn't left me feeling so broken. I want to be in a relationship again, but I'm afraid of putting myself out there."

"It's hard to do that, especially when you've been put through the wringer. But if you don't try, you'll never know what's possible. You might miss out on the greatest thing that ever comes your way."

Sophia bit her lip. She knew she was being a bit of a mess, but Patience was her soft place to fall. She could tell her anything. Her insecurities. Her fears. The highs and the lows. Her sister always understood where she was coming from. She grounded her.

"You don't have to figure out any of this today," Patience reassured her. "Have you ever thought of simply having fun with Caleb?" She let out a mock cry of horror and slapped her hand over her mouth. "Or is that a dirty word?"

"It's definitely something I haven't had in a long time," Sophia admitted. "But Caleb makes me want to be spontaneous. I haven't wanted to walk on the wild side for a long time."

"Oh, really? Tell me more." Patience leaned over and put a hand to her ear.

"We kissed at work the other day," she admitted. Just saying it out loud made her feel sheepish.

Patience let out a loud squeal. "Get out! I want details! The more, the better."

"There's not much to tell, but on a scale of one to ten it was off the charts. And we were alone in the photo studio, so we were a little bit discreet."

"Look at you, making out with Hattie's grandson during your first week at Yukon Cider. I absolutely love this side of you." She put up her hands and said, "Grrrrrr" as if she were a tiger growling.

Sophia swatted her sister's hand away. "I don't know if it was the wisest move, but you know what? Kissing Caleb was the most exciting thing that's happened to me since Lily was born. It made me feel alive, and I can't feel sorry about that. Not by a long shot."

Patience was right. She needed to live a little while she still could. Reaching out to Caleb about dinner would be a great start.

When Sophia texted Caleb to ask if he was interested in having dinner with her on Sunday night, his response was immediate. Her only stipulation was that it would have to be dinner at her house due to Lily. As the son of a single mother himself, Caleb understood that Lily's needs came first, and he wouldn't want it any other way.

Caleb arrived at Sophia's place carrying a huge amount of takeout he had picked up in town. Not knowing what her favorite food was had been a bit challenging, but he'd decided to go with Italian and Mexican. The scent of the food had taunted him during the drive over, serving as a reminder that he hadn't eaten since noontime. Because his hands were so full, he was forced to lean on the doorbell with his elbow.

"I come bearing food. Lots and lots of food," Caleb

announced as Sophia greeted him at her front door. He paused for a moment to drink in the sight of her. Even in jeans and a cardigan she looked incredible.

"Whoa. Let me take some of that so you don't drop it," Sophia said, reaching for one of the bags. She ushered him inside, then gracefully kicked the door closed with her foot.

Once they were in the kitchen, Caleb placed the food down on the counter and let out a sound of relief. Maybe he had gone a bit overboard with the food, he realized as soon as he saw how much space the bags took up on the counter.

Sophia placed her bag down and turned to him. "You do realize it's just the two of us, right? Lily is having a love affair with chicken nuggets. That's pretty much all she eats."

"She ate ribs at dinner, didn't she?" he asked, remembering how the little girl scarfed down a hearty portion.

"That's an exception, especially since Auntie P made them."

"Well, then, I hope you're as hungry as I am," Caleb told her.

"I'm a bit peckish." Sophia peeked in the bags. "What do we have here?"

"Mexican from Fiesta and Italian from Amore's. Consider yourself lucky. I almost ordered wings from Northern Exposure," he confessed, chuckling.

She shook her head. "You should definitely bring the leftovers back to Hattie's place. I can't imagine we'll eat all of this." Sophia took out plates and glasses from the cupboard. "Lily," she called out as she began taking the food from the bags.

"Tacos. Empanadas. Rice and beans. Meatballs. Garlic knots. Chicken parmigiana. And for dessert, churros." Caleb rattled off the items as if he were a chef who'd made the meals.

Just then Lily ran into the kitchen and headed straight for Caleb. She let out a cry of delight as she wrapped her arms around his legs. "Caleb!"

"Princess Lily," he said, bending down to lift her up in the air.

"I missed you," Lily said, placing her arms around his neck and kissing him on the cheek.

"I missed you too," he said, smiling. What was it about kids that made grown adults feel like they could vault over tall buildings? How could her bio dad not want to spend every waking hour with this little gem? He tried not to judge people he had never met, but Sophia's ex was a total punk in his opinion.

"Lily, we're about to eat. Do you want to try some of the food Caleb brought over?" Sophia asked.

"Mmm. I don't know," Lily answered with a shrug. "Did you bring chicken nuggets?"

She was looking straight at Caleb, waiting for an answer.

"No, I'm sorry, but I would have if I had known you loved them so much," Caleb said. Rookie mistake. He'd forgotten kids loved chicken nuggets. That's what happened when there weren't any littles in his family tree.

"But I did bring some chicken parm, which is yummy chicken with red sauce and mozzarella cheese." He rubbed his stomach and made a funny face that immediately generated giggles. "Yummy in my tummy."

"I wanna try," Lily said, causing Sophia's eyes to widen.

"That's music to my ears," she said as she placed utensils down beside the plates before organizing the platters in the middle of the table. "Take a seat, Lily."

Caleb pulled out a chair so Lily would sit down, then he pushed her chair in.

"Let me make a plate for you," he said as he sat down

beside her. "Let's start with the chicken parm. If anything else looks good, just let us know, and we'll put some on your plate." Sophia, who was sitting on the other side of Lily, leaned over and cut up her chicken into small pieces.

"Okay," Lily said, lifting a forkful of chicken parm and putting it in her mouth.

Caleb and Sophia waited with bated breath for her verdict.

"So, do you like it?" Sophia asked, pausing before she took a bite of her own food. Sophia had filled her plate with a little bit of everything, just like he did. This food smelled too good not to sample.

"I don't like it," Lily said, wrinkling her nose. After a few beats she yelled, "I love it!"

Caleb and Sophia looked at each other and shook their heads.

"Yes!" Caleb said, raising his palm so Lily could high-five him.

"Thank you," Sophia said in a low voice. He had to admit that it felt all kinds of wonderful to have enticed Lily out of her chicken nugget comfort zone. He could see the satisfaction on Sophia's face, and it made him happy. Lily completed her meal by taking several bites of a taco and eating half a meatball.

After dinner they ate the churros, with Sophia pulling out some vanilla ice cream from the freezer to top them off.

"Lily's practically falling asleep at the table, so I'm going to bring her upstairs," Sophia said, lifting her from the chair.

"Can I help?" Caleb asked.

"No, I'm good, but if you can pack up the leftovers, that would be great. You can take them home with you," Sophia told him. "Although you can leave the rice and beans for me. I love 'em."

Caleb got to work as soon as Sophia headed upstairs

with Lily. By the time he was finished packing up the items, Sophia was back in the kitchen.

"That was fast. No bedtime story tonight?" he asked. He stacked the leftovers and placed them in a bag, making sure to leave the rice and beans in the fridge.

"Nope. She was out like a light by the time her head hit the pillow," Sophia said, a smile twitching at her lips. The love she felt for Lily was evident in every single gesture, smile, and softly spoken word.

"How about some sangria?" Sophia asked, reaching into her fridge and pulling out a chilled bottle.

"I would love some," Caleb said. "Let me grab the goblets." He rooted around in her cabinet, quickly finding them.

A few minutes later they were in Sophia's great room, sitting on her couch and drinking sangria. The room was light and airy, with cream-colored walls and floor-to-ceiling windows.

"Lily is a great kid," Caleb told her. "I don't spend a lot of time with little ones, but she's a great one."

Sophia took a big sip of her sangria. "That means a lot to me. It's so true what they say. Once you bring a child into the world, everything shifts."

"I totally get that. And everything else fades away in comparison to her needs and wants." How often had his mother said this to him and his brothers?

"Exactly. I still have aspirations, but if things aren't good with Lily, then nothing is right with me."

"I'll toast to that," Caleb said, lifting his glass in the air and clinking glasses with Sophia, who'd raised her goblet to meet his.

"I received a very cool call today," Sophia announced, barely able to contain her excitement. She was wiggling around in her seat and looking at him as if she were holding on to the world's biggest secret.

"Tell me more," Caleb said, getting a kick out of her being so eager to tell him something.

"By some extraordinary stroke of luck, I was asked to do a photo session with Malina Blackrock." Sophia covered her mouth with her hand and let out a strangled scream.

"What? Are you serious? She's a superstar." Malina was an indigenous Alaskan singer who had catapulted herself to fame and fortune all over the globe. She was a local girl with humble origins, having grown up in Seldovia.

"I know!" Sophia said in a raised voice. "It's such a random thing. She's on fire as an artist. Can you believe it?"

Caleb shook his head. "Nothing in life is random. Growing up, my mom drilled it into our heads that what will be, will be. Meaning that this is happening for a reason. Most of all, you deserve this gig."

"That's sweet of you to say."

"I'm not being kind. Just truthful. You're very talented, which is why your name is out there generating buzz." He reached over and entwined his hand with hers. "Take this opportunity and run with it. She's not the only one who's on fire."

Sophia responded by playfully fanning her face with her hand.

"Seriously, it's like I said earlier. Lily is the center of my world. If she's proud of me, that means I've succeeded."

"So, what's the story with you and Lily's dad? If I may ask." Caleb didn't even bother to hide his curiosity. He figured she was just as curious about his infamous relationship with the Taylor twins. At some point he knew that particular topic would crop up. He just hoped he was ready to tackle it head-on.

"Of course you may ask." Sophia took a long sip of her sangria. "Well, do you want the short version or the detailed one?"

"Whatever you're comfortable with. I just want to know more about you and what brought you to this point, especially your journey as a single mom."

Sophia was blown away. She had never met a potential romantic partner who had wanted to know about her past. Not even the father of her child. None of them had expressed any interest whatsoever. She was touched by Caleb being so intentional toward her.

She took a steadying breath. "I met my ex, Donny, about six years ago. We were together for two years. Honestly, everything was going great until I took a pregnancy test, and it was positive." She winced as the painful memories crashed over her.

Caleb frowned. "I'm guessing he didn't take the news very well."

"Bingo," she said, running a fidgety hand through her hair. It wasn't easy to talk about, but she wanted to get closer to Caleb. She wanted to tear down her walls with a sledge-hammer. They had been up for so long, and she knew on some level it was impeding her growth. "Even though we had talked about a future together—engagement, wedding, kids. Then all of a sudden he became a ghost. He stopped communicating with me, and he didn't show up at any of my prenatal appointments." Her stomach clenched. "I didn't want to believe it, but I could feel that he was pulling away from me."

"That had to be confusing and painful," Caleb said.

"It was. I was months away from giving birth, and my partner was completely MIA. When I found out I was having a girl, I was with Patience. He was nowhere to be found when I went into labor." Tears stung her eyes, but she blinked them away. She had cried enough tears over Donny's behavior. Now her sorrow was for Lily. Lily's father wasn't a reliable man, and she worried constantly that he would smash Lily's heart to smithereens.

"My sister always showed up for me, but *he* should have been there. He should have been holding my hand and feeding me ice chips. Even if he decided that he didn't want to be with me anymore, he still should have shown up."

"I-I can't believe he treated you that way," Caleb sputtered. The look of disbelief on his face turned to anger. "What kind of man abandons his partner and baby?"

"Well, according to him, he hadn't asked to be a father." She let out a snort. "Lily wasn't planned, so I wasn't expecting the news either. But I embraced the fact that I was going to be a mother. And, honestly, she's the very best thing that has ever happened to me."

For a moment the kitchen was eerily silent. Neither one said a word.

"Sophia, you're not only a strong woman, but you're an incredible mother raising a wonderful little girl." He placed his hand over his heart. "I'm in awe of you."

Sophia ducked her head down. Making eye contact with Caleb after she'd spilled her guts would make her feel too vulnerable. Telling him about Donny made her feel as if she'd bared her soul.

"Aww, shucks," she said, trying to sound lighthearted. "If I'd known that, I would've told you weeks ago." She let out a shaky laugh that didn't sound at all genuine. There was nothing funny about what she had just told him, and they both knew it.

"I see you, Sophia," Caleb said, reaching out and grazing his knuckles across her cheek. "And I don't think I've ever laid eyes on anything as beautiful or as real." Caleb leaned over so that their lips were mere inches away from each other. "I want to kiss you so badly, but I need to know that you want this too."

Sophia nodded. She licked her lips in anticipation. "Yes, please."

He encircled her waist with both of his hands and pulled her against his chest. Once she was there, Sophia tilted her head upward just as Caleb's lips brushed over hers. She parted her lips in response, inviting him in.

As the kiss heightened and soared, she inhaled the scent of him—something rugged and woodsy like cedar. Caleb's hands were solid and grounding.

This kiss wasn't just explosive. There was sweetness too, a kind of tenderness that made the moment even more amazing. A feeling of security swept over her. She wasn't sure that she'd ever responded to a kiss this way or needed someone as much.

By the time they pulled apart, Sophia's mind was nothing but mush. This man was like a five-alarm fire.

"So, you owe me your story, Caleb. I'm all ears."

"Another time, okay? It's getting late, and I've got an early shoot tomorrow with a really demanding photographer." He leaned in and whispered, "I hear she's a bit of a diva."

She let out an outraged sound and playfully swatted him. "Absolutely not. She doesn't have a diva-like bone in her body."

"For which I am very grateful," Caleb murmured as he swept another kiss on her lips. Although this one was short and sweet, it left her equally breathless.

Once she had walked him to the front door, Sophia said, "Good night, Caleb. See you tomorrow."

"Night," he said as he dipped his head down and brushed a kiss on her temple.

She was definitely going to hold him to his promise to tell her his story. Sophia knew now that there was way more to the story regarding his stint on the reality show. And she wanted to know why he seemed slightly guarded with regard to his heart.

CHAPTER TWELVE

"It's about time we talked," Xavier said as he sat back in his chair and crossed his hands thoughtfully in front of him on his desk. It was their Friday lunch hour, and Xavier had called an emergency meeting for the Stone brothers.

"We talk all the time," Caleb said, unwrapping his turkey-bacon sandwich from the plastic wrap and taking a huge bite.

"But not about our mindset regarding Yukon Cider. We've been avoiding this discussion," Landon said. He dug into his own lunch, two Caesar wrap sandwiches and a large bag of chips. For someone so lean, Caleb was noticing Landon could really pack it in.

"We've all been busy," Caleb told them. He didn't know why, but he felt a little defensive. Making a decision about whether or not to stay and run the company was getting more complicated by the day. In the beginning, their grandmother was just a fuzzy memory from their childhood. But after living and working with Hattie for the past months, she was now permanently tattooed on their hearts. It was hard to believe that she hadn't always been a presence in their lives.

"This is important stuff, so we have to make time to discuss it," Xavier said, sounding like the older brother that he was. This was Xavier's sweet spot. Taking charge and leading the way. Now that he was engaged to True, Caleb was curious about his thoughts on the matter.

"You're right," Caleb conceded. "Time is ticking away."

"So, where do you stand?" Landon asked, looking at Xavier.

"It's tough because I'm engaged to True now and we're going to be living in Moose Falls, at least for the foreseeable future. I can't see True wanting to relocate, especially with Jaylen still in school." He reached for his Coke and took a swig of it. "That being said, there's still the question of whether or not I see myself running Yukon Cider, along with the two of you."

"Honestly, that's the enticing part," Caleb admitted. "Working alongside you knuckleheads." Neither of his brothers objected to his use of the K word, since they all knew it was meant as a term of endearment.

"It's been nice being back together again and living under the same roof," Landon acknowledged. "Working at the lab got lonely, especially when everything went south."

It made Caleb angry just thinking about what Landon had been put through. He was the smartest brother and had always been dedicated to academic and scientific pursuits. His work at Abbott Laboratories had ended with his integrity as a scientist being questioned. He had been thrown out of the lab on his ear and accused of manufacturing data. All of his research had been confiscated.

All three of them had gone through rock-bottom moments in the last few years, with Xavier suffering through an injury that had ended his NFL career. He had also been dumped by his fiancée, Heather, who had been cheating on him with his friend and teammate. Thankfully, Xavier had met True, the love of his life, here in Moose Falls.

"It has been nice," Caleb recognized, "but we all came here with goals in mind that we haven't met. I just don't want to lose sight of that." He had come to Alaska with the express purpose of exploring Hattie's inheritance and rediscovering his past in Moose Falls. On some level he had always figured that he and his brothers would sell Yukon Cider once they had met the requirement set by Hattie to work at the company for a year. His big dream was to carve out an acting career for himself in California. If he chose to stay and run the company, those dreams would go up in smoke.

"You're right about that," Landon said. "I'm more determined than ever to get my good name back in the scientific community. I was scapegoated by the laboratory, and I'm not letting them get away with that."

"Good for both of you for holding on to those dreams," Xavier said. "Before coming here I desperately wanted to get back in the NFL world, even though I knew my playing days were over. I couldn't let go of that dream of football glory."

"Until you met True," Caleb said. Everything had changed for Xavier on that fateful day. She had turned his world upside down and broken down all of his walls.

"And the rest is history," Landon said with a flourish. "Love. Engagement. All the feels in the world."

Xavier nodded. "My situation is a little different because of my commitment to True, but the fact remains that we have to make a unanimous decision. If we don't, it goes to charity."

"While giving it all to charity would be honorable, this is our grandmother's life's work," Landon said passionately. "Carrying on her company after her…passing would be upholding her legacy. I'm not going to lie. That would be pretty powerful."

"I feel guilty about disappointing Hattie, even though she might not be around to see our decision," Caleb said, feeling glum about their options. On one hand, he hated the idea of giving up on his dreams; while on the other hand, he didn't want to feel like he had thrown away a family legacy. "Yukon Cider means something to the folks here. We mean something to them. They've welcomed us to town with nothing but goodwill." He winced. "I hate even thinking about their reaction if we sell."

"And Hattie's," Landon said, his eyes welling up. "She might haunt us from beyond like in one of those spooky movies."

Caleb and Xavier tried to hold it in, but they both burst out laughing. In his mind's eye all he could see was Hattie's ghostlike figure reprimanding them in her harshest tone. Landon was always so dramatic with his words that it was hard to take his comment seriously.

Landon made a *tsk*ing sound as they continued. "You two are the worst. Laughing at our grandmother's demise is pretty low." He stood up and grabbed his brown paper bag and crumpled it up.

The more Caleb tried to stop laughing, the harder he howled. Ditto with Xavier. There was no way in the world they were finding humor in Hattie's terminal illness, but something about Landon's referencing her as a ghost sent them into hysterics.

"I'm out of here," Landon fumed. His face was flushed, and his movements were jerky. Caleb was used to the telltale signs that his younger brother was upset. Being the youngest had often left Landon feeling a little out of sorts. He was also more sensitive than Caleb and Xavier, often taking things to heart.

"Hey, Landon. Don't leave. We were only letting off steam," Caleb said, trying to explain their laughter. "We weren't being cruel to Hattie."

"We're all under a lot of pressure whether we realize it or not," Xavier said, gripping Landon's arm to keep him from storming out. "There's so much at stake here, and we're all afraid to make a wrong move. Plus, knowing Hattie's dying adds an extra layer, an emotional one. We've all grown close to her, and that factors into our decision."

Xavier was saying all the things Caleb himself was thinking and feeling. His older brother had a knack for speaking eloquently from the heart. He could see Landon softening and lowering his defenses. They were all under a huge amount of stress, and it was healthy to offset it with laughter.

"I-I just didn't think it was very funny," Landon muttered. "We're going to lose Hattie and, as a result, nothing will ever be the same again."

And here it was. Landon was emotional about what was going on with Hattie. No matter how much they tried to carry on as if nothing was catastrophically wrong, there was this huge shadow hanging over them. How were they supposed to make such a monumental decision about Yukon Cider, knowing what their grandmother truly wanted them to choose? For a moment he envied Xavier. Having True as his future wife gave him more of a reason to stay in Moose Falls and run the company. But, as they knew, their decision had to be unanimous. As brothers they all needed to be on the same page regarding the decision so there weren't fractures in their relationships.

"No one or nothing." It was what Daisy had always told them since they were small. No one or nothing could get in the way of what the three Stone brothers had.

"Point taken," Caleb said, putting his hand on Landon's back. Sometimes he forgot how his brother was—loyal to a fault. He would have reacted the same way if he'd thought someone was disrespecting him or Xavier. And that was just one of the many reasons to adore Landon.

"We need to keep talking about our decision and keep the lines of communication open," Xavier said. "It's the only way we're going to make it through this and come to an amicable decision that we can all live with."

"Agreed," Caleb said, knowing that with each passing day they were coming closer to having to make a decision. And it wasn't going to be easy, much like today's tension-filled lunch. There would be strain and disagreements and discord, but eventually they would be in accord. They had to be. Brothers Stone above all else. All for one and one for all.

There were a lot of things Caleb didn't have figured out, but he knew one thing for certain. No one would have laughed harder than Hattie if she'd heard Landon referencing her as a ghost coming from the beyond to haunt them. That was the type of woman she was. His grandmother was always able to see the humor in situations, and he loved her for that more than words could express.

In Sophia's experience, when it rained it turned into a tsunami. A flat tire on her way to Yukon Cider had resulted in her sitting in a cold car while waiting for emergency roadside service. While rushing inside the Yukon Cider building, she had missed a step and fallen, landing on her butt. Now, she had just gotten off the phone with Lily's sitter, Yolanda, who had suddenly taken ill. From the sound of it, she was suffering from the flu, which meant Sophia didn't have

coverage for her photo shoot tomorrow with Malina Black-rock in Anchorage. Thankfully, her dad was able to go to her house today and relieve Yolanda, but tomorrow he was going to be out of town on a trip with friends. It wasn't as if she could bring a four-year-old with her on a professional photo shoot. And it wasn't likely that Yolanda was going to recover from the flu overnight.

She was wracking her brain and coming up empty. Despite her issues with Donny, she would ask him in a heartbeat, but his schedule as an EMT didn't permit him to take time off at the last minute. There was literally no point in asking.

It was massive bad luck that this once-in-a-lifetime opportunity was falling apart right before her eyes. Nothing was more important in her life than Lily, but yet and still, she wanted this opportunity to come to fruition. Who knew when another chance like this one would come along?

A knock at her studio door dragged her from her thoughts. She definitely needed a distraction from her current situation. Sophia was starting to feel sorry for herself, and years ago she'd made a vow never to get stuck on the pity train. It never led anywhere good.

"Come in," she called out, her stomach doing flip-flops at the sight of Caleb in the doorway. This was the perfect pick-me-up. Just seeing him made her feel better.

"I hope this isn't a bad time to stop by," he said, dimples on full display.

Sophia sat up straighter in her chair. "Of course not. It's nice to see you." Even though her brain was telling her to play it cool, another part of her wanted Caleb to know she appreciated this impromptu visit. It was hard not to feel excited when he was in her orbit, even in the midst of a bad luck day.

"I come bearing gifts," he said, advancing toward her

desk and holding out a small brown paper bag. She felt a little jolt as his fingers brushed against hers.

"Something smells good," Sophia said as she opened the bag. A big fat chocolate chip cookie sat inside. "Oh, my goodness. How did you know these are my favorite?"

"Aren't they everyone's?" he asked, smiling.

"If they're not, they should be," she said, pulling out the cookie and splitting it evenly in half. "Here you go. Halfsies."

"I bought the cookie for you. Sharing isn't necessary," he said, taking a seat in a chair by her desk.

"I'm about to take a gigantic bite out of this, and I don't want to eat alone." She pushed his half of the cookie toward him.

"If you insist," Caleb said. He immediately took a bite and let out a satisfied sound. "Almost as good as my mom makes."

Sophia bit into her half and sighed. "This cookie is good enough to almost make me forget this dumpster fire of a morning."

Caleb frowned. "You look a bit stressed. What's going on?" he asked, leaning forward in his chair.

She let out a ragged sigh. Although a part of her didn't want to unload her problems on Caleb, another part of her yearned for listening ears. "My shoot with Malina isn't going to work out the way I planned," Sophia told Caleb, doing her best to sound unbothered about the situation. It was actually one of the most devastating career disappointments she had ever faced. There was nothing she could do about it, but being this close to a huge career opportunity only to have it slip through her fingers was heartbreaking.

"Why not? Malina didn't back out on you, did she?" The fierce expression etched on Caleb's face was endearing. He looked as if he was ready to wage war on her behalf.

"No, it's nothing like that. It's Lily. I don't have anyone to watch her tomorrow. My sitter suddenly took sick," she explained. "And my dad is going on his annual fishing trip on Kachemak Bay with his buddies. I know he'd cancel if I asked, but I can't do that. He's looked forward to this trip all year."

"How about Patience? Can she swing it?" Caleb asked, his brow furrowed.

"She's out of town herself on assignment." Patience traveled where the stories took her. This week she was in Nome writing a piece on the Iditarod Race.

Caleb shook his head. "There's got to be a way."

Frustration flooded her. Opportunities like this one were rare. Being asked to photograph a famous Alaskan singer was an honor and a privilege. She couldn't imagine being asked again if she canceled at the last minute.

She bit the inside of her cheek to stop herself from screaming. Life wasn't always fair. And even though she was eager to boost her career, Lily always came first.

"Any way Lily's dad could watch her?"

Sophia swallowed past the huge lump in her throat. "I could ask him, but as an EMT it's near impossible to get time off at the last minute. I need to just put my big-girl panties on and tell them I can't do the shoot." Sadness enveloped her. Why couldn't things ever work out for her?

Caleb reached out and took her hands in his. "Sophia, that can't happen. You've got to do the shoot. I can watch Lily."

"What? You can't be serious," Sophia sputtered.

"I wouldn't make an offer like that if I wasn't." He made a face. "And acting so mystified at my offer is a tad insulting, just so you know."

"But how would that work?" Her mind was racing. She

wanted this opportunity so badly she could taste it, and the last thing Sophia needed was to get her hopes up. What did Caleb know about watching a four-year-old?

"I, Caleb Stone, will watch Lily while you fly out to Anchorage. I'll entertain her, cook for her, play dolls with her." He grinned. "I'll be a veritable Mary Poppins."

Sophia chuckled at the visual image Caleb's comment brought to mind.

"Caleb, do you really cook?" she asked, surprised that he would even offer. For some reason she couldn't imagine him at a stove, even though he would look all kinds of hot wearing an apron.

"Of course I do. Daisy made sure all of her boys could cook. She said it was her gift to our future partners."

"I like your mom's style," Sophia said with an approving nod. "What's your signature dish?"

"Bourbon chicken or my famous slow cooker mac 'n' cheese. I'll let you decide when I invite you for dinner." He playfully winked at her, distracting her for a moment from the issue at hand.

"That sounds nice, but back to Lily. If you're serious, I'll be taking an early morning flight and getting back early evening." She bit her lip. "Do you think that you can handle her for that length of time?"

"Of course I do," he said, sounding extremely confident. "Lily and I are buddies. It'll be a piece of cake. And a nice way to spend a Saturday."

Sophia didn't know what he was imagining watching a four-year-old would be like, but she trusted him to keep Lily safe and secure. And from the sound of it, he would feed her and keep her entertained.

"She's four, Caleb," Sophia pointed out. "Nothing with that age group is a piece of cake. They fight against nap time.

A temper tantrum can happen at the drop of a dime. And one minute they love chicken nuggets and the next they're yucky."

"We'll be fine. I'm creative and funny, not to mention that I bring the fun. We're going to have a blast." Caleb rubbed his hands together. "Matter of fact, I might become her favorite sitter of all time."

"You're all those things and more," Sophia said, feeling warm and fuzzy about his generous offer. Not only did it salvage her photo shoot with Malina, but he was also making her believe that she could count on him in a crunch. This was different from anything she had ever experienced in the romance department. Even with Donny she had never been able to rely on him in difficult situations. Caleb Stone was a unique kind of man.

"I appreciate you," she said, coming from her side of the desk toward the other side where he was seated. Caleb stood up, as if sensing she needed to hug him.

She reached up and placed her arms around his waist and leaned against his chest, hugging him for all she was worth. Being in his arms felt safe, something she hadn't experienced before in a man's arms other than her dad's. Sophia didn't know where this thing was headed with Caleb, but for the moment he was making her feel that anything was possible.

CHAPTER THIRTEEN

Caleb looked at the clock on the kitchen wall and ran a hand over his face. How was it possible that it was only ten a.m.? He had shown up at Sophia's house at the crack of dawn so she could catch her flight to Anchorage. Even at that early hour, Lily had been awake and eager to see him. He had been relieved that the little girl hadn't shed any tears at her mother's departure.

He'd already fed Lily, watched *Bluey* cartoons with her, gotten her dressed, and fixed her hair. Now what? Despite his boasting to Sophia, he was stumped.

Why had he thought that he'd be fine? Lily was running him ragged, and he was coming up empty with ideas on how to keep her entertained. She had so much...energy, like the Energizer Bunny. When was she going to run out of steam? He would make lunch for her, then desperately pray she went down for a nap.

Frankly, he was the one who absolutely needed a nap.

Why had he thought this would be a cakewalk? He had wanted so badly for Sophia to have the chance to do the photo shoot with Malina that he may have slightly exaggerated his babysitting skills.

By the time twelve-thirty rolled around, he was feeling a bit desperate. He had fixed a nice lunch of chicken nuggets and steamed broccoli with apple sauce and pita bread. Lily had devoured her entire plate, then asked for seconds. But the meal had been like fuel for her. Instead of settling down for nap time, she was revved up and ready to take on the world. Caleb was running after her as she zipped around the house like a roadrunner.

When she finally slumped over on the couch and fell fast asleep, Caleb pulled out his phone and called his brothers. Xavier picked up the call first, then Caleb patched Landon in.

"Hey, what's going on?" Landon asked. "What's with the three-way call?"

"I have an emergency," Caleb said, not wasting any time getting to the heart of the matter.

"Seriously?" Xavier asked, sounding stunned.

"As a heart attack," Caleb answered.

"Aren't you... babysitting?" Landon pressed.

"Yes. Yes, I am," Caleb said in a strangled voice.

"Did you call 911? Is it Lily?" Xavier asked, sounding slightly panicked.

"No, no, it's nothing like that," Caleb said, trying his best to reassure them. He didn't want a full-blown panic on his hands.

"Then what is it?" Xavier pressed, sounding impatient.

"Double-oh-seven," Caleb said, pulling out the big guns.

"What's the address?" Landon asked.

Caleb quickly gave Sophia's address and hung up. The bargain he had with his brothers stipulated that no explanation was necessary once you invoked the numbers 007. It was tried and true. They had only pulled it out a handful of times in moments of dire emergencies. Caleb figured this situation qualified, since he was over his head and drowning fast. He had no idea what he was going to do with Lily for the next six hours. She was sleeping a bit fitfully, and he sensed she would soon be waking up from her mini nap.

Not ten minutes later, the doorbell buzzed, and he let out a sigh of relief.

"Reinforcements," Caleb said as he wrenched the door open. He had never been so happy to see Xavier and Landon in his life. "I'm so stoked to see you, I could almost cry."

They didn't waste any time stepping inside Sophia's house. Both of them were looking around, as they weren't quite sure what to expect.

"So, what's the emergency?" Xavier was looking at him with a good deal of suspicion on his face.

"Shh. Lily is sleeping," Caleb said, raising a finger to his lips. The last thing he wanted was for Lily to pop up and start running him ragged again. She was a great kid, but having a few moments of peace and quiet was pretty awesome.

"Is she sick or something? Because you do realize neither one of us is a doctor." Landon threw up his hands. "Start talking, Caleb. Tell us what's wrong."

All of a sudden he felt pretty sheepish. Maybe he was overreacting.

"I think I'm in over my head if I'm being completely honest," Caleb admitted. "Lily is an amazing little girl, but I literally am already exhausted. And I promised Sophia I would be a rock star sitter for her daughter, so I need your help."

Both of his brothers were frowning and shaking their heads.

"I can't believe you invoked double-oh-seven for a babysitting situation," Xavier said, letting out a hissing sound like air escaping tires. "You're definitely getting soft in your old age."

"Taken down by a four-year-old," Landon said, letting out a snort. "Who would've thunk it?"

He should have known that his brothers wouldn't understand. When was the last time either one of them had babysat a small child? The answer was never.

"You guys have no idea of how much stamina a four-year-old has or everything I've done to keep her entertained," he said huffily. Humph. They had no business judging him when they had no experience of their own with little ones.

All of a sudden Lily was standing in the hallway, stretching her arms over her head.

"Caleb! Let's play dollies," she cried out. The nap must have done her a world of good, because she was totally reinvigorated.

"Oh, no," Caleb said, groaning. "She's awake!" He was speaking in a hushed tone so Lily wouldn't overhear him. The last thing he wanted to do was hurt her little feelings.

Xavier poked him in the side with his elbow. "Don't be such a wuss." He went over and bent down in front of Lily. "Hi, I'm Xavier, Caleb's older brother. And this guy here," he said, pointing at Landon, "is our baby brother, Landon."

"Hi there," Landon said, waving in her direction.

"Hi," Lily said, moving toward Caleb and tugging on his hand. "Come on, Caleb. It's playtime." She turned toward Xavier and Landon. "Let's play dress-up."

Caleb shot his brothers an imploring look. "Yeah, let's all play," he said. "Please."

The next thing he knew, Lily was pulling him toward the playroom with his brothers in tow. Within minutes she had dressed them all in her fancy dress-up clothes. Big straw hats, flouncy skirts, tiaras, dresses, and lacy shawls. He was grateful that there was no one present taking pictures of them on their cell phones. If he looked half as ridiculous as his brothers did, the photos could be used as blackmail pics.

When his cell phone buzzed, Caleb wondered if it was Sophia calling to check in on Lily.

"Hey, Sophia," he said once he saw her name pop up on the caller ID. "How's Anchorage?"

"Everything's going well, but my flight has been delayed, so I won't be getting home by dinner. I hope that's not a problem," she said. He could hear the uncertainty in her voice, and all he wanted to do was reassure her, even though he was still doubting his babysitting skills.

"Sophia, I've got this," he told her. "Lily is playing and smiling and well fed. We're good here."

He could hear Sophia let out a sigh of relief on the other end. "That's great to hear. I can't wait to tell you all about the photo shoot."

"Me too. Safe travels, Sophia," Caleb said before ending the call.

He could feel Landon's eyes on him.

"You're good with Lily," Landon said in a low voice as he moved closer. "You'll make a great father one day."

So many emotions washed over him upon hearing Landon's comment. A part of him had always figured he wouldn't be any good at being a dad, since he was still a bit broken by his own experiences with Red. Even though he had worked hard to convince himself that he had moved past the issues of parental neglect, at times like this Caleb knew he hadn't. Maybe it wasn't possible to heal certain wounds.

"Nah, I don't think so," he said. He wished he felt different, but it was always hard for him to imagine himself in that role.

"Why not? Because of Dad?" Landon's brown eyes were full of questions.

Caleb shrugged. "You know how it is. It's one of my biggest insecurities, thinking that I'm not going to be any good at fatherhood because of our absentee dad."

"You're forgetting something," Landon said, the corners of his mouth lifting in the hint of a smile. "Our badass mom. She was both mother and father to us. And she taught us well."

"You're right," Caleb admitted. Daisy Stone had played both roles for him and his brothers. And she had shown them everything they would ever need to know about parenthood. Landon's reminder served to buoy his spirits. It wasn't inevitable that he was going to be a flop at fatherhood.

"I know I am," Landon said, just as Lily came over and pulled them back toward her play area.

"Do you know how to make a French braid?" Lily asked, looking around at the three of them.

"Definitely not," Caleb said. "Sorry, Lily. I wish that I did."

"Sorry. I don't think so," Landon said.

They all turned to look at Xavier. He looked slightly uncomfortable. "I may know how to make a French braid." He sounded incredibly sheepish.

"You do?" Caleb asked. He shouldn't be surprised at all. It seemed as if there wasn't a single thing his big brother couldn't do. But a French braid? That was news to him.

He shrugged. "My ex-fiancée taught me."

It totally made sense since Xavier's ex, Heather, was a supermodel who had cared a lot about hair, makeup, and clothes.

"Okay, it's time to play hair salon," Lily said, reaching for Xavier's hand and tugging on it. The excited expression stamped on her face caused a squeezing sensation in the center of Caleb's chest.

"She never slows down, does she?" Xavier asked as he allowed himself to be led away.

"Told ya," Caleb said, grinning. Thankfully, he'd been vindicated.

By five o'clock, both Xavier and Landon were exhausted and in need of a break.

"Thanks for the help, guys," Caleb said, "but I can take it from here. I appreciate the rescue."

"You didn't even need it," Landon said. "As I said before, you're great with Lily. She clearly adores you."

"The feeling is mutual. She's one amazing kiddo," Caleb gushed. As much as he had felt overwhelmed earlier, being with Lily had actually been fun. Having Xavier and Landon present had given him a boost of confidence.

"And Lily's mother?" Xavier asked. "You must think a lot of her if you agreed to watch her daughter like this."

Caleb nodded. "I do. She's everything I never knew I needed or wanted at this point in my life. So far it's pretty casual, but I like being around her. I miss her when she's not with me. Like now," he said, running a hand over his face. "I can't wait to see her tonight."

"Sounds pretty serious to me," Xavier said, locking eyes with Caleb.

"I'm not looking for serious. We're just having fun hanging out," Caleb said, holding up his hands. He wasn't sure who he was trying to convince, himself or Xavier. Even as he said the words out loud, his heart was telling him something different. "Just meeting someone like Sophia is enough for me. A great Moose Falls surprise."

"Yep," Xavier said, grinning so wide it seemed as if his face might crack wide open. "That's what I thought when I met True." Xavier and Landon exchanged a pointed look.

Caleb scoffed. "Not everything has to result in falling in love and an engagement." Even as he said the words, he experienced a funny feeling in the pit of his stomach.

"So, are you kicking us out?" Landon asked. "I thought

you would at least feed us." He rubbed his stomach and looked around the kitchen.

"Good point," Xavier said. "You're the best cook out of the three of us. What are you making?"

"You're welcome to stay, guys. I'll start on dinner right now," Caleb suggested. He loved that they both wanted to stay for supper. Now he wouldn't have to feel so guilty about dragging them away from home.

"And we'll hang out with Lily," Landon said. "I don't know about the two of you, but I love *Bluey*. I'm hooked."

"As long as we don't have to do another round of makeup, I'm good," Xavier added. Caleb didn't think this was the time to tell him that he still had traces of glitter on his face.

"I'm baaaack from the potty," Lily said, spreading her arms wide as if she was expecting a standing ovation.

"Good girl," Caleb said, leaning down and patting Lily on the shoulder. He couldn't believe how well Lily was behaving around him and his brothers. Although she and Caleb had been building a friendship, she hadn't known Xavier or Landon at all. And now they were all getting along like a house on fire. Sophia had done a marvelous job in raising this sweet and spunky child. Being with Lily had been a blast, although challenging. He admired Sophia more than ever for parenting so successfully as a single mother. Next time he would have to eat his Wheaties to keep up with her.

Whoa! He was starting to think about next times. Maybe he was getting a little ahead of himself. Becoming a part of Sophia and Lily's world was serious business. For all he knew, this was a one-off.

Caleb made dinner for all of them while Landon, Xavier, and Lily chilled out in the playroom watching television. Beef stir-fry with rice and veggies, a big Caesar salad, and cornbread. The meal was a hit, especially with Lily, who said it was like going out to eat. Bless her little heart. She was a bona fide sweetheart. After they ate, Xavier and Landon said their good nights, with Caleb thanking them profusely for hanging out with him and Lily.

It didn't take Lily long to drift off to sleep after Caleb read her two books—*The Little Mermaid* and *Brown Sugar Baby*. As he tucked the blanket over her and made sure her night-light was glowing, he stepped back into the hallway, leaving the door open a crack.

Caleb grabbed a Coke and settled in the den with the television on. A little after eight he heard the jingling of keys as Sophia let herself in the house.

"I'm in the den," he called out, standing up and greeting her in the entryway.

She let out a beleaguered sigh. "Home sweet home."

"It's good to see you," Caleb said, encircling her waist with his arms and pulling her into a kiss. Caleb was so excited to have her back in Moose Falls, back in his arms. He wasn't used to missing anyone or having a little ache in his soul.

"Why don't you sit down and put your feet up?" Caleb suggested, gently leading her toward the oatmeal-colored couch. "I'll make you a cup of tea so you can tell me all about your amazing day."

"Sounds like heaven," Sophia said, sinking into the couch and putting her feet up on the coffee table.

A few minutes later Caleb was back with a mug of chamomile tea. Sophia was sitting back with her eyes closed, and for a moment he wasn't sure if she had dozed off. Sensing his presence, she opened her eyes and reached out for the mug. Caleb made himself comfortable next to her, watching her as she took a big sip of her tea. She let out a blissful sound and placed the mug down on a coaster.

"So, don't keep me in suspense. How was it?" he asked, impatient to hear details from Sophia's day.

"It was pretty epic," she confirmed. "Malina was amazing. Down to earth. Funny. Magnetic. The pictures turned out so well I can hardly believe it." She ran a hand through her dark, wavy hair. "She was so kind to me and said some really complimentary things. When I showed her some of the images, she was truly moved by them. Tears and all."

"Of course," Caleb said. "She was probably blown away by your skills."

Sophia chuckled and swatted at him. "I can't tell if you're being serious or not, but I'll take the compliment."

"That's how it was intended, Sophia." He grazed the side of her face with his knuckles. "Face it. Your talent speaks for itself. That's why Malina wanted you for this assignment."

"Pretty soon you're going to give me a swollen head," Sophia said, chuckling. She motioned with her hands. "Keep the compliments coming."

Her lids were closing, and her words sounded a bit jumbled. She was exhausted from her whirlwind trip.

"Hey, why don't you get some shut-eye?" he suggested. "It's been quite a day for you."

She let out a yawn and covered her mouth. "Oh, I'm so sorry. I really am beat, and this upcoming week is important. We need to do our on-location shoot and wrap up this campaign."

Caleb was a bit surprised. The campaign was rolling along like a freight train. "It's going at warp speed. I'm no expert, but this is fast, isn't it?" He had a bit of a perspective since he'd been a cast member on *Love Him or Leave Him*, although he knew marketing a product was different from promoting a reality show.

Sophia bit her lip. "I know. I have a hunch that Hattie is

trying to wrap things up before her health declines even further. She wants to see this come to fruition before she goes. Most of all, Hattie wants to see you repping Yukon Cider."

Caleb was a bit speechless. He hadn't even considered that possibility. Hattie had lots of life in her yet.

"Hattie's not going anywhere. That lady is the toughest woman I've ever known," Caleb said. He could hear the defensive tone in his voice.

Honestly, it gutted him to think that his grandmother was trying to get her affairs in order before she passed on. Feeling this way was ridiculous, since Hattie's impending death was the very reason he was here in Moose Falls. Sometimes he felt as if he were operating in reverse. Instead of leaning toward accepting the inevitable, Caleb was chafing against the reality that Hattie wouldn't be around a year from now. His chest was suddenly tight, and he was feeling a bit panicky. What was going on with him? None of this was new information, but all of a sudden it was hitting him like a ton of bricks.

"Caleb, are you okay?" Sophia asked in a soft voice. "I'm sorry if I spoke out of turn. The situation with Hattie must be agonizing, especially since you two are so close."

"I'm fine," he said, standing up from his seat. He wasn't really feeling fine, but it wasn't Sophia's fault. "But it's getting late and you need some sleep."

"If you like, I can make lunch for you tomorrow. It's the least I could do after you saved my bacon. How about it?" she asked.

"I'm not one to turn down a lunch invitation from a pretty girl," Caleb said, flashing her a smile. "Mama didn't raise no fools."

Sophia made a move to get up, and he stopped her with a gentle hand on her shoulder. "I can see myself out, Sophia.

You get some rest. I'll see you soon." He pressed a kiss on her forehead and beat a fast path toward the door.

Caleb knew that he hadn't done a good job at hiding his feelings about Hattie. There was something so sobering about the fact that Hattie might be trying to put finishing touches on her legacy before her illness worsened. Would it be weeks? Months? It hurt his heart to think about losing his grandmother. Slowly but surely he was putting things in perspective. He thought back to how heartbroken he had been after losing Abby, and although it was a different type of love, it paled in comparison to what he was feeling now.

Caleb inhaled a deep breath as he stepped outside into the chilly night air. It was so cold he could see his breath in front of his face. As he drove back to Hattie's house, his mind was racing. He was starting to experience a sense of belonging here in Moose Falls. He was no longer a stranger getting reacquainted with his childhood hometown. He enjoyed his work at Yukon Cider and the many friendships he'd developed with his colleagues. Living with his brothers under Hattie's roof took him all the way back to his younger years, when he woke up in the morning and looked out of his bedroom window to the sight of majestic snowcapped mountains. Words couldn't describe the way that northern lights shimmered and pulsed in the skies. While his relationship with Red was far from close, they were on solid ground. And Hattie—feisty, irrepressible Hattie—easy to love and tattooed on his heart for all time.

And now, he was establishing a bond with Sophia and her daughter. It was nothing like anything he had ever known. He hadn't expected this thunderstruck feeling, this desire to spend every waking moment with her. In actuality, he'd been running from the mere prospect of catching feelings for anyone. But now he knew with a deep certainty that he wasn't in love with Abby anymore.

Up to this point he hadn't allowed himself to admit the depth of his feelings for Sophia. He was falling for the gorgeous single mom, and it scared him to death.

CHAPTER FOURTEEN

After Caleb left her house, Sophia forced herself to get up from the couch, even though she could easily drift off to sleep right here. Sophia locked up, turned off all the downstairs lights, and trudged up the stairs. Quietly, she stepped into Lily's bedroom and walked over to her bed. Her daughter was sleeping like an angel, peacefully curled up with her teddy bear in her arms. The night-light softly illuminated Lily's brown skin, making it glow.

"Good night, sweet girl," she whispered, leaning over and placing a kiss on her temple. Lily was sleeping so soundly she didn't even stir. The love she held in her heart for Lily was so strong and powerful it made her feel weak in the knees.

As she fell asleep, Sophia had a picture in her mind of Caleb—his infectious smile, his dimples, and his warm brown skin. The way he looked at her as if she were all that mattered in the world. She drifted off thinking about him.

The following morning, Lily was up and at 'em right after Sophia herself woke up. Her daughter couldn't stop talking about the events of the previous day and how much fun it was.

"I had three sitters," Lily told her over breakfast.

"Three?" Sophia asked as she took a big gulp of her coffee.

"Yep," Lily said, smiling as she ate a spoonful of her cereal.

Sophia frowned at her. "What were their names?"

"Caleb was the boss. Umm," Lily said, as if trying to remember.

"Was one Landon?" Sophia asked.

Lily nodded before slurping down her cereal milk. When she finished, there was a milk mustache above her mouth. "And one was called X something."

"Xavier, right?" Sophia already knew the answer. The three Stone brothers were as thick as thieves. A contemporary Three Musketeers.

"Yeah, but I couldn't say his name, so he said I could call him X," Lily told her. "We had so much fun."

The fact that Caleb's brothers had helped watch Lily cracked Sophia up. Clearly, Caleb had needed reinforcements. Sophia couldn't blame him. Lily could be a whirlwind at times. Being responsible for small children wasn't for the faint of heart. According to Lily, they had all been amazing caretakers. She had been very impressed with their willingness to play dress-up.

Sophia was still chuckling about it as she got ready to host Caleb for lunch. Instead of cooking anything elaborate, she'd prepared some teriyaki salmon, jasmine rice, and a big salad. Promptly at twelve-thirty, Caleb arrived, carrying two bouquets of flowers. Lily came racing to the door, chanting Caleb's name as soon as she laid eyes on him.

"Lily," Caleb said, scooping her up in his arms and hugging her. "Long time no see."

"I just saw you yesterday," Lily said, looking up at him with wide eyes.

Caleb and Sophia chuckled at the confused sound of her voice.

"Right you are," Caleb said as they walked toward the brightly lit kitchen.

Since Lily had already eaten her lunch, Sophia and Caleb sat down by themselves at the butcher-block kitchen table while Lily colored in the playroom. It was cozier in here than in the larger dining room. The table being set for two lent an intimate vibe to the space. Sophia laid out the food and the place settings, along with tall glasses of iced tea.

"I like the flavor of this," Caleb said after taking a bite of the salmon.

"Thank you. I marinated the salmon in teriyaki sauce," Sophia said. "It really does taste nice."

"Thanks for inviting me over," Caleb said. "I know weekends are precious."

"Of course. It's my pleasure. Lily tells me that you had company yesterday," Sophia said, her lips twitching with laughter. Ever since finding out, Sophia had wished she could have been a fly on the wall. The thought of Caleb watching Lily was adorable, but knowing it had been the Brothers Stone as a babysitting crew was magnificent.

A guilty expression came over his face. "Busted. I hope that was okay. Now I'm thinking maybe I should have asked your permission before I invited them over." Caleb looked nervous.

"No, that's fine," she reassured him. "I trust your judgment, Caleb. Otherwise, I wouldn't have let you watch Lily or stay at my house. Landon and Xavier are great. I'm really happy True and Xavier are getting married."

"Phew," Caleb said, letting out a breath. "I have to admit, taking care of a four-year-old is much harder than I imagined." He made a face. "She ran me ragged."

Sophia burst out laughing as an image of an exhausted Caleb chasing Lily ran through her mind. "Been there, done that," Sophia said. "I could apologize, but you were pretty insistent about watching her." She took a sip of her iced tea. "And if I haven't thanked you profusely enough, I'm incredibly grateful for your help yesterday. Lily thinks you hung the moon."

"As Hattie would say, she's the bee's knees as far as I'm concerned."

Caleb's comment caused a warm sensation to flow through her. Lily deserved to have as many people as possible in her world who held her in high esteem.

"As a mom, it's always heartwarming when someone values your child. So thank you for seeing Lily." Not everyone enjoyed children, so this was another green flag as far as she was concerned.

"You've been great about letting me into your world, Sophia."

"Well, I was sort of hoping you would return the favor. I haven't forgotten. You owe me a story." Sophia hoped she wasn't overstepping, but she wanted to know what had gone down with Abby. The real scoop that the reality show hadn't depicted. He'd promised to tell her, so she was holding him to it. If their relationship was going to deepen and flourish, he had to peel back the layers. She sensed that if she dug a little, she would hit pay dirt and discover so much about him that he didn't normally share.

Caleb fidgeted with his hands. "To tell you the truth, I hate talking about this, but I know you must be curious after what was shown on television."

"Believe me, I get it. Making ourselves vulnerable in relationships isn't easy. And then to have it all blow up in your face must've been excruciating."

He shrugged, his sweater taut against his chest. "Maybe I'm just embarrassed that I thought Abby and I were the real deal and, much to my surprise, it was anything but authentic."

Sophia could hear the pain laced in his voice and it gutted her. What had Abby done to him? Anger swiftly rose up inside her. Poor Caleb!

"I think loving is what we were put on Earth to do, so you should never feel embarrassed or foolish about having given yourself wholly and completely to another person," Sophia told him. Honestly, it caused a groundswell of tenderness toward him to wash over her.

"When I went on the show, I never imagined making it all the way to the finals. I honestly did the show because I was told by my agent that it would be a great way to get exposure that could lead to acting roles. Famous last words." His jaw clenched tightly. "I really liked Gillian. She was beautiful, smart, and funny. And I truly believed she'd come on the show in the pursuit of love. But as time went by, I knew that I wasn't falling for her. Yet every week she kept picking me to go forward. Behind the scenes, I was falling for her twin sister, Abby, who was on location with us and had a small role on the show." His eyes lit up. "I don't know how else to say it, but I was drawn to her. We could talk for hours about everything under the sun. Movies. Food. Our favorite musical artists. I'd never vibed with anyone like that before."

"Wow," Sophia said. Caleb's story was intriguing, and she was following along with rapt attention. How wrong she'd been to judge him.

"Abby and I started spending a lot of time together away from the cameras, so no one really knew that we were connecting. She was sweet and kind, and she made me believe that I could do just about anything." He wrinkled his nose. "Confessing that I wanted a professional acting career has never been easy, but she was so encouraging and enthusiastic. Everything felt as if it was falling into place so effortlessly."

"You fell in love with her," Sophia said. It was clear from the look on his face and the softness in the way he said her name.

He nodded. "I fell for her hard, like someone knocked me over the head with a ton of bricks. We were in love and planning a future together. Or so I thought," he said, quirking his mouth. "At the same time I was advancing on the show. I kept telling Abby that I needed to bail on the show so we could be together. I didn't want Gillian to get hurt or end up being blindsided, and I knew everything was coming to a head. There were a few episodes where I tried to push her in another direction, but she always picked me." A huge sigh slipped past his lips. "And then Gillian discovered Abby and me together while the cameras just happened to be running. Abby came out smelling like a rose." He let out a brittle laugh. "And I ended up stinking to high heavens."

Sophia frowned. "Do you think they were in cahoots?"

He leaned forward and splayed his hands on the table. "Well, think about it. They framed me as the bad guy, got explosive ratings for the show, then parlayed the drama into a spin-off featuring both of them. It's the only thing that makes sense to me."

Twin Shot at Love was a brand-new reality series featuring Abby and Gillian's attempts to find love after betrayal. Part of the narrative was that Caleb's cheating ways had wounded both of the twins and damaged their relationship. They had both courted the media with their tales of woe and their desire to love and be loved.

"Did you ever try to talk to Abby about all of this?" Sophia asked.

He ran a hand across his jaw. "She cut me off completely. Changed her cell phone number so I had no way to reach her. A few of the guys from my season let me know that she'd made some noise about a restraining order if I tried to get in touch with her." Caleb shuddered.

"That's pretty diabolical," Sophia sputtered. "They extended their fifteen minutes of fame at your expense. Not to mention smearing your good name."

Caleb made a face. "One hundred percent. They took my pain and used it as a springboard into a lucrative contract. I think they were both in on it, setting themselves up as the victims and me as the Love Rat."

Sophia was horrified that the twins had gotten away with it. "And no one has ever pointed a finger at them or cast doubt on their story."

"Nope," Caleb said before downing the rest of his iced tea. "It made for good TV and stellar ratings. That's all that matters to some people."

"I'm so sorry this happened to you," Sophia said, tears misting in her eyes. What kind of woman would treat a man like Caleb in this horrific manner? He had given Abby his love, then had those feelings thrown back in his face. Not to mention the fact that his reputation and budding career had been trashed. Life could be so unfair.

"It's okay," he said with a shake of his head. "Actually, it's not okay, but I've managed to move on from it. Hopefully, I've grown as a person."

Sophia got up and went over to his side of the table. She placed his head between her hands. "You're an incredible man, Caleb Stone. She didn't deserve you." Her body trembled with outrage for what he'd been through. She ached with sadness for him.

Caleb placed his arms around her waist and pulled her

down onto his lap. Sophia looped her arms around his neck and gazed into his eyes. "My taste has matured since then."

"Oh, really?" she asked, meeting him halfway in a blistering kiss that seemed to take them both by surprise. Sophia knew that she was falling for Caleb, and it was far too late to make an exit plan. She wanted to take away all the hurt and restore his belief in love. She placed her hands on both sides of his neck, tenderly grazing her fingers against his skin. As the kiss soared and crested, Sophia didn't want it to end. She wanted to hold on to this moment as long as she possibly could. Her mouth opened and their tongues met, savoring, exploring, each other. She melted into him, sucked into a vortex of pure need.

"Mommy." Lily's little voice rang out in the stillness, startling both of them. Sophia swung her gaze toward the entryway where Lily was standing, a confused expression on her face. "Why are you kissing Caleb?"

Caleb and Sophia pulled apart at the sound of Lily's voice, despite the fact that it might have been the hardest thing he'd ever done. The look of shock on Sophia's face told him that she wasn't used to her daughter catching her in the act of smooching.

"Lily! I-I thought you were coloring," Sophia said feebly.

"I was," Lily said, "and I wanted to show you my picture." She held up a brightly colored drawing.

Sophia let out an exaggerated gasp. "Oh, that's fabulous. A masterpiece. You're my little Picasso," she gushed, holding her hands to her cheeks.

Caleb let out a whistle. "No one told me you were an artist."

"Why were you kissing?" Lily asked again, looking back and forth between them. Clearly, their attempt at distraction wasn't working.

"Umm, well I—" Sophia began, fumbling with her words.

"Lily," Caleb said, interrupting Sophia. "Sometimes when grown-ups really, really like each other, they want to spend time together. And when they're with each other, they kiss to show each other just how much they like each other."

Lily looked up at him with her big brown eyes. Sophia was totally tongue-tied by his side.

"Does that make sense?" Caleb asked, reaching out and squeezing her hand. Lily nodded and said, "Yes. And I don't mind," in a solemn little voice.

"Thank you for that," Caleb said, trying not to laugh. Lily seemed to be rather serious about the whole matter.

Lily gifted him with a beatific smile and held out the drawing toward him. "For you," she said, ducking her head down.

"Can I get a hug?" he asked. "This is a great present."

Lily didn't hesitate to hold out her arms and fall into his. Hugging Lily made him feel protective. She was so little and innocent, full of goodness and light. A scent of vanilla and soap clung to her. He totally understood why she was the center of Sophia's world.

When he let go of Lily, she gave him another smile and skipped off toward the playroom. Caleb looked down at his drawing, a smile twitching at his lips.

"She's something else, but I'm guessing you already know that," Caleb told Sophia.

"She's everything," Sophia said, tearing up. "Thanks for stepping in like that. I had no idea how to answer her, and that never happens to me. It just makes me realize that as she gets older, the questions are going to get harder."

"I agree, but you've got this. Lily adores you, and you're a nurturing and loving mother. A child couldn't ask for a better home in which to thrive." He placed his arm around her shoulder and pulled Sophia against him. She had the same strength as Daisy—raising a child on her own and doing it like a rock star.

"You're going to give me a swollen head, Mr. Stone," Sophia said, leaning her head on his shoulder. They sat like this for a few minutes, comfortable in the silence that stretched between them. Caleb was content in a way he hadn't experienced before. He didn't need to be doing anything at all with Sophia in order to feel this way. No bells or whistles. No fancy clubs or the glare of the spotlight.

Being on reality television had done a number on his self-esteem. Sophia was enough to silence that little voice inside him that told him he wasn't worthy of a happy ending.

Despite the winter thaw in Moose Falls, temps were still chilly as Caleb posed for Sophia's camera at an outdoor shoot by the town's historic waterfall. The last time he had seen Sophia had been a few days ago at her house when Lily had walked in on them. Even though they'd just been kissing, Sophia had been a little freaked out. Lily had never seen her kissing a partner before, not even her dad. And the little girl had later peppered Sophia with endless questions. He had to admit to being relieved that he hadn't been present for the grand inquisition.

Like the true chicken he was, Caleb couldn't handle such intense questioning. Being a sitter he could do, but being grilled by a four-year-old was out of the question.

His current backdrop was the gorgeous mountain range—craggy, towering mountains that seemed almost surreal.

He couldn't remember ever seeing anything so beautiful in his entire life. The sky—a pristine robin's-egg blue—only heightened the effect. Judging by the sounds Sophia was making as she checked the photos on her camera, the end result was amazing.

"Just a few more," Sophia called out. "Let's get some shots with you on the snow machine with Hazel."

It always cracked Caleb up that snow mobiles were called snow machines here in Alaska.

"Sounds good," he said, rubbing his hands together. Thankfully, he had been given thermal gloves to wear during the shoot. Otherwise, his fingers would have been frozen to the bone. This photo shoot was shaping up a little differently than the previous one. This time he had a costar. Hazel Alexander was a model hired for the shoot due to Hattie's belief that a romantic storyline might enhance the campaign. With black shoulder-length hair and stunning cheekbones, Hazel radiated model vibes.

Caleb and Hazel were led over to the snow machine by Sophia's assistants, Max and Laura. The married couple had been working as a team for a decade, working on brand campaigns and enhancing the shoots with their experience in photography.

Caleb sat down on the snow machine with Hazel sitting in front of him, striking a pose as Sophia snapped away. Sophia called out compliments, praising them for nailing the shots. Although Hazel was a stunning woman, all Caleb could think about was the woman behind the camera. He loved watching her in action. Her movements were fluid and graceful. Poetry in motion. She was giving him the confidence to be completely at ease and in control of his own image. It was a nice feeling to be creative and finally have some autonomy.

For the longest time he'd been keeping a lid on the part of him that wanted the spotlight. He'd come out of his experience on the reality show feeling as if he should stuff all of his aspirations down into a dark hole and never pursue them again. He had changed his mind after licking his wounds. Now he still harbored hope that he could turn things around and pursue an acting career.

As the shoot concluded, Sophia and her team gave them a standing ovation.

"I think we've got it," Sophia called out. "We've got some great stuff here."

Caleb gave Hazel a hug. "Nice working with you, Hazel. Let's hope we created a little magic on camera." So much was riding on this.

"Same," Hazel said with a grin. "It's been a lot of fun."

Caleb wasted no time making a beeline in Sophia's direction. Whenever she was in a five-mile radius, he just wanted to be as close to her as possible. Hazel was a stunner, but he hadn't even thought twice about her.

"Hattie's going to be really pleased with these photos. We got a little bit of everything," Sophia raved. "You and Hazel's chemistry was off the charts."

"She's sweet, but I think my chemistry with the photographer is much more intense," Caleb said, resisting the urge to give her a celebratory kiss. Since they were on a shoot, he knew that showing his affection in that way would be crossing a line. He wasn't going to do anything to jeopardize Sophia's professional reputation. She had worked tirelessly to make a name for herself in the industry and her efforts were beginning to pay off.

He would be content just to admire her from a foot away. She was wearing an adorable white parka, a matching hat, and dark jodhpur-style pants. Her brown cheeks were rosy from the cold, and she'd stuffed her long tresses under her hat.

"I have an idea," she said. "Have you ever gone snow machine riding?"

"I can't say that I have," Caleb said. "I was a little too young when we left here to be able to ride."

"Well, there's still enough snow to do it. We could hit the trails and see some scenic views."

"That sounds like my kind of fun," Caleb said. "Just tell me when and where."

"Lily is spending the weekend with her dad, so I have some free time on my hands," Sophia told him. "I can pick you up at Hattie's house."

"How's everything going with that situation?" he asked. Sophia hadn't told him anything more about the custody issue, and he hadn't wanted to broach the subject.

"Things have been quiet on that front, thankfully," Sophia explained. "I'm hoping his custody talk was just a passing fancy. I don't need or want any drama."

"I hear that," Caleb said. "I've had enough drama for several lifetimes. Who knew my life in Moose Falls would be so chill?"

Sophia grinned at him as she packed up her gear. "Alaska is a very chill place."

He couldn't agree with her more. Lately he'd been asking himself if he could imagine himself becoming a permanent resident of Moose Falls. At moments like this one, it wasn't hard to envision at all.

Caleb helped Sophia carry her gear to the work van. They headed back to Yukon Cider, where Sophia focused on checking the images from today's shoot and comparing them to the ones she had previously taken. Caleb popped in the pics. He gave off star vibes. It wasn't just his good looks either. He projected an effortless cool, the sort that was hard to come by. He radiated confidence. Every instinct told her that he was going to soar in this campaign. The public was going to love him, and by extension, the new hard cider product. The commercials would be icing on the cake.

Sophia couldn't help but wonder if Caleb would stay in Moose Falls once this campaign blew up. After all, it was his dream to become an actor. The reality show hadn't been a great stepping stone, but this Yukon Cider campaign could give him a shot at fame. She'd seen it happen before with ad campaigns and models who became personalities. The thought of losing Caleb made her pulse race and gave her an uncomfortable gnawing in her belly.

It would hurt to lose him just as they were starting to build something. But he deserved to live out his dreams. And even if it killed her, she would cheer him on.

By the end of the week, she had taken all of Caleb's campaign photos and filmed two commercials. She wasn't sure which of them was more excited about the upcoming ads. Sophia knew this was going to be a career high for her, and that felt exciting. Yukon Cider was a quality company, and if this campaign was successful, she might have a strong future with the company. That would help her establish a secure foundation for Lily, which was all she had ever wanted in this world.

When Saturday rolled around, Sophia handed Lily over to Donny for an overnight visit. Although it wasn't easy, Sophia put her big-girl panties on and smiled at her daughter as if she were going on a grand adventure. She gave an Oscar-worthy performance. Thankfully, Lily enjoyed spending time with her dad, which made the situation more palatable. Sophia knew from her own life and experiences the importance of daddy–daughter time. If Donny had decided to spend more time with Lily, then she needed to encourage it and try to minimize any conflict. He needed to prove to her that he could be a consistent, responsible parental figure in their daughter's life before she agreed to grant him joint custody.

While Lily was away, Sophia planned to spend the day with Caleb. She had dressed in the perfect gear for snow machining—a lightweight snowsuit—advising Caleb to do the same. There was still a lot of snow on the trails despite the spring thaw. She had grown up snow machining with her dad, and it was something she truly enjoyed. And she wanted to share this pastime with Caleb.

When she swung by Hattie's house, Sophia didn't even have to step out of her vehicle. Caleb was at the front door in minutes, raring to go. He quickly made it over to her truck and stepped up into the passenger seat. "Good morning," he greeted her, along with a wide smile. Sophia had to hand it to Caleb. He always had a positive outlook and a cheerful disposition. She wondered if that was part of a coping mechanism from a chaotic childhood torn apart by divorce and moving away from everything he'd ever known. Smiling through the pain.

"Morning, Caleb," she said warmly, giving him a subtle once-over. He was decked out in snow pants, a navy turtleneck, and a lightweight parka. As usual, he looked amazing.

"Thanks for picking me up," he told her. He held up a brown paper bag. "Landon baked some chocolate chip cookies, and he insisted we take some along with us."

"Aww, that's sweet of him. I love that he bakes," she gushed. The idea of Landon up to his elbows in flour and chocolate chips was heartwarming.

"Well, I helped," Caleb quickly added.

"Did you?" Sophia asked. "What was your role? Taste tester?"

"How did you know?" he asked, chuckling.

"I just had a feeling," Sophia said, laughing along with him. She would love to have seen him as a little kid. She just knew he'd been mischievous and one of a kind.

She heard a rustling sound, and out of the corner of her eye she saw Caleb digging into the brown bag. "Want a bite?" he asked. A quick look confirmed that he'd already dug into one of the cookies.

"It's kind of early for a cookie," she answered.

He let out a gasp. "Seriously? Is that even a thing? In my world it's never too early for a chocolate chip cookie." He let out a moan of appreciation as he bit into the treat. The aroma of chocolate wafted over to her, serving as a temptation she couldn't easily ignore.

"Wow. It's so rich and gooey," Caleb said in a garbled voice.

"Gimme some of that," Sophia said, holding out her hand.

"You sure? I wouldn't want you to sacrifice your principles on my account."

She let out a little growl. "If you don't break me off a piece of that chocolate deliciousness, we might never make it to JR's."

"Okay, okay," Caleb said as he handed over half of the cookie. Sophia kept one hand on the wheel and took the cookie from Caleb. Instead of biting into it right away, she lifted it to her nose before taking a huge whiff.

She took a bite, letting out a little sound the moment the flavors hit her tongue. "Oh, my goodness. This is incredible. Like seriously amazing."

"Why, thank you. Landon and I make a good team."

"These cookies are bakery worthy," she raved, taking little nibbles so she could savor the experience. "I'd love the recipe."

"Hattie's recipe," Caleb said. "She handed it over under strict orders that it was for our eyes only."

"Aww, bummer. I totally get it, though. My dad has so many secret recipes they could fill a cookbook. If they weren't secret, that is."

Conversation flowed easily between them in the truck. There wasn't a single moment where the conversation lagged or became stalled. They shared a good rapport, and he made her laugh like no other. There was so much about Caleb that she found to be endearing. It was both scary and exciting to realize the depth of emotion he brought out in her.

When they arrived at JR's Snow Patrol, there was a short wait to rent the snow machines. It was a crisp, gorgeous day, so she wasn't too surprised that other folks wanted to take advantage of the weather. After renting helmets and the snow machines, they headed over to the area where the snow machines were located.

"If you've ever ridden an ATV, this is pretty similar," Sophia explained. "As long as you understand the basic mechanics."

"Yep. ATVs are big in Arizona. We grew up riding them as teens," Caleb said. "Those were some great adventures."

"Well, you're going to love this. I promise," Sophia told him.

Sophia gave Caleb a detailed overview, explaining the mechanics and how to accelerate and brake. He picked everything up quickly, seemingly at ease with the snow machine. When they started off on the trail, Sophia advised Caleb to go in front of her so she could watch him until he found his groove. As they set off, she reminded him to watch his speed and let her know if he wanted to take a break. The trail was easily marked with colored dots based on the difficulty level. They were starting off on the beginners' trail, then planning to switch to intermediate. Sophia figured the difficult trail could be attempted on another day. There was no point in pushing it. After a while they switched over to the intermediate trail, with Caleb having increased his speed. He was doing fantastic. A real pro, even though it was his first time.

All of a sudden Caleb's snow machine abruptly accelerated rather than braking as they reached a fork in the trail. Caleb let out a yell, and the snow machine lurched forward. Seconds later the machine crashed into a bush, sending Caleb flying into the air. He landed with a thud in the snow. Sophia hit the brake and jumped off her machine, running to Caleb's side. He was lying on his stomach, appearing very still.

"Caleb!" she shouted, shaking him. "Are you all right?"

She wasn't breathing properly until he let out a groan and turned on his side. Signs of life. She had been imagining the worst.

"Oh, wow. That was a complete face-plant," he said, lifting his snow-covered face up from the ground. He looked like the abominable snowman, covered in the fluffy white stuff.

"Does anything hurt?" she asked, grabbing ahold of his elbow. "Let me help you get up."

"I might need a kiss to make it better," he said, pointing to his lips. Feeling relieved, Sophia kneeled down and swept a kiss against his frosty lips. Caleb placed his hands on her arms and pulled her down so that she was next to him in the snow. Despite the cold temps, their kiss warmed her up, making Sophia forget all about the cold. As the kiss soared and deepened, she felt a fluttering sensation in her chest. This man made her feel more alive and present than she had ever felt in her life other than the day Lily was born.

"Do you need help getting up?" she asked, still worried about any potential injury.

"I'm fine, just took me by surprise," he said, standing up under his own steam. He looked over at the snow machine resting against the bush. "I hope it's okay. JR might not be too happy with me if I wrecked one of his machines."

"It looks fine to me," Sophia said, giving it the once-over.

"Then let's get back to it," Caleb said, grinning. "I'll let you lead for the rest of the trail."

"Are you sure you're okay to continue? You might have a few bumps and bruises tomorrow."

"Are you kidding me?" he scoffed. "I'm a Stone brother. Bumps and bruises come with the territory." He laughed as he jumped back on the snow machine. He tested it out by slowly reversing, then putting on a little speed.

"In that case we can finish the trail then loop back to our starting point. Sound good?"

Caleb gave her a thumbs-up, and she took off with him following at a safe distance. He had rebounded quickly from the incident with his snow machine. Once they reached the end of the trail and headed back to JR's shop, they both pulled over to turn in their snow machines.

"That may have been the coolest thing I've done since coming back to Alaska," Caleb raved. "Thanks for the invite. I can't wait to tell Xavier and Landon all about it."

"You're welcome. There's nothing quite like it if you ask me," Sophia said. "The view. The feel of the cold air against one's cheek. The feeling of flying through the air."

"Literally," Caleb said with a deadpan expression before

bursting into laughter. She chuckled along with him, enjoying the fact that he could laugh at his snow machine mishap.

She pulled out a thermos from her bag and lifted it in the air. "Snack time. Hot cocoa coming right up!"

Caleb rubbed his hands together. "Oh, I'll definitely have some of that to warm my insides."

"I'm really sorry about your fall off the snow machine. You were such a good sport about it," Sophia said. Caleb could so easily have gotten hurt. Wearing a helmet and being in great shape had really helped him.

"No worries. The only thing hurt was my pride." He chuckled, showcasing pretty white teeth. "I'm not a fan of embarrassing myself in front of someone I'm dating." He playfully hid his face with his hand while holding his hot cocoa in the other.

Dating? It was nice hearing him confirm what they were doing. In past relationships she had "dated" men who had their own lingo for what was going on between them. Hanging out. Hooking up. Passing time together. Netflix and chilling. Now that she had Lily, she couldn't afford to be so cavalier. Although she was gun-shy about romance, the truth was that she wanted to be in a committed, loving relationship. She had worked very hard to ignore this reality, but just seeing other couples like True and Xavier find their happily-ever-after cemented the fact that she wanted her own.

"I could get used to this!" Caleb said, looking around the wooded area. "This must be the most pristine air I've ever breathed in."

Sophia nodded. "It's as close to perfect as it gets. You and your brothers must have loved living here as kids. There was always so much to do. Skating. Skiing. Sledding. Hiking."

A wistful expression passed over his face. "We loved living in Moose Falls. It all ended rather abruptly with the divorce and all. We moved to Arizona, which is the very opposite of Alaska." A sigh slipped past his lips. "I missed the snow and the cold and wearing sweaters."

In her mind's eye Sophia could picture an adorable, pint-size version of Caleb. He would have stood out in a crowd. Charming and hilarious.

"We must've crossed paths as children, right?" Caleb asked. "This town is pretty small."

Sophia let out a raucous laugh. "Maybe, but I think that I would have remembered you if we had. For a while after my parents divorced, I went to live with my mom in Homer, so we probably missed that connection."

Caleb scrunched up his nose. "To this day I hate that word. The D word."

She reached out and touched his gloved hand. "Why? It's just a word."

"Not to me. It's the thing that changed everything in our lives. It's the reason we had to leave Moose Falls."

"I get it. For me it was almost a relief from all the stress around the house. Other than having to live in Homer for a few years, it wasn't horrible." She bit her lip. "I just wish that my dad had found someone else to love. He's been alone all this time."

"Have you ever asked him if he's looking for love? He might be content being single."

"I've hinted a few times, but he always shuts me down," Sophia admitted. It wasn't a comfortable topic with her dad even though they shared a tight bond. Sophia had a hunch that her dad didn't want to be vulnerable in a relationship again. Of all people, Sophia understood that predicament. Once bitten, twice shy. Donny had taken a bite out of her that had left permanent marks. Putting herself back out there wasn't easy.

But meeting Caleb made Sophia want to take a chance. If she didn't, she would always regret it.

"My mom has been single for a long time and, honestly, it doesn't bother her. I think her rationale is that she had a big love and in the end things didn't work out."

"What about Red? I don't know him very well, but I don't recall hearing him linked up with anyone here in town."

"I have no idea. Our relationship was nonexistent for many years. Our entire childhood basically after we moved to Arizona," Caleb explained in a tone laced with sorrow. "I can't imagine being an absentee father. Why did he allow that to happen?"

"Sounds like something the two of you might want to spend some time repairing," Sophia suggested.

"We're working on it, but it's slow going. I want to ask him so many things, but the words just keep getting stuck in my throat."

"Why do you think that is?" Sophia asked. She was finding out more and more about this man as time progressed, and this was baffling. He wasn't bashful or awkward, so why was he having such a hard time talking to his dad?

"Because a part of me doesn't want to know the answers," Caleb said. "Sometimes it's better just to stick your head in the sand." He shrugged. "Sometimes the truth hurts."

CHAPTER FIFTEEN

The snow machining adventure with Caleb couldn't have gone any better, Sophia thought as she sat down in her breakfast nook to eat her toast, blueberries, and scrambled eggs. He was such a fun person to be around. Yesterday he had peeled back his layers and shown a side of him that was vulnerable. Talking about his childhood and his relationship with Red had been a bit of a surprise. Listening to him had given her so much insight into the things that had shaped him. She had slept in this morning but had awoken thinking of Lily, only to remember she was with Donny until noon. Lily had only been away for less than twenty-four hours, yet Sophia missed her little girl like nobody's business. Her heart and mind were all over the place. Making sure Donny was in his daughter's life was important, but she resented the fact that she always had to be the bigger person.

When Donny brought Lily home, Sophia threw her arms around her as if she hadn't seen her in weeks. Lily tugged Donny by the hand and brought him into the house.

"I want to show Daddy my dollhouse. Okay?" Lily asked,

practically dragging Donny through the house and toward the playroom.

"Sure thing," Sophia said, clenching her teeth. She was working overtime trying to pretend as if nothing were wrong. Lily needed to see a united front between her parents at all times. Sophia didn't even want to make eye contact with him, knowing she might end up glaring. She was trying her best to be cordial, but all she could think about was his threat to sue for custody after doing the bare minimum with his daughter. It would never sit right with her.

Sophia sat in the den while Lily exuberantly showed off her dollhouse to Donny. She had to hand it to him. He always made their daughter feel special and loved. It was a damn shame that his presence in her life was so erratic. Lily would have benefited greatly from him being around more. She lit up with excitement every time he was around. Sophia didn't want Lily going through life with daddy issues and searching for love in all the wrong places.

After about twenty minutes, the sound of the playroom door being shut followed by Donny's approaching footsteps caused her to swing her gaze toward the doorway. He was standing there, shifting uncomfortably from one foot to the other. She had no intention of making things easy for him. If he had something to say to her, he just needed to spit it out.

"I have something for you. Here," Donny said, stepping closer and handing her an envelope.

"What is this?" she asked, tensing up. Was he serving her custody papers in her own house?

"Open it," he said. "It's not what you think." He shoved his hands in his jean pockets and watched her. With his dark hair and deep-set eyes, he looked like a brooding bad boy.

She opened the envelope and pulled out a check. She took

a quick look at it, letting out a surprised sound at the large amount. She swung her gaze up to meet Donny's. "What brought this on?"

"I want a fresh start with my daughter, and that means I have to make things right with you," he explained, his voice quavering. "I'm trying to play catch-up."

Sophia was so floored by Donny giving her this check for back child support that it rendered her speechless. He didn't sound cocky or brash; he sounded sincere. Although she was happy he had finally done the right thing, she had to wonder what had really changed. Why was he making this grand gesture?

"Better late than never," she said, deciding on the spot not to thank him for something he had been obligated to pay her for quite some time now. She already knew that he thought she was a pushover. No need to prove it by thanking him.

"Lily told me that you have a boyfriend." Donny uttered the words as a statement and not a question.

Boyfriend? Sophia found it hard to believe her four-year-old had used that word. She had the feeling Donny was putting words in her daughter's mouth to go on a fishing expedition. Anger rose up inside her. Was he gathering information for his custody case?

"Yes, I'm seeing someone," she responded. "That shouldn't be a problem." Donny should understand, since he'd always had a partner in his life, going from one relationship to the next. She did feel better now that he was married to Zora, so Lily wouldn't have to be subjected to a parade of girlfriends.

"So he's watched her for you?" He made a face. "Lily told me something about a day when you were away for work."

"Yes, that's true. He watched her when my family couldn't step in and I had a work commitment."

"You could have asked me. I'm her father."

She counted to ten. "Every time I've asked you, there's been an issue with your job. Am I wrong?"

Tension crackled in the air.

"You just don't want to give me a chance, do you?" he asked, frowning.

She threw her hands in the air. "Where is this going, Donny?" She wished that he would just get to the point. He seemed upset and was clearly probing into her private life.

"You can't just replace me in our daughter's life." He spat the words out angrily. His mouth settled in a hard line.

"What are you talking about?" Sophia sputtered. "I'm not trying to replace you."

He looked as if he might explode. "I'm still her father, and I haven't forgotten about joint custody. My lawyer's going to serve you with the paperwork to make things official." His body was trembling. His eyes glistened with anger.

"Whatever, Donny. Bring it on. You have a lot to answer to if and when you take this to court. Giving me a fat check doesn't change that."

"You're not the only one who has rights," Donny muttered right before turning around and heading out of the kitchen. Moments later she heard the front door close behind him.

She let out a sound of frustration that caused Lily to come running from the playroom. Her daughter looked up at her with innocence brimming from her eyes.

"What happened?" Lily asked.

"Nothing, baby, I stubbed my toe," she fibbed. There was no way she could justify telling a four-year-old that she was frustrated with her father. She had vowed a long time ago not to badmouth Donny to their daughter.

"Oh, no! You got a boo-boo," Lily said, raising her hands to her cheeks. She began blowing kisses at Sophia.

"I'm okay, sweetie," Sophia said, pulling Lily against her

and holding her tight. She needed this embrace right now. Being around Donny's negativity was exhausting, but getting a hug from Lily fed her soul.

Lily patted her back. "Okay, Mama," she said before racing back to her playroom.

"Thanks, sweetie," she called after her. She pressed her hand against her chest and began to take shallow breaths.

At moments like this, Sophia felt as if she were still grieving the loss of Donny. She wasn't in love with him anymore, but it hurt to have lost someone who had been so important to her. Having a child with someone established a lifelong bond. In a perfect world she and Donny could be friends post breakup and not adversaries. She shouldn't have to question his motives in seeking more time with Lily.

Donny used to be her friend, lover, and partner in crime and silliness. She hadn't even seen him change, nor had she been prepared for the transformation. It had happened in the twinkle of an eye, before she'd even realized it was occurring. She barely recognized him anymore.

And, as she continued to grow closer to Caleb, the reality scared the life out of her.

Love was a frightening proposition. It was the most unpredictable force on the planet.

People didn't always stay the same. They changed. And sometimes it wasn't for the better. What if the rug was pulled out from underneath her again when she least expected it? What if Caleb decided not to stick around Moose Falls once Hattie was no longer alive? It was too late for her to play it cool and pretend as if his leaving wouldn't tear her apart.

She was falling in love with Caleb, and there really wasn't anything she could do to prevent it from happening. *But* she could be proactive and try to protect herself *and*

Lily from having their hearts shattered into a hundred little pieces.

By the end of the work week, word got around Yukon Cider that test audiences were raving about the new campaign, with a particular emphasis and enthusiasm for Caleb as the spokesman. There was a palpable buzz in the air at the company. Caleb couldn't help but get excited, even though the campaign hadn't officially rolled out yet. Sophia was getting kudos too, especially from Hattie, which made him happy. She deserved every bit of praise, and he knew how much it meant coming from his grandmother. Like everyone else in Moose Falls, she thought Hattie was the be-all and end-all. Truthfully, he had a serious case of shero worship when it came to his grandmother.

And now, he was heading to Cosmic Bowling Alley for a boys' night out with the Brothers Stone. Once he parked and headed inside, Caleb made a beeline to the counter to pick up his bowling shoes.

Hanging out with his brothers never got old. It didn't matter where they were or what they were doing. Xavier and Landon were his best friends, and there weren't two other people in the world he would rather spend time with. Sophia's face flashed before his eyes. She was rapidly becoming one of his favorite people. She was probably a master bowler who won every single game she played. The thought of her bowling a perfect ten and jumping up in the air with excitement caused a grin to tug at his lips. He could honestly say that he wished Sophia were here tonight.

When he'd finished getting his shoes, Caleb heard Xavier calling his name. He made his way over to lane four, where his brothers were waiting.

"It seems congratulations are in order," Xavier said, holding up a can of Yukon Cider in the air. "Raise your cups, boys."

Landon and Caleb held their cans of hard cider in the air and clinked them together.

"To Caleb, who never met a mirror he didn't like," Landon quipped, earning him a jab in the ribs by Caleb.

"Hey, play nice," Caleb protested.

Xavier chuckled and continued by saying, "To Caleb, who always thinks he's the best-looking guy in the room."

"Charming. Is this a surprise roast or something?" Caleb asked, fighting off feelings of annoyance. "You two are hilarious."

"No, seriously, we're really proud of you, and we want you to know that," Landon said. "Wherever this takes you, we support your dreams."

"Here, here," Xavier said, letting out a loud whistle. "Way to represent for the Stone family, Caleb."

Caleb's cheeks flushed with pleasure at the sincerity in his brothers' voices. He could hear the love and respect emanating from them. More than anyone else other than their mother, Caleb valued their praise above all. They both knew how Caleb had struggled to find a sense of purpose and pride in himself. And they knew his dreams too—the ones he'd confided in the hours after lights out when secrets had been whispered and shared.

Xavier cleared his throat dramatically. "So, I wanted to ask the two of you knuckleheads if you wanted to be my best men." Although Xavier tried to lighten the ask by injecting a little humor, Caleb could hear the raw emotion in his voice.

Caleb and Landon shared a glance. They both knew how monumental this moment was. Xavier had been on the cusp of getting married once before, only to have his entire world crash and burn. He'd come to Moose Falls jaded about love. His journey to finding happiness and love everlasting with True had been epic. Even though it was their tendency to joke around as brothers, they both knew this wasn't the time or the place.

"I thought you'd never ask," Caleb quipped, reaching out and hugging Xavier.

Landon followed suit and said, "It would be an honor. We love both you and True."

The three of them hugged it out for a moment, knowing that soon things would shift in their lives. It was inevitable, since Xavier was settling down and devoting himself to True and Jaylen. Caleb was ecstatic that his older brother had found his other half, but he couldn't deny the tiny part of him that hated the idea of losing Xavier. Sure, they had always been close, but he'd been living in California while Xavier was in Arizona. Being in Moose Falls and living under the same roof had been a bonding experience.

"I hope I'm not interrupting anything." A honeyed voice rang out, causing the three of them to pull apart. True was standing there with Jaylen, a huge smile gracing her face. Xavier's face lit up with the purest smile Caleb had ever seen. If he hadn't known it before, he knew it now with a deep certainty. Xavier was deeply in love.

"I was wondering when you would show up," Xavier said, reaching for True and pulling her into an embrace. True stood on tiptoes and placed her lips on Xavier's.

"Get a room, people," Jaylen said in a raised voice. He rolled his eyes dramatically.

Caleb and Landon burst out laughing. Jaylen was one of the coolest kids around. He was sweet and loving. Clearly, he'd seen a lot of PDA between his sister and Xavier. Whenever the newly engaged couple was together, they couldn't keep their hands off each other.

Xavier and True pulled apart. Xavier's lips were twitching with suppressed laughter. Xavier always took Jaylen's comments in stride. Caleb knew he and Jaylen got along really well, with Xavier being the coach for Jaylen's football team.

"Jaylen," True said in a warning tone.

"What? I'm just keeping it real," the young boy said. He looked over at Caleb and Landon. "Am I right?" he asked, seeking support. He held up his hand, waiting for a high-five. At the risk of True's displeasure, Caleb slapped his hand, followed by Landon.

"Seriously?" True asked. "Ganging up on me, huh?"

"No worries," Xavier said, encircling her waist with his arms. "I'll always be team True."

A chorus of groans erupted from Jaylen, Caleb, and Landon as Xavier dipped True into another kiss.

"Not again," Jaylen griped. "We know you two are googly-eyed over one another. We get it!"

At least one of the Stone brothers had his future carved out. Caleb still felt as if his own was a big question mark.

"Look who's here," True called out, looking at a spot in the distance.

Pure joy shot through him at the sight of Sophia strutting toward lane four. In reality, she probably wasn't strutting, but the way her body was moving was definitely a sashay.

Figure-hugging jeans and a navy-colored long-sleeved tee lent her a casual vibe. She was ready to bowl and hang out with them. He couldn't be any happier.

Caleb knew he was grinning wildly at the sight of her. *Keep cool*, he reminded himself, knowing his brothers would laugh their butts off if he took a page from Xavier's playbook and got handsy with Sophia. In his heart of hearts Caleb wanted to walk over and plant a big, fat kiss on her lips, but he wasn't sure they were at that stage of public acts of affection.

What was going on with him? Hadn't he just teased Xavier about his smooch session with True? Okay. He knew what this was. Endorphins. He was being inundated with a rush of feelings that took him back to when he'd fallen for Abby. Was that what this was? Was he falling in love with Sophia? The thought made him feel as if he were gasping for air.

"Sophia. What are you doing here?" he asked, walking to meet her halfway.

"Am I not supposed to be here?" she asked, stopping in her tracks, then making a pivoting motion as if turning around to leave.

"No," he said quickly, reaching out and gently grasping her by the arm. "I'm just surprised."

"True invited me. Hope that's okay." For a moment she appeared uncertain, looking around the bowling alley.

"It's more than okay. It's a happy surprise," he said, smiling down at her. He leaned down and whispered, "Matter of fact, you made my week by showing up."

Sophia grinned back at him. "Now that's what I want to hear."

"Where's the princess?" Caleb knew getting coverage for Lily wasn't always easy, so he was really stoked she'd made it out tonight.

"At the moment Lily is being spoiled by Aunt Patience. Tonight they'll be painting their nails and having pizza."

"We're not painting any nails, but I can promise you pizza," Caleb said.

"The way to a girl's heart is definitely through pizza," Sophia said, walking beside him as they headed toward the group. Xavier and Landon greeted her with enthusiasm.

His brothers sent him loaded glances behind Sophia's back, driving the point home that they were still stuck in elementary school.

True immediately gave Sophia a hug, and the two began to chat in animated fashion. Caleb loved the graceful slope of Sophia's neck and her genuine, oversize grin.

"The two of you look good together," Xavier said in a low voice.

Caleb let out a throaty laugh. "Sophia would look good no matter who she's standing with, but the two of us together..." Caleb let out a low whistle. "We're a smoke show."

Landon shook his head. "You're too much. Like, seriously. Way too much."

True clapped her hands together. "Let's divvy up into teams. Girls against guys."

"We're not an even number," Landon pointed out.

"We are now," True said triumphantly as Jaylen walked over to the group.

"Not fair," Xavier shouted, waving his arms around.

"What's the matter?" Jaylen asked. "I'm just a kid."

Xavier looked around the group with his mouth hanging open. "Are you kidding me? Does no one else have a problem with this? He's a ringer," Xavier explained, his eyes wide. "I smell a setup."

True went over to her fiancé and planted a kiss on his lips. "It's going to be okay, Xavier. Stop being so competitive. This isn't the Super Bowl or anything."

Jaylen held his hands up. "Just a little friendly competition. Don't sweat it, Coach. Isn't that what you always tell us on the field?"

Xavier sputtered. "Jaylen is an amazing bowler. How about we swap him for Landon?" he asked, pointing at his baby brother.

Caleb let out a hoot of laughter at the outraged expression on Landon's face.

"Hey," Landon protested. "That's pretty foul of you. I have decent bowling skills."

"Not like the kid's," Xavier muttered. He turned to True. "Let's just get the ball rolling."

Despite a hard-fought battle, the all-men's team lost to Sophia, Jaylen, and True's team. Caleb loved every minute of it. Sophia cheered him on when it was his turn, eliciting groans from her teammates. He loved the way she let out a little squeal and jumped in the air every time she had a high score. Her enthusiasm was contagious. Sophia made him feel all warm and fuzzy inside. She was a woman who had a lot on her plate, including the new wrinkle about her ex trying to get joint custody, but she still managed to radiate joy.

"Careful," Landon said, "if you stare any harder, you might bore a hole straight through her."

"I like watching her," Caleb admitted. It made him happy, which would sound way too corny if he said it out loud. This feeling had been a long time coming. He had never imagined that he would meet anyone in Moose Falls who would evoke these strong emotions.

"That could sound creepy, but I'm just happy to see you back in the game," Xavier said, patting Caleb on the back. "I like her for you."

His chest tightened at Xavier's words. The thought of things becoming serious with Sophia made him nervous. It gave him flashbacks to his disastrous relationship with Abby and how it had broken him. He'd never imagined that he would be ready to wade back into the waters with anyone this fast.

Afterward, they sat down and ate pizza and chicken wings as Jaylen cracked them up with knock-knock jokes.

"Xavier," Jaylen said. "Knock, knock."

"Who's there?" Xavier asked.

"A little old lady."

"A little old lady who?"

"I didn't know you could yodel," Jaylen said, throwing his head back and cracking up at his own joke.

Xavier nodded approvingly. "That's a good one." He clapped him on the shoulder.

Seeing Jaylen and Xavier's tight bond drove home the point that Xavier was building a life for himself in Moose Falls. He would be a father figure for young Jaylen. And considering the fact that he had helped Daisy raise him and Landon, Caleb knew Jaylen couldn't ask for a more dependable and solid influence in his life. Xavier possessed all the qualities to make an outstanding dad.

Caleb was sitting at the end of the table next to Sophia. He had the feeling his brothers and True were sitting a discreet distance away from them in order to give them a little privacy. They hadn't been at all subtle about it, which he thought was pretty nice of them.

"I love seeing your brothers so excited for you," Sophia said as she filled her plate with slices of cheese and pepperoni pizza. Throughout the evening they had mentioned the campaign and Caleb's role in it.

"I hope you know that your talent is the real star of the campaign," Caleb told her. "You've got skills, girl." From the photos he'd seen, Sophia had worked her special brand of magic and made him look rugged, suave, and a bit out of reach.

Sophia grinned. Her cheeks flushed at the compliment. "That's sweet of you to say. We worked really well together, which I appreciate." She let out a chuckle. "You'd be surprised how many people I photograph get swollen heads and turn into divas. I think a lot of good things are going to be coming your way, Caleb, as the campaign rolls out." Sophia had a knowing expression on her face.

Caleb sure hoped so. Life had taught him that nothing was promised, and there was no point in counting his chickens. He wasn't in control of any of this.

"It's a bit premature, but I'll take the enthusiasm and good vibes." He made a face. "I haven't had anything in a long time to feel proud about. Being on the reality show was supposed to be my big moment, but I think it's safe to say I crashed and burned." He took a big bite of his pizza slice, then washed it down with some water.

"I'm happy to see you've come full circle. Being the face of Yukon Cider is a big deal. Did you know they've never had a spokesmodel before?"

Caleb felt a warm sensation in the center of his chest.

"Hattie did tell me that, and to say I'm honored is an understatement. I'm not sure that I've ever led the way in anything before." He shrugged. "Xavier was always first in every way imaginable. First kiss. First date. First to graduate."

Sophia's grin lit up her entire face. "Well then, even better. Your very own first."

"Growing up, I always felt overshadowed by my brothers and their accomplishments. I wasn't an athlete or a scholar. That made it really hard for me to figure out my place in the scheme of things."

Being the middle child hadn't always worked out well for him. With Xavier being a football star and Landon excelling in academics, he'd always felt that he wasn't special. Being loved by his family had made him feel safe and secure, but he'd always wished he hadn't felt so lost.

"This might be your time. Who knows where this might

lead," Sophia said in a spirited tone. He loved her enthusiasm and the optimistic way she viewed the world. Even though she tried to project a tough girl image, she was in actuality all tenderness and warmth.

He let out a chuckle. "I felt that way before when I went on *Love Him or Leave Him*. That didn't exactly work out the way I imagined." His experience in the world of reality television was one of the main reasons he was always careful not to set his hopes too high. If he did, it meant he had a long way to fall if things went wrong.

"In my experience, life rarely does." She raised her soda to her mouth and took a swig. "I never imagined I would be raising a child on my own, but sometimes the things we never expected turn into our biggest blessings." She let out a throaty chuckle. "Sounds corny, but it's true. Life has so many twists and turns."

"No, it doesn't," he said, nodding, "it sounds amazing. My mother used to say that something wonderful is always waiting for us around the corner."

"Your mother sounds like a national treasure. I bet she misses her boys a lot. I can't imagine ever being away from Lily even when she's all grown up." A thoughtful expression crossed her face.

"My mom is already planning her next trip out here," Caleb told her. "I'd love for you to hang out with us so you can get to know Daisy. She's a trip."

"That would be nice," Sophia murmured. "I love a strong woman."

He had surprised himself by broaching the subject of his mother and Sophia spending time together. Caleb really wasn't one to introduce the women in his life to Daisy. Matter of fact, he never had, other than a few high school girlfriends. He wasn't sure where things were going with him and Sophia, but he hoped her feelings were growing, along with his own. Lately, he'd been picturing himself settling down in Moose Falls. He was growing more attached every day to this quaint little Alaskan town. And to Sophia.

Could he really give up a career in Hollywood to work for Yukon Cider?

Although the idea of giving up the thing he'd always thought he wanted for another shot at love terrified him, the idea of losing Sophia scared him even more.

CHAPTER SIXTEEN

In the weeks after the campaign rolled out, it became abundantly clear to Sophia, and everyone else in creation, that Caleb Stone had star power. Social media was abuzz with chatter about his dark good looks and magnetic personality. As a photographer, Sophia knew that certain people popped on camera and came vibrantly alive. Caleb was one of those individuals. And the public was eating him up with a spoon. It was too soon to know if sales of the new product had been positively impacted, but hope buzzed in the air.

Sophia was getting a lot of accolades as well for the campaign, but she knew Caleb was the true star of the show. She was just happy to have been a part of the process. So far, working for Yukon Cider was a dream job, one that allowed her flexible hours and a generous salary. Seeing this campaign soar filled her with pride and a wild sense of joy. Her life was getting better by the day. She had grown so much in the last four years.

Caleb's past on *Love Him or Leave Him* was mentioned, but not focused on, as he had feared. This, she realized, was the best news possible for his future. Being on the show had tarnished his image. Being the ambassador for Yukon Cider was a golden opportunity to turn things around. Sophia couldn't help but wonder what was next for Caleb. Would this catapult him back into a world that had chewed him up and spit him out? Or would he stick around Moose Falls? He did seem exceptionally close to his grandmother. Perhaps he would choose to honor her wishes and make a life here in Alaska.

"Penny for your thoughts?" Her father's voice drew her out of her thoughts as he walked into her kitchen as she washed dishes from lunch. Spending time with her father always made Sophia happy, and with a scheduled day off, she'd wanted to treat him to a meal while Lily was at preschool. Their strong bond was one of the main reasons why she wanted to keep an open mind. There had always been a kernel of hope in her heart that Donny would grow into his fatherhood role and become the type of presence in their daughter's life that Lily deserved, one like Sophia had. She had to admit that he'd stepped up in the last few months. He was putting his words into actions and keeping his promises.

"You might have to raise your rates," she teased. "I'm thinking some pretty deep thoughts, I'll have you know."

"Care to talk? I'm always here to listen to my girls." Skip looped his arm around Sophia's waist. Sophia turned her head toward her dad and pressed a kiss on his cheek.

"I'll take you up on that. Why don't you put the kettle on, and we can chat over tea and some of the oatmeal raisin cookies you brought over?"

"Sure thing," Skip told her, turning away from her to begin making the tea. Sophia quickly finished up the dishes.

She sat down at the table just as a teacup and saucer were

placed down in front of her, along with milk, lemon, and sugar.

"Thanks, Daddio," she said as she blew on the steaming liquid.

"My pleasure," he said, sinking down into a seat across from her with his own cup.

"This is about Caleb," she explained. "I think about him all the time now."

Skip smiled at her, little creases forming at the sides of his mouth. "And is that a bad thing?" he asked.

"I'm not sure," she said, shrugging. "When I met him, I thought he was just a big ol' flirt with zero substance. I judged him unfairly."

He let out a snort. "Based on that reality show, I presume."

"Yes," she said with a nod. Guilt had taken hold of her. It had been pretty shallow to judge Caleb before she had ever met him. She really should have known better, since a lot of reality shows were scripted or shot in a way to make certain participants look like they were villains. And viewers ate it up with a fork and spoon.

He had texted her a little while ago about taking her out to lunch, but she'd told him that she was busy. Even though she would have loved to see him today, maybe it was important for her to take a little step back from him before she tumbled over the edge.

"Having met Caleb, I can only tell you that he struck me as one of the good ones," her father told her. "A really decent guy." He knitted his brows together. "Are the two of you an item?"

"I think so. Sort of. Ish." She bit her lip. "We're definitely seeing each other, but neither one of us has put a label on it."

Skip shook his head. "I miss the old days when things were more transparent. Back in the day we didn't have to scratch our heads about it. When I met your mother, I made it clear that she was my girl and I was her guy." His voice cracked a little bit, causing a pang in Sophia's heart.

"Oh, Dad," she said, reaching out and patting his hand. "I know you've been through it with Mom."

"And so have you, sweetheart. If I could have, I would have taken every ounce of heartbreak and put it on myself." His face crumpled, and he appeared to be fighting back tears. "It's agonizing seeing one's child so broken, all because she fell in love with the wrong person."

"My heart healed from that experience, but I'm wary now of falling for Caleb. He might not be sticking around Moose Falls," she said. "If he leaves, it's going to be really hard for me."

"Have you asked him what his plans are? That might help."

"Not in so many words. I know there's an inheritance at stake and ownership of Yukon Cider, but I don't know the particulars. And I can't pry into his family's business like that. To make matters more complicated, he's always wanted to be in the entertainment industry. That's the whole reason he went on that stupid show in the first place."

Skip chuckled. "Umm, so now it's a stupid show? You watched it faithfully every week. Some might say you were the show's number one fan."

"That was before they did a number on Caleb," Sophia said in a raised voice. "They could have portrayed him in a way that didn't demonize him, but they wanted over-the-top ratings and a scandalous storyline, all at his expense. If only they had shown his strength and humor, along with his compassion and drive. Things would have been so different. The audience would have fallen in love with him."

Her father studied her from across the table. His expression softened. "Like you have?"

She swallowed past the huge lump in her throat. Even though she'd been worrying about falling in love with Caleb, the truth was radiating from her father's eyes. He'd come upon the realization before she had.

She was madly, wildly, deeply in love with Caleb Stone.

Caleb was trying not to be annoyed by the fact that Sophia had just turned down his lunch invitation, citing a prior engagement. Was she really unavailable, or was Sophia blowing him off? A groan of frustration slipped past his lips. Why was he acting like such an idiot? Sophia was an honest person, and there was no reason for her to lie. A part of him knew that he was looking for problems when none existed. It wasn't at all like him to have self-doubt when it came to women.

He let out a snort. Prior to finding his passion for acting, wooing females had been Caleb's number one skill. He was ashamed to admit it now, but he'd been proud of that particular claim to fame. He had been a lady's man, to say the least. He'd evolved enough to know that he had needed to be good at something. Anything, simply not to be mediocre.

Perhaps his current angst was karma biting him in the butt. For so many years he had played with women's heartstrings, never making sure that their feelings were protected. His relationship with Abby had been cosmic payback. He'd been put through sheer agony as a result of giving his heart away to someone who hadn't truly wanted it.

And now things had come full circle.

Caleb didn't want to have all of these feelings swirling around inside him, but they were impossible to ignore. He didn't want to count on Sophia being in his life when he'd vowed to never place his faith in a woman again. That's when the rug got pulled from underneath a person. That's when one made a fool of oneself. And Caleb didn't want to go out like that. Not again. Been there, done that. He had the scars to prove it.

The last thing Caleb wanted to do was hurt Sophia with his indecision. His life was in limbo at the moment, and he couldn't offer her anything of substance. Perhaps he was becoming a better man because he was actually thinking about how his actions would affect Sophia. He cared about her.

Being in Alaska for a year had been part of the agreement with Hattie. Time was flying by, and before they knew it, he and his brothers would have to make a huge, life-altering decision about Yukon Cider. Would Moose Falls be a good fit for him long-term? He thought it could work out, but a niggling thought was bothering him. He'd never managed to quash his dreams of making a name for himself in the acting world. Oh, he knew that it might never work out for him to become a big Hollywood name, but he would be content to find work in the industry. Would he be able to let go of his big dream in order to pursue other aspirations right here in town?

His phone buzzed, and he frowned at the screen, not recognizing the number that popped up. He impulsively decided to pick up the call, figuring he could always block the number if it was a telemarketer.

"Hello," Caleb said.

"Is this Caleb Stone?" the voice on the other end asked.

"Yes, this is Caleb." His tone was crisp and no-nonsense.

"This is Eddie Maynor. I'm a talent agent."

Caleb froze. "I-I know who you are," Caleb responded. His heart was thundering in his chest. Was he being punked? Why would Eddie Maynor be calling him?

"I hope you're doing well, Caleb. I'm calling because I'm interested in offering you representation. I'm a big fan of your Yukon Cider campaign."

"Wow," Caleb said, feeling a bit blown away by this unexpected call. "I'm a bit surprised at the call. I haven't had an agent in a minute."

"I'm aware. You were working with Rodney Tolliver, weren't you?" Eddie asked.

"I was," Caleb admitted. Their relationship had soured after his disastrous stint on *Love Him or Leave Him*. "He hasn't repped me for quite some time."

"Well, Caleb, I would love to fly to Alaska and discuss this over a meal and some hard cider. How does that sound?"

"I'm open to it, but not promising anything," Caleb said. "This time around, I'm going to weigh my options."

"Hey, let's just meet up and see what happens," Eddie said, sounding agreeable.

"I'll call you if I decide on whether I want to take the meeting," Caleb said.

After the call ended, Caleb sat for a moment marveling at how swiftly things could turn on a dime. He didn't want to get his hopes up, but this opportunity could be life-changing. The campaign had gone viral, and he was being referred to as the Yukon Cider Hottie. Hattie was getting a serious kick out of that nickname. And if he was being honest, he was savoring it as well. Who could blame him? For so long his name had been dragged through the mud, and he hadn't been taken seriously within the industry.

Red had invited him and his brothers to hang out with him this evening. Xavier was busy with Jaylen, and Landon had caught a bad cold, so neither one of them was available. Because he was still trying to find his footing with his father and build a relationship, Caleb accepted the invite. Maybe he could do a little digging and get some answers about Red's vanishing act and the reasons his marriage had fallen apart. This would provide him with a perfect opportunity to open up a discussion with his dad.

How could he truly move forward with his own future if he didn't even understand his own past? When he was a kid, before the divorce, he'd idolized Red. Caleb remembered how he had been his dad's shadow, trailing around after him like he was the Earth, moon, sun, and stars. All of that had shifted once his parents split up.

When he was a kid, his father would often take him to the movies when they lived in Moose Falls. It was how Caleb had developed his love of all things Hollywood at an early age. Red had been a big fan of classic movies like *The Wizard of Oz*, *Blazing Saddles*, and *Chinatown*. He had even taken his son to see *The Godfather* once, which had become Caleb's favorite film. They had tried to keep it a secret from Daisy due to the onscreen violence, a fact that made him laugh out loud whenever he thought about it. Like a true bloodhound, his mother had found out anyway and laid into Red something fierce. To this day, he remembered the feeling of sitting in the darkened theater and watching the drama unfold. Red had given him a window into the world of make-believe and he'd loved it.

The classic being shown this evening at the theater was a movie called *Carmen Jones*, another gem, featuring Harry Belafonte and Dorothy Dandridge. They were Black actors from the 1950s who had made a splash in Hollywood with their good looks and talent. Caleb had seen the movie on numerous occasions, but watching it on a big screen like this never got old. It was cool being able to spot new details he'd never noticed before. The movie was based on the opera *Carmen*, which he'd once seen in New York City, and he'd never realized that the two main leads had their singing voices dubbed.

"Large popcorn, right? It comes with free refills," Red asked, wiggling his eyebrows.

"I'll never say no to movie popcorn with lots of butter on it," Caleb said. "And a soda. Need something to wash it down with."

"You and your popcorn," Red said, chuckling. "I used to have to buy one just for you because you didn't want to share."

He laughed along with Red. "Believe it or not, I remember that," Caleb said. "Those movie outings were the best. Probably some of the most memorable moments of my childhood. That's when I fell in love with cinema."

Red looked sheepish. "I'm glad that I could give you that at least."

An awkward silence stretched between them. Caleb didn't know what to say. Was this his father's way of acknowledging his deficits as a father and the fact that he hadn't been around? He kept his mouth shut rather than disputing Red's comment. He hadn't told any lies. Love of cinema was one of the major things he'd passed on to Caleb. They both knew there should have been so much more.

They headed into the theater and immersed themselves in the movie for the next two hours. There weren't many places on Earth that Caleb felt more comfortable. The reclining seats and the heady smell of popcorn wafting through the theater. The hush in the air just as the movie began to play. Every single time it gave him a rush.

When the final credits rolled, Caleb wanted to stand up and cheer in the darkened theater. As the lights came on, he and Red exchanged a look that signified their deep appreciation of the film. No words were needed between them.

When it came to cinema, they had always been on the same wavelength.

"Dinner at my place? I have some chicken, collards, and black-eyed peas that I made earlier. And some cornbread. Enough to feed a small army," Red said, a hopeful expression on his face.

"Say less. I never turn down collard greens," Caleb said, his stomach grumbling. Red had always had a way around the kitchen. Bittersweet memories of his parents cooking together flashed in his mind. At one point their home had been a happy one.

Caleb followed his father to his house, which was the same family home they had all lived in during their years in Moose Falls. The ranch-style home had been the perfect size for their family of five. He couldn't help but wonder why Red had held on to the house all these years. Perhaps he was way more sentimental than Caleb realized. Perhaps he'd built up this image of Red based on his past actions that wasn't necessarily accurate.

Once they were inside, Caleb helped Red heat up the food and gather their plates and utensils. They sat down in the kitchen, forgoing the dining room, since it was just the two of them. Caleb had worried things would be awkward between them because they really hadn't hung out alone. Red had hosted him and his brothers for dinner, but Xavier and Landon had helped to make things less tense. So far they were vibing really well together. Red told such interesting stories, and due to his travels, he knew a lot about the world that Caleb hadn't yet experienced.

"If you get the chance, explore Bali and Ireland and Vietnam. There are so many corners of the world to check out," Red gushed. His entire face lit up with excitement, to the point he almost resembled a little kid.

"Sounds amazing," Caleb said. "As soon as I can, I'd love to see the world."

Sophia would also love an opportunity to travel. She would be over the moon taking pictures of incredible sights like the Taj Mahal or Stonehenge. Maybe an African safari or the fields of lavender in Provence. He could picture seeing the world with her, with Lily in tow. A wistful feeling swept over him. Although it would be nice, was it realistic? She had a life in Moose Falls raising her little girl and doing all the responsible things that came with motherhood. And he had to keep his eye on the prize—a career in show business or bust.

Now that he had Red's full attention, Caleb needed to broach a sensitive topic with him. Hopefully, his father would be receptive and it wouldn't put a damper on the evening.

"Can I ask you something?" Caleb leaned across the table.

Red pushed his plate away and wiped his mouth with a napkin. "Ask me anything. I'm an open book."

Caleb hesitated. This wasn't an easy topic to broach with his father. A huge divide stood between them despite a recent thawing due to their return to Moose Falls. There were just too many things Caleb was still confused about.

"I've got some questions that have been weighing on me. What went down with the two of you? Did you cheat on my mother? Is that why she left Alaska with us?" The words tumbled off his lips before he could second-guess the wisdom of bringing up this topic.

Red looked at him with an air of complete bewilderment, his mouth hanging open. "Wh-what? You cannot be serious. Why would you ask me something like that?"

"Because of the way she left with us and never came

back. Plus, she shuts down our questions whenever we've asked."

"I see that you've been stumbling around in the dark about this," Red said, running a hand over his face.

He shrugged. "We've had to fill in the blanks ourselves. We were kids, and no one told us anything, although we witnessed a lot of arguments and felt the tension in our household."

Red splayed his hands on the table. "Listen to me, son. I would never have stepped out on your mother. She was the most magical, brilliant person I had ever encountered in my life. I was shocked she even went out on a date with me, let alone agreed to marry me." He let out a brittle laugh. "She was like a shooting star in the night sky."

"So you really loved her?" Caleb asked. Even as he spoke, Caleb already knew the answer. Although the memories had faded over time, he knew his parents had loved each other deeply.

"Absolutely. Madly. Profoundly. There's never been another." He thumped his chest with his palm. "I take the blame for all of it. I wasn't present. I took her for granted, and I didn't appreciate the beautiful life we'd made and the family we created." He let out a tortured sigh. "Whenever problems came up, I vanished, physically and emotionally."

Caleb was shocked to see tears in his father's eyes.

"I don't know if Daisy would be okay with my telling you this, but it's my story too, I suppose." He bit his lip. "Daisy had a miscarriage."

"Mom was pregnant after Landon? Why didn't we know that?" he asked, flabbergasted.

"We were planning to tell you boys at the three-month mark, but she lost the baby a few days before we reached that milestone." He shrugged. "Perhaps it was too painful for her to ever tell you and your brothers about the loss, even when you became older."

"So...how did that lead to the end of your marriage?" Caleb asked, frowning. "It's tragic, but not insurmountable."

"I couldn't handle seeing her in such emotional pain, so I left her in the lurch. I did what I'd always done. I took off." He put his head in his hands. "There was no coming back from that, although Lord knows I tried."

"I-I can't imagine leaving her like that if you loved her." Caleb's mind was racing. He knew his father had dealt with childhood trauma after witnessing his father's tragic death while mountain climbing. But that didn't excuse Red for abandoning his wife during a health crisis.

"I'll always be ashamed of that, Caleb. Do you remember me showing up in Arizona?" Red asked, his features creased with anxiety.

"Vaguely." He had a fuzzy memory of Red standing in the doorway of their house with presents in his hands.

"Your grandpa wasn't too happy to see me," Red said, quirking his mouth.

Caleb could imagine! His grandpa had been a feisty but loving man who was overly protective of his only daughter. From what Caleb had gleaned, Grandpa Joe had objected to Daisy marrying Red in the first place. He'd never fully trusted him due to his wealth and position, fearing that he would hurt Daisy. He had been more than happy to open his home in Arizona up to them when they'd left Moose Falls.

"Come to think of it, neither was your mother." He visibly winced. "Trying to fix things after they're irretrievably broken is almost always impossible."

"I imagine so," Caleb murmured. Relationships were hard in general. Fixing a damaged one would be like trying to glue back together something that had shattered into a hundred little pieces.

"Caleb, if you're ever lucky enough to find the one, hold on to her. Treat her right. Listen to her worries and fears so she doesn't have to shoulder them all by herself. Don't ever take love for granted."

Caleb was blown away by Red's honesty and vulnerability. One never knew what lurked inside the human heart. He was finding out things about his father that he had never known before this moment. They had never talked like this up to this point, and now Red was speaking from the heart and revealing so much about himself.

"You still love her, don't you?" Caleb asked. He was pretty sure that he already knew the answer, but he wanted to hear it from Red's lips.

"Always," Red answered. "That will never change. But I'm not harboring any illusions that we'll get back together. That was once in a lifetime."

As he headed back to Hattie's place, Caleb tried to process everything he'd learned today from Red. He felt closer to his father than he had ever felt in his life. Red's experiences deeply moved him. He'd lost it all due to fear and neglect and being blind to the needs of his partner. Caleb hated what it had done to his mother, but he also felt a huge amount of compassion for Red. He had realized all his wrongs, but it had been too late to salvage his marriage. While he, his brothers, and Daisy had been together, his father had been alone. He wasn't letting Red off the hook either. He was simply giving him grace.

Above all he was realizing that love, true love, endured. And if a person was lucky enough to find love, it was worth holding on to with all one's might.

On his way home, he made an impromptu stop for

flowers. Something was telling him that he needed to heed
Red's advice. His feelings for Sophia were increasing by
leaps and bounds. He was falling in love with her. The idea
of building something lasting with her and telling her how
he felt was a terrifying thought, but the idea had crept into
his brain more than once. And even though the concept of
forever scared him, the idea of losing this incredible woman
frightened him even more.

CHAPTER SEVENTEEN

When the doorbell buzzed, heralding Caleb's arrival, Sophia beat a fast path to answer the door. She'd been eagerly looking forward to having a date night with Caleb. As soon as she pulled open the door, a sandalwood aroma drifted under her nose.

"Come on in from the cold." She invited him in with a hand gesture.

"Don't mind if I do," Caleb said, rubbing his hands together. "I'm still getting used to this unpredictable weather."

Caleb was right. Alaskan weather, even with spring approaching, was a bit on the temperamental side.

"The flowers you sent are gorgeous," Sophia gushed the moment she saw Caleb at her front door. The floral delivery had arrived at her house earlier, giving her a boost. "Thank you again for being so thoughtful." She had immediately texted him a picture of the bouquet so he would know they'd arrived.

"I'm glad you like them," he said, dipping his head down and placing his lips over hers.

They had plans tonight to head to Northern Exposure for a little dinner and dancing.

Lily was with her dad tonight. When Donny had come to pick up Lily, there had been zero attitude and no bravado. He'd been quiet, as if he had something on his mind. That was the best-case scenario as far as Sophia was concerned. The less he said, the better, especially with Lily around. Their daughter had big ears and a habit of listening in on grown folks' conversations.

Not a snowflake was in sight as Caleb drove them over to the tavern. The night sky was stunning with a smattering of twinkling stars and a sliver of a moon. She let out a sigh. Nights didn't get more perfect than this, especially with Caleb at her side. He entertained her with Stone brother stories during the ride, causing her to clutch her stomach with laughter.

"You can't be serious," Sophia said after hearing one of his tales about a plot to make a skunk the family pet.

He glanced over at her with a knowing look. "I swear it's true. It took my mom days to get the skunk smell out of the house."

"And what happened to the skunk?" she asked, still chuckling at the thought of them trying to make a skunk a new pet and bringing the animal home.

"Mom had to call a place that rescues animals and places them back in nature," he answered, making a face. "I swear, just talking about it brings that funky smell back."

"Eww, that must've been awful," Sophia said. Skunk odors were some of the worst smells in nature. Her own mother would have lost her cool if she and Patience had done anything like that.

"Well, it was and it wasn't. Flower was an amazing pet, if only for those few short hours."

"Flower, huh?" she asked, her lips twitching. The Stone brothers must have been hilarious.

"Of course, in honor of the legendary Flower from *Bambi*. He was pretty iconic," Caleb explained. "The name was an homage."

"Of course it was." Sophia shook her head. "You boys sure kept your mom busy."

Their household must have been full of mischief and fun. And an abundance of love and brotherhood. She would love one day to give Lily a sibling or two and to fill her own household with the energy of a bunch of kids. If so, she would pick the father of her children more wisely. Next time, she would choose someone who didn't bail at the first opportunity. Someone who meant it when he told her that they were forever.

When they arrived at Northern Exposure, Caleb quickly came around to the passenger side and opened the door for her. This was simply more confirmation that Daisy Stone had raised her sons right. She couldn't recall a single time anyone had done this for her. Score! Not only was Caleb an Alaskan hottie, he was a true gentleman. He gently took her by the arm and helped her out of his vehicle.

Caleb wrapped her hand in his as they walked toward the entrance. True immediately spotted them as they were seated at a table by one of the waitstaff.

"Hey! It's great to see the two of you at the tavern. Date night?" True asked, her gaze swinging back and forth between them.

"Yeah, we heard there's a great band playing here tonight," Caleb said, looking around. "Where's Xavier? I thought we might see him here."

"He's supposed to be here, but he may have gotten tied up at work," True said. "I think he had a meeting with Hattie. I was hoping Landon would show up. It would be great to see him come out of his shell."

Caleb let out a laugh. "Good luck with that. My little brother isn't really social, and he doesn't like to dance."

"Well, he can just sit at a table and look pretty." True winked at them. "There are plenty of ladies in Moose Falls who are into his nerdy science guy vibe."

Caleb grinned. "He's a good one. Sensitive and warm-hearted. Whoever ends up with him is going to be one lucky lady." He put a finger to his mouth. "Don't tell him I said that. We like to give him a hard time, but we think he's pretty amazing."

Sophia loved the protective tone in Caleb's voice. He was such a solid guy. Her initial impression of him had been way off base. She was a bit proud of herself for falling for such a wonderful man. After Donny she'd vowed to watch out for signs of potential issues since she had ignored many in that relationship. In retrospect she knew that she'd gone along to get along, especially after falling pregnant with Lily. Because she had been deeply affected by not having both parents in the home, she'd wanted her daughter to have better. But, from what she had learned from the experience, living in a home torn apart by tension and indifference was never healthy for a child. So far, she was holding things down as a single mother and doing a pretty kick-ass job at it.

"I'll send Bonnie over to take your order," True said before heading toward the bar.

A few minutes later Bonnie came over to their table. She was their waitress tonight.

"Hey there, guys," Bonnie said with an ear-to-ear grin. "Good to see you here tonight."

"Hi, Bonnie," Sophia said, warmed by the woman's enthusiasm. She wasn't sure there had ever been a time when Bonnie hadn't been pure sunshine.

"Bonnie," Caleb said. "Nice to see you as well. I'm having fun working with Tucker at Yukon Cider. That dude keeps us in stitches."

"That's my guy," Bonnie said proudly. "He's a real keeper."

It was nice seeing Bonnie so in love after everything she had been through. Truly, it gave Sophia hope that she too could wind up in a faithful, loving relationship that went the distance. With Caleb now in her life, she couldn't help but dream about him filling that role. She just had to keep believing and not give in to doubts and insecurity.

"So, do y'all know what you want to order?" Bonnie asked.

She took their order without even writing it down—an app of chicken wings, an order of slow braised ribs with rosemary mashed potatoes, and salmon with truffle fries and green beans. For drinks they both ordered iced teas.

"Coming right up," Bonnie said. "The music is going to start in about forty minutes, so you'll get a chance to eat first."

"Good deal," Caleb said as Bonnie walked off to put in their order.

Sophia inhaled the aroma of the food emanating from other tables. "I can't wait to eat, if I'm being completely honest. The food smells incredible."

"I've never been disappointed. True takes great pride in Chef Ito's fare."

Laurie Ito was an award-winning chef hired by True to inject new life into the tavern's menu. She had succeeded way beyond True's wildest hopes. Anyone who wrote Northern Exposure off as just being a bar was mistaken. In the last year eating at the tavern had become a culinary experience.

Sophia looked around in awe. Over the years True had

made major changes to Northern Exposure, all for the betterment of the establishment. She could only imagine that things would keep evolving, now that True owned the tavern. This place was her pride and joy. It was nice to see that hard work and dedication paid off. She thought of her own career path in the same manner. The sacrifices she'd made were now beginning to pay off.

Their drinks and appetizer came, followed by their delicious entrees. Sophia ate with gusto, not bothering to hide her appetite. It was nice feeling so comfortable with Caleb that she could scarf down her food without worrying about being dainty. She'd dated men in the past who seemed to think women should just exist on water and air.

"Chef Ito really put her foot in that," Caleb said, wiping his mouth with his napkin and pushing his empty plate to the side.

"She sure did," Sophia agreed. "Let's make sure to tell True how much we enjoyed the food."

"She's doing such a bang-up job here. I know my grandmother is beyond proud," Caleb said. "As we all are, but they have a special relationship."

"As do you," Sophia said, carefully watching his expression. Lately she had noticed a pensive expression etched on Caleb's face whenever the topic of Hattie came up. She imagined he was wrestling with the inevitability of losing her, even though he rarely discussed it with her.

He ducked his head and looked at the table. "I never imagined that we would build such an unbreakable bond. She's the real cherry on the sundae as far as I'm concerned."

"You should tell her that," Sophia blurted out. *While you can.* Although the words rattled around in her head, she stopped short of saying them. Caleb didn't need any reminders that Hattie was slipping away from them. He saw her every day at home and at Yukon Cider. Saying those words would just be rubbing his nose in it, and she couldn't do that to him.

"Maybe I will," he told her before standing up and holding out his hand to her. "Let's dance." The band had begun playing a few minutes ago, and couples were now filling up the dance floor. Although she did want to shake what her mama gave her, Sophia had the feeling that Caleb was using dancing as a diversion from talking about his grandmother's decline.

"I thought you'd never ask," she said as he pulled her to his side and brought her into the middle of the floor.

"I want everyone to be able to admire my beautiful girl," Caleb said in her ear, drawing her against him as they began to move.

Being held in Caleb's arms gave her a feeling of security that she'd never known with a romantic partner. He was solid and strong. He cared about her. She felt it deep in her bones. And he was a total smoke show.

They moved in time to the music—a slow song by Alicia Keys—their bodies in perfect sync with the band's rhythms. Although there were other couples on the dance floor, to Sophia it seemed as if it were only the two of them. She wrapped her arms around his neck and melted into him, feeling as if all was right with the world. As far as she was concerned, it didn't get any better than this.

Suddenly, the flash of lights in the darkness blinded her. She heard snapping sounds, one after the other, followed by more intense flashes of light. Sophia put her hands up to shield her eyes.

What in the world was going on? After a few moments of feeling dazed and confused, it hit her. Someone was recording them. Taking pictures of her and Caleb. She could only think that they were being pranked by someone.

Caleb raised his arm up and shielded her from the glare of the bulbs. She grabbed onto him, fighting against a sensation of dizziness. He placed one arm around her, and she felt herself being held against a rock-solid chest. All of a sudden the lights came on, and she squinted to see what was going on. A camera crew. A group of people focused on them. A woman was standing next to them—a very striking, familiar-looking individual.

Caleb's voice rang out in a sharp tone. "Abby! What in the hell are you doing here?"

Caleb's knees nearly buckled at the sight of Abby Taylor, the woman who had torn his heart out of his chest and fed him to the wolves during the filming of *Love Him or Leave Him*. Was he having an out-of-body experience? There was no way Abby was standing mere inches away from him in Alaska of all places. *Was there?*

Caleb felt disoriented as Abby stood so close to him, surrounded by a camera crew. Someone had turned on the lights in the tavern, so there was no mistaking the sight of his ex-girlfriend. She was looking up at him with that same butter-wouldn't-melt-in-her-mouth look that he'd fallen for hook, line, and sinker during their time together.

"Hey! You don't have permission to film in here," True shouted above the music as she came storming over to them. "I'm the owner, and this is out of line."

Why was Abby here with a camera crew? And why had they been filming him and Sophia?

"Are those cameras still rolling?" he asked, trying to make sense of things. His anger and frustration were rising exponentially.

"We wanted to capture you in an unguarded moment," Abby explained.

Abby was still as beautiful as ever with shoulder-length black hair that gave her a sophisticated air. Her skin was the color of almonds. When they had been together, she hadn't been into makeup or designer clothes. She'd changed since the last time he had seen her, with a new, sleek hairdo and upscale clothes. He had a feeling the makeover was due to her starring in the spin-off show.

But what was she doing in Moose Falls, Alaska? She still hadn't given him any explanation.

Before he knew what was happening, Abby flung herself against his chest. He was so stunned, he froze and let the memories sweep over him. The scent of her coconut body lotion rose to his nostrils, as did a floral scent from her hair. He tried to disentangle himself, but Abby was holding on to him for dear life. With what felt like superhuman strength he managed to remove her arms from around his waist.

She was looking at him with puppy dog eyes. "Caleb! I've missed you, and I came all this way to Alaska to see you."

"And you brought a film crew with you to document it?" he asked, frowning. He didn't know exactly what was going on, but his Spidey senses were on full alert.

"I'm sorry to ambush you, but I wasn't sure you'd want to see me if I reached out. The show wanted everything to look natural." Abby had a tendency to talk in a baby voice, and at the moment it was like nails on a chalkboard. Grating and annoying.

His jaw nearly dropped to the floor. "The show?"

"Yes," she said solemnly. *"Twin Shot at Love."* She shot him a beatific smile. "Have you seen it? I'm one of the stars, along with Gillian."

Did she seriously think he was watching her new reality

show where she and her twin were looking for love? This had to be a joke. One look at her face dispelled that notion. She was dead serious.

"No, I haven't checked it out, but I'll put a reminder on my phone," he responded, biting the inside of his cheek to stop himself from going off on her. She couldn't hurt him anymore, so he didn't need to lash out.

"Who is *this*?" Abby asked, blinking like an owl. He had the feeling she was trying to bring on the waterworks for sympathy.

Sophia! In all the mayhem he had totally forgotten that Sophia was standing beside him. He turned to look at her. Sophia stood with her arms wrapped around her middle. She was tapping her foot on the wood flooring. He was a bit surprised there wasn't steam coming out of her ears.

"Oh, don't mind me," Sophia muttered. She wasn't even making eye contact with him. Was she blaming him for Abby turning up at Northern Exposure? This was the last thing he would ever want in a million years.

Caleb wished he could focus on Sophia, but he needed to deal with Abby before he did so. There would be ample time later to make things right with Sophia.

Caleb fought against a rising sense of frustration. Abby was dodging his questions and trying to deflect. "Abby, it's actually none of your business who she is. Let's focus on the gigantic elephant in the room. Why are you here?"

"You really don't know?" Abby asked. "I'm here for you, Caleb. I want you back."

Sophia let out a loud groan. "Oh my god! Gimme a break. How long has it been? Two years?"

He appreciated Sophia having his back, but he didn't want her to even engage with Abby. Abby clearly had an agenda, which he still hadn't quite figured out. What if she got Sophia tangled up in her mess?

"Sophia, I've got this," he said, trying not to sound too curt. Her eyes widened, and her mouth settled in a hard line.

"Can we have a few minutes alone?" Abby asked, glaring at Sophia.

Caleb felt like a deer caught in the headlights. He opened his mouth, then shut it. What could he even say to Abby at this point? When it had truly mattered, she had turned her back on him and thrown him under the bus. Thanks to her betrayal, his name and reputation had been trashed. All because she'd wanted to extend her fifteen minutes of fame.

How many nights had he gone to bed wishing that Abby would take him back and say how wrong she'd been? Back then he would have jumped for joy over her tracking him down and expressing her feelings like this. But that was then, and this was now. He had Sophia. She was honest and solid, the very opposite of Abby, who'd done nothing but lie to him throughout their relationship.

"I'd rather not, Abby," he said. And he meant it. There was nothing Abby could say to him in private that could sway him in any way. Without even realizing it, he'd completely moved on. He was miles and miles away emotionally from the days when he'd been in love with her.

"I want you to be on the show with me," she said, a pleading tone in her voice. "Imagine how much the viewers would eat it up if we got back together. The ratings would be through the roof."

And there it was. Abby and her film crew were here to lure him back to California to be on her reality show. She didn't love him. He was fairly certain she never had. The only thing honest about her was what she'd just said about wanting him on her show. For ratings. For more fame. It was sickening and utterly despicable.

"Abby, I don't have time for this nonsense. I'm sorry

you've wasted time traveling all this way to Alaska, but I actually have a life here in Moose Falls that I really love. Something tells me you know I'm the spokesman for Yukon Cider's new campaign." He locked eyes with her. "Isn't that part of the reason I'm suddenly on your radar?"

She didn't even need to respond. He could see the truth emanating from her eyes. This time around he wasn't hurt. She no longer had the power to bring him to his knees. And that gave him such a rush that he thought he might explode from happiness.

"I feel sorry for you, Abby. Chasing reality show fame isn't ever going to bring joy into your life." He shook his head at her.

Her face fell, then seconds later her expression hardened.

"So now you're full of yourself because you've got a little buzz as a cover model?" She let out a brittle laugh. "Who are you to look down on me? It wasn't so long ago that you wanted to be reality show famous."

She was right. Back then he'd believed that being a contestant on the show would catapult him into fame and fortune. For a while that's all that had mattered to him. He'd had blinders on, fueled by a desire to make it in the entertainment world.

"The thing is, I've grown up since then. Maybe it's time you do as well," Caleb said.

Suddenly, True stepped toward Abby so that they were practically nose to nose.

True's expression was fierce. "Caleb is too nice to tell you to go, but you need to vacate the premises. Leave. Scram. Kick rocks."

Abby appeared flustered. "Who are you to tell me to leave?" Abby asked.

"I own the place, so I reserve the right to choose my

clientele." True perched a hand on her hip. "You've out-stayed your welcome. We're really nice here in Moose Falls, but you crossed the line."

"Don't you know who I am?" Abby asked, with her hand at her throat.

"I have a vague idea," True said, "but I really don't care." She turned toward Caleb. "Do you?"

He folded his arms across his chest and rocked back on the heels of his shoes. "Not even a little bit."

Abby let out an outraged gasp and turned around to leave. He didn't think he had ever seen her so horrified or at a loss for words. The jig was up, and she knew it. Her entire MO in the past had revolved around using him, and he wasn't going down that road again. Not in this lifetime or any other.

"And take your camera crew with you," Caleb yelled after her.

True followed behind Abby and the crew, making sure they left the tavern. "Don't let the door hit you where the good Lord split you," she called out.

Caleb looked around, wanting to make sure Sophia had witnessed the way Abby had been dispatched from North-ern Exposure. He was proud of himself for dealing with her head-on and not falling back into old patterns.

The truth was, he didn't love her anymore. He was a one-woman man, and all of his affection was squarely focused on Sophia. This felt like a triumph.

Only thing was, he couldn't seem to find her. She wasn't anywhere in the vicinity or hanging out by the bar. Had she stepped into the ladies' room?

"True! What happened to Sophia?" he asked as she came back and began breaking down tables. "Where did she go?"

True quirked her mouth. "She left."

"What do you mean she left?"

"Did I stutter? I think she got tired of watching your reunion with your ex. She probably felt like a third wheel."

"Nothing was going on between us," he protested. "I was surprised to see her, that's all. And I had zero interest in her plan to get back with me."

True sucked her teeth. "I'm going to keep it real with you. You let that woman hug you for way too long." She shook her finger at him. "That may come back to bite you in the butt."

"That's ridiculous," he said, feeling heated. He wasn't the one in the wrong here. Abby had shown up without warning and blindsided him. He'd done his best to handle the situation without making a huge scene. He was now a representative of Yukon Cider, and with a film crew rolling, he really would have gone viral if he'd gone off. Under the circumstances, he thought he'd done a damn good job at containing Hurricane Abby.

"Don't blame the messenger," True said as she went about the business of closing up the tavern.

Caleb ran a shaky hand over his face. True's intel, combined with the dazed expression that had been on Sophia's face when the cameras began to flash, didn't bode well. No woman ever left a date night if things were going well. And it was a first for him. He'd messed things up badly with Sophia, and he had no idea how he was going to fix it.

CHAPTER EIGHTEEN

At some point, Sophia thought, she was going to have to respond to Caleb's multitude of texts and phone calls. But at the moment she was still stewing. What had gone down last night at the tavern didn't sit well with her. The unexpected appearance of Abby Taylor had left her feeling confused, unsettled, and angry. Of course she'd been jealous and insecure about her own place in Caleb's life, but she could have dealt with those feelings if Caleb had handled things better.

Sophia hated feeling this way. The emotions the situation had brought to the surface were a painful reminder of how she'd felt in the past. She knew Abby from reality television, and she was a beautiful woman who projected grace and gentility. She was the type of woman who could easily wrap people around her finger, as she had done with Caleb in the past.

Maybe this was all her problem, and it had nothing to do with Caleb. But she couldn't stop thinking of the way he'd looked with Abby planted against his chest. He hadn't seemed indifferent to her. He hadn't pushed her away. And then he'd dismissed Sophia when she had tried to help. Taking off had been a bit childish, but she had been so hurt, and it had been an attempt to protect herself. She didn't want to be hurt again, didn't want to love a man who might still be in love with someone else.

A knock on the door drew her from her thoughts, providing a temporary reprieve from stewing over the situation. She was expecting Donny to return with Lily any minute now. Sophia wasn't sure that she had the strength to deal with any negativity today, especially after last night's drama. All she really wanted to do was go back to bed and draw the covers over her head. But it was mommy time and she needed to put on a smile. There really wasn't any time right now to wallow in her feelings. Later this evening, she told herself, she could curl up in front of the television with a glass of sangria and dissect every moment from the encounter with Caleb's ex.

As soon as she pulled the door open, Lily came rushing into her arms.

"Mommy, I missed you," she said, bursting into tears. One look at her daughter told a huge tale. Lily had dark shadows under her eyes, and she appeared to be exhausted.

"Hey there, Lily. There's no need to cry, sweetheart. I missed you too," she said, pulling Lily against her.

"I'm hungry," she said with a wail. "I want mac 'n' cheese."

"Because you refused to eat breakfast or lunch," Donny pointed out, making a face. "I tried to get her to eat," he said feebly.

"Okay, Lily, settle down," Sophia said, placing a kiss on her cheek. "I'll fix you a bowl from your leftovers," Sophia said, making eye contact with Donny. He had a discouraged look stamped on his face, accentuated by his slumped shoulders. "Donny, why don't we talk while Lily eats."

He nodded without saying a word, his jaw tightly clenched.

A few minutes later and Lily was sitting happily at the table, eating mac 'n' cheese and applesauce, and drinking a cup of chocolate milk. For the moment, all was right in her world.

Sophia turned toward Donny. "Let's go in my study," she suggested, leading the way down the hall. This way they could talk in private without listening ears.

Once they were in the room, Donny sank down onto a love seat while Sophia sat down on the couch. She was going to let Donny lead the conversation, even though she was eager to find out what happened during the overnight. It wasn't like their daughter to act like this.

"In case you were wondering, she had an awful time. I think she might just hate me," Donny muttered.

"What happened?" she asked, feeling stunned. "She loves spending time with you." This was a first. Lily had never been upset after a visit with her dad.

"She kept telling me she missed you, which I totally understood, but then she wasn't listening to or engaging with me. I guess you could say she shut down," Donny explained. "And her room, which she used to love, was now too pink and too big. Nothing was making her happy."

Sophia ran a hand through her hair and let out a sigh. He might as well have been talking about someone else's child. Lily loved pink. And she had told Sophia on numerous occasions how much she loved her bedroom at her daddy's house.

"She might have just been having an off day," Sophia told him. Even though she and Donny weren't at a good place with each other, she hated this turn of events. He looked despondent. She wanted Lily to be a happy, well-adjusted child who enjoyed the time she spent away from Sophia.

He held up his hands. "You win. Lily made it clear that

she's not ready to be with me half of the time." He held up his hands. "Don't worry. I didn't say a word to her about joint custody, but her actions spoke volumes. She's not ready for things to change so drastically."

She narrowed her gaze as she looked at him. "What are you saying, Donny?"

"I'm not going to fight our custody agreement. It makes no sense to force something that isn't working."

He had changed his mind about fighting for custody! Relief flooded through her. The idea of being engaged in a court battle had been unnerving. But she didn't feel as elated as she would have imagined. If Lily wasn't happy, then Mama wasn't happy.

"First of all, I don't consider this winning. You and Lily having a good relationship is beneficial for all of us, especially Lily. I hate that you wanted fifty-fifty custody, but it has nothing to do with my being against you." She took a deep breath. "The truth is, you haven't earned the privilege yet. You need to understand that simple fact. Second of all, giving up on your daughter isn't cool, Donny."

He blinked back tears. "What do you want me to do? I-I'm trying to make up for lost time, and it's difficult to have a door slammed in my face." His voice trembled. Uncertainty radiated from his eyes.

"I want you to keep trying," she said fiercely. "You don't think I get frustrated being a single mother? Everything isn't always peaches and cream, I can tell you that. But I never give up, because to do so would be to turn my back on our daughter. And I'll never do that." She locked gazes with him. "And neither should you."

His brow furrowed as he studied her. "Why are you encouraging me to be involved with our daughter? After all I've done and failed to do?"

"Because it's the right thing. And that always trumps anything else," Sophia said.

Donny stood up. "I'm not going for fifty-fifty custody." He twisted his mouth. "I'm going to spend some time building a solid foundation for my relationship with Lily. That's all I want, to make up for the things I failed to do before now. Zora and I plan on having kids, and before that ever happens, I want to be the father I should've been from the beginning. I just want to be a part of her life and for her to know that I was present."

"I respect that, Donny," Sophia said, standing up to face him.

"I'm sorry, Sophia. For everything I put you through and for letting Lily down. I know it might be hard to believe, but those days are over."

She heard something laced in his voice that made her believe him. Maybe she needed to believe that redemption was possible.

"Is it okay if I say goodbye to Lily?" he asked.

"Of course," she said, following at a discreet distance as Donny found Lily in her playroom and exchanged a heartfelt embrace with her. Lily appeared to have forgotten all about whatever had been bothering her, and she wrapped her little arms around Donny with enthusiasm.

"I love you, Daddy," she said, gifting him with a heart-warming smile.

"I love you, bitsy," he said, pressing a kiss on her cheek before turning back toward the entryway.

Donny left without any more discussion about their daughter. They had said all they'd needed to say and reached common ground.

Sophia was stunned by this sudden turn of events. Donny had revealed himself to her in a way she'd never seen before. He'd been incredibly emotional and transparent.

And with that realization, something settled in her chest. For so long she had been angry at Donny for the way he had treated her during their relationship. His failings as a father had infuriated and saddened her. But now she saw what she'd never seen before. Vulnerability. She had always known he loved Lily, but now she saw regret and a desire to turn things around. She didn't believe he had earned the right to joint custody, but as he'd just said, Donny would always be her baby girl's father. He needed to be in Lily's life. She would do everything in her power to support their relationship.

Maybe, just maybe, things could be different moving forward, if for no other reason than her daughter's best interest. She wasn't absolving him of anything. She actually didn't even have to like him as a person. They simply had to work together to benefit Lily. Based on their heart-to-heart conversation, things were definitely moving in the right direction. And for that, she was incredibly grateful.

Caleb didn't like the idea of bombarding Sophia with calls and texts, but he figured it was better than showing up unannounced at her doorstep. And hashing things out at work wouldn't be professional. The last thing he wanted was for his colleagues to start talking about them having a falling-out. He let out a ragged sigh. Hattie wouldn't approve of any workplace drama at Yukon Cider. Maybe he was just being paranoid. For all he knew, Sophia had been tied up with Lily and other responsibilities. Her world didn't revolve around him.

A last-minute decision to head downtown to pick up lunch turned out to be a wise one. He was able to enjoy the gorgeous scenery along the way. The melting snow had given way to verdant green grass and budding plants and flowers. Signs of spring in Alaska were everywhere. The sun was shining in a perfectly blue sky. When the weather got a bit warmer, he wanted to take Sophia to the falls for a romantic picnic. It had been a special place in his childhood, and the memories were some of the strongest ones he'd held on to from the past.

The downtown area was charming, resembling a quaint Alaskan postcard. All of the shops were brightly colored with decorative signs and awnings. Tea shops, a bookstore, restaurants, and clothing stores. The movie theater was nestled between the library and a candy store. Moose Falls emitted a heartwarming, quaint vibe, the kind of place people sought to settle down in. He stopped in his tracks on the sidewalk, feeling a bit dazed.

What had made him randomly think about settling down in Moose Falls? It wasn't something that had been on his bucket list before. All he'd ever really aspired to was to pursue an acting career. But his heart was shifting him in a new direction. Who ever said one couldn't have it all? He didn't have to limit himself to just being one thing, he realized. Like Hattie always said, the world was his oyster. He was happier than he'd been in years doing the print ads for Yukon Cider and making commercials.

Craving a sandwich, Caleb headed to Sam's, a shop that had been in Moose Falls since the 1950s. The owner, Sam Parks, had opened the establishment at the tender age of eighteen. With pluck and grit, Sam had turned the sandwich shop into a go-to spot for residents and tourists alike. Sam's boasted a wide range of offerings, but he specialized in all kinds of salmon sandwiches.

He parked his car out front and made his way inside, taking his place in the line. He wasn't surprised that the place was busy, but his heart leaped at the sight of Sophia standing at the front of the line. Caleb would recognize the gentle slope of her neck and the tilt of her head as she studied the menu anywhere. When she turned around and spotted him, her eyes widened in surprise.

She slowly walked over to him, her expression shuttered. Sophia held up her hand and waved at him. "Hi, Caleb. Fancy meeting you here." She folded her arms across her chest.

He would have greeted her with a kiss, but her body language wasn't encouraging him to be affectionate. Her shoulders looked rigid with tension. For all intents and purposes, she was putting up a wall.

"Hey, Sophia. I've been blowing up your phone. Why haven't you called me back? Everything okay?" he asked in a low voice. He didn't need the other customers to overhear their conversation. Before they knew it, their names would be on blast all over town. That's how small towns worked. This one was no different.

She shrugged. "I had some stuff going on with Lily and my ex that I needed to wade through." He could see the evidence of strain on her face. Slight shadows rested under her eyes.

"Are you okay?" he asked, reaching out and running his thumb across her cheek.

"I'm fine," she murmured, not making eye contact with him.

He removed his thumb from her cheek, stuffing his hands in his pockets.

"You're upset with me. I can feel it. This is about the other night, isn't it?" he asked, gently grabbing her by the hand and pulling her outside.

The temperature outside was a bit brisk, but having

privacy was worth the chill in the air. Caleb didn't want anything standing between him and Sophia. He needed to fix the situation right away before things took a turn for the worse. If life had taught him anything at all, it was not to allow issues to fester.

"I apologize for making you feel as if you didn't matter when Abby and her crew showed up," Caleb said. "I should have just taken your hand and gotten us out of there. Forgive me. I'm an idiot for not doing that."

She shoved her hands in her pockets. "Just being there with you and Abby made me feel confused about where things stand between the two of you. It didn't seem finished." She shrugged. "Just a feeling I had." The defeated tone of her voice gutted him.

Caleb vehemently shook his head. "It's dead and buried. There's nothing between us," Caleb answered. "That ended a long time ago."

"So you're not still in love with Abby? There's not some little part of you that wants to be back with her?" He could hear the stress in her voice. Emotion vibrated in every syllable.

"Absolutely not!" Caleb said vehemently. "That's the furthest thing from the truth."

"I watched the two of you talking, and it seemed like there was a lot of emotion between you." She bit her lip. "And feelings. Things got so intense between you that I was an afterthought. You seemed to forget I was even standing there watching the whole thing go down. You have no idea how that made me feel."

"I'm sorry if our encounter made you feel bad, but I had no idea she was going to travel all the way to Alaska to find me," he told her. Frankly, he never imagined that he would lay eyes on her again. Nor had he wanted to.

"Did you know she's still here in Moose Falls?" Sophia

asked. There had been several sightings of Abby and her film crew all over town, a fact that infuriated Caleb. Abby was still an opportunist chasing reality show fame. And now she was messing up his love life.

"I heard that, but it really doesn't concern me. Abby and I are over. Her coming to Moose Falls wasn't about me. This was her last-ditch effort to use me for her reality show. There's no way I'm riding that train again."

"Well, that's a relief," she muttered.

Had Sophia thought for a single second that he'd be down for that type of nonsense? She knew all about his abysmal experience on reality television. Why would he ever agree to put himself through that again? Trying to be patient, Caleb slowly counted to ten in his head.

"Yes, I'll admit that things got a bit chaotic, especially with the TV crew there, but I never once forgot you were right there with me. Until you did a disappearing act on me."

"That wasn't my best moment, Caleb, but...I was uncomfortable. The whole situation made me realize that I have no idea where we stand, the two of us. I don't even know if you'll be around six months from now. And whether you are or aren't is your decision, but I have to protect myself too."

"Protect yourself?" he asked. "Against me?"

"No, I didn't mean it like that," Sophia said. "It's not on you, but I need to focus on Lily and not on a relationship that may not be going anywhere."

Ouch! Was this really how she felt? Or was she simply reacting to the Abby drama that had gone down at Northern Exposure? Either way she was taking backward steps away from him. And it hurt like hell.

He threw his hands in the air. "What's going on here, Sophia? It's like you're pulling away from me as we speak."

He lifted her chin up so their eyes could meet and connect. "Stay with me, Sophia. I know you've been hurt before. So have I. I'm not going to do that to you. To us."

Sophia was chewing on her lip. "But that's not something you can promise me," Sophia said, her voice cracking. "I can't fault you for that, but I don't want to be in that dark place again, Caleb."

"Why are you thinking the worst?" he pressed. It was as if seeing Abby had opened up a host of problems that he hadn't even seen coming. "Things got uncomfortable, but it doesn't have to change what we have. What we are to each other."

"This isn't all your fault. I went into this with my eyes wide open, and I just think I'm not ready to take all of this on."

"Sophia," Caleb said, knowing she was right about not making promises. People hurt the ones they loved all the time in relationships despite their best intentions. He wasn't going to push the point. Caleb sensed Sophia was at a breaking point, close to tumbling over the edge. Even though it was the last thing he wanted to do, Caleb understood that he needed to give her time and a little bit of distance. Hopefully, she would realize that they were worth fighting for.

"Caleb, I need to head back to work for a meeting," she said. Sophia headed inside and grabbed her sandwich, then strode toward the parking lot without sparing him another glance.

As he watched her walk away from him, he was hit by a huge realization. The feeling crashed over him in unrelenting waves. He was head over heels in love with Sophia.

Maybe he should have told her and somehow found a way to convince her that Abby was his past and she was his future. But how could he say that to her when she'd been so closed off to listening to him? He was human, after all. He didn't want to be rejected by the woman he adored.

The best he could do at this moment was give Sophia some space until she was ready to hear him out. In the meantime, Caleb worried that his heart might just shatter all over again.

CHAPTER NINETEEN

As Sophia drove away from Sam's, tears streamed down her face. Although she had spoken her truths, she wasn't sure if she'd been fair to Caleb. Just because she had fallen in love with him didn't mean he had to feel the same way or profess his undying love for her. Even though secretly she'd been looking for something that would cement her position in his life, he'd stopped short of making a commitment to her. Maybe she was being ridiculous, but her heart was on the line here.

Sophia had felt her breathing getting choppy during her talk with Caleb. The idea of Caleb still being in love with Abby had been painful to discuss with him, but she was proud of herself for being honest about her suspicions. If heartache was coming her way, she was heading it off at the pass. Better to walk away from Caleb than to get dumped or blindsided.

Who was she kidding? Not having him in her life would be its own circle of hell. Just driving away from him caused her stomach to clench up and her palms to moisten. She

missed him already. It felt as if she'd closed a door on him,
and it caused a painful twisting sensation in the region of her
heart.

Caleb had accused her of putting up a wall between them.
He had been very intuitive about her feelings. She needed to
protect herself in a way she had failed to do with Donny.
Otherwise, she would be in a world of hurt. She'd been foolish to get wrapped up in a romance with Caleb. He was like
a comet flashing through orbit at the speed of light. Holding
on to someone like that was near impossible.

After she headed into the Yukon Cider headquarters,
Sophia made her way toward the conference room, telling
herself to stay strong. What doesn't kill you makes one
stronger, right? She'd loved and lost before. Somehow she
would get through this.

She needed to focus on her career and building a life
worthy of her daughter. Now that Donny no longer wanted
joint custody, she could breathe a little easier on the home
front, but she still had to keep her eyes on what mattered
most. And that was Lily. She didn't want to get her heart broken again if Caleb decided to leave town. Even if it turned
out that he wasn't interested in reuniting with Abby, Caleb
was now in a perfect position to launch an acting career, one
that would take him far away from Alaska and ownership of
Yukon Cider.

"Sophia!" Hattie's voice exploded in the small conference room. "Good afternoon."

"Hi there, Hattie," Sophia said warmly. Seeing Hattie
always made her feel joyful, even in the middle of heartache.
She couldn't help but notice the oxygen machine Hattie was
walking around with and the raspy sound of her voice. In her
terminally ill state such things were to be expected, but they
were shocking nevertheless.

"I can't wait to go over some exciting news with you," Hattie said as she sat down at the head of the table in a plush leather chair.

Sophia clapped her hands together. Now was the perfect time to hear good news.

"I'm intrigued. Don't keep me in suspense," Sophia said. "Did you and Jacques run off to Vegas and tie the knot?" Although she was teasing, Sophia wouldn't put it past Hattie to do the unexpected. YOLO was her mantra, after all.

The sound of Hattie's tinkling laughter filled the air. "No, I didn't, but why didn't I think of that? It would certainly make everyone's jaw drop."

"Gotta keep 'em guessing," Sophia said, winking at Hattie.

Hattie splayed her gnarled hands on the table. "Sophia, I called our meeting today to congratulate you on your work on the campaign. It's been a smashing success. Not only did the advertisement go viral, but my grandson is making a name for himself. And this time it's in a good way."

"That's exciting, Hattie. I had a lot of fun shooting Caleb, and I'm not at all surprised that people responded to him the way they have," Sophia said. "It's not just his looks, as I'm sure you know. He films really well, which made my job easy. And his personality pops."

Hattie's gaze narrowed as she looked at her. "It warms my heart to hear you speak so well of him. He's a very special young man."

"He is," Sophia conceded. "I don't think I've ever met anyone like him." And she knew that she never would again. Her heart constricted just thinking about Caleb.

Hattie drummed her fingers on the table, making a staccato sound. "There's an opportunity to do a tour featuring Caleb. It would be a great chance to increase our visibility in markets that historically haven't been purchasing our ciders."

"That's a really great idea. Have you told Caleb?" He would be delighted at the idea of hitting the road to rep Yukon Cider.

Caleb would never be content to stick around Moose Falls, not after going viral almost overnight. Honestly, she couldn't blame him. Who wouldn't grab hold of the brass ring if they were in his position? It was all he'd ever wanted. She was happy for his success, especially since he was now being portrayed in a positive light. The focus wasn't on his reality show past but on the present.

"I haven't told him yet," Hattie said. "He knows how well the campaign is doing and that sales are way up. I wanted to know if you're interested in going along for a few weeks? I know it might be tricky with your little one, but I think it'll be a great opportunity for you."

Could she really go on tour with Caleb and keep things platonic? This was the problem with mixing business with pleasure. Sophia adored her position at Yukon Cider. She finally felt valued and respected as a photographer. This opportunity was allowing her to soar and make a new life for herself.

"I-I'm not sure that would work out," she admitted, breaking eye contact with Hattie. Her boss was too perceptive. She would definitely pick up on the fact that something was wrong. She was desperate to keep things professional and not burst into tears.

"What's wrong, Sophia? I thought that I might be imagining things, but you look lower than an ant's belly."

"It's nothing," Sophia said, trying to keep her chin up to meet the older woman's gaze. Rookie mistake! There was something about looking into Hattie's soulful brown eyes that made her tear up. Despite her best intentions, she was falling apart at the seams.

"Oh, sweetheart, please don't cry." Hattie dug in her bag and took out a tissue. She handed it to Sophia, who dabbed at her eyes.

"I'm sorry, Hattie. I promise you, I'm usually more professional," Sophia said. Embarrassment washed over her, threatening to drown her.

Hattie waved her hand in the air. "Don't you dare worry about that. I value you and your work. That's not going to change over a few tears."

Sophia's voice shook. "I don't think things are going to work out between me and Caleb," she admitted. "And if you can't tell, I'm pretty heartbroken about it."

"May I ask what happened? I heard one of the twins showed up the other night at the tavern." Hattie let out a growl. "If I'd been there, I would have run her out of town with just my cane."

Sophia chuckled at the image. "I would have given anything to see that. Seeing her with Caleb brought up every insecurity that I have about myself. And it made me doubt my relationship with him and whether he's truly ready to move on with me."

"I can see how her showing up would have shaken you, but if you really care for Caleb, that shouldn't have been a deal-breaker." She arched an eyebrow in Sophia's direction. "Should it?"

"I don't want to get hurt again," she blurted out. "I went through the emotional wringer with Lily's dad, and I just can't go down that road again."

Hattie nodded. "Forgive me, but it sounds like Caleb is paying the price for your ex's missteps. That's not only unfair, but it's downright foolish."

Sophia let out a little gasp. Hattie was nothing if not outspoken.

"I'm saying this with love and affection, Sophia. Caleb is a good man who's wild about you. The two of you make an incredible pair." She frowned. "Yet you're going to let his ex and a fear of getting hurt stand in your way?

"Life ends up hurting us, one way or another. I can't describe the pain I felt when my husband died in an accident. It was unexpected and well before his time. I've always thought he should have passed at the age of one hundred after trekking in the Himalayas. But that's not the card I was dealt."

"I'm so sorry, Hattie. That's terribly sad." Sophia couldn't imagine losing so tragically someone she loved.

"Unfortunately, that's life. My point is that we can't always shield ourselves from getting hurt. So I understand that you feel the need to protect yourself, but if you cut the person you love out of your life, what have you gained?"

"Is it so obvious that I love him?" Sophia asked, dabbing at the moisture in her eyes.

"It's crystal clear to me," Hattie said. "And my eyesight is pretty bad. Just saying."

Sophia began to chuckle, with Hattie laughing along with her. She couldn't believe that she was able to chuckle while feeling such sadness, but Hattie had a spectacular way of boiling things down to their most essential parts. Her body shook with laughter until her stomach ached.

Hattie was right. Life brought pain to everyone. And it would be ridiculous for Sophia to think that she could shield herself from that reality. She'd be cutting off her nose to spite her face if she walked away from Caleb out of fear and her insecurities. What kind of role model would she be for her own daughter if she didn't embrace love, no matter where it took her?

"You know what, Hattie? When I grow up, I want to be

just like you," Sophia said, reaching out and grabbing hold of Hattie's hand.

"As far as I'm concerned, you're well on your way," Hattie said, grinning with pleasure.

If you're ever lucky enough to find the one, hold on to her. Red's voice crashed over Caleb like a tsunami, reminding him of what the stakes were. This wasn't the time to fade into the background or step aside. He was a Stone brother. He wasn't going to give up and walk away with his tail between his legs. These past few days without Sophia had been miserable. He couldn't go on like this.

Hold on to her. He could hear Red's voice again, precious words of wisdom from a father who had been absent for most of his life. How odd was it that he was now playing such a monumental role in Caleb's life? Because of Red, Caleb was going to lay it on the line with Sophia, the way he should have done the other day.

When he drove up to Sophia's house, Caleb saw that her truck was parked outside. Score! She was at home. At least this part of his master plan had gone smoothly. Now he just needed to speak from the heart. For a few minutes he paced back and forth in front of Sophia's door trying to gather his thoughts. What if she sent him away? Rejected him again? Caleb wasn't sure he had the strength to deal with it head-on.

All of a sudden the door swung open. Sophia was standing on the doorstep, her long hair swept up in a high ponytail and wearing matching pink sweatpants and sweatshirt. She looked enticing and wholesome at the same time. All he wanted to do was scoop her up in his arms and kiss her silly. But that would have to wait until later.

"Are you just going to pace back and forth, or are you going to come inside?" Sophia asked with a tilt of her head. "It's cold out here."

She waved him into the house, and he brushed past her as he walked inside, immediately smelling the aroma of freshly baked chocolate chip cookies. The overall effect served to make her home seem even cozier.

"Where's your mini me?" he asked, surprised that Lily hadn't come running to the door.

"She's on a playdate with her friend Ashton," Sophia said. "She'll be home soon."

"Abby's gone. I saw her face-to-face and made sure of it," Caleb told her. "She's on a one-way flight back to California. Her and her film crew."

Sophia let out a surprised sound. "She is? I'm shocked that she gave up so easily after coming all the way here."

"I'm not. She knew that there was no point in sticking around. I wasn't going to film the show with her, nor was I interested in rekindling our romance." He quirked his mouth. "Something tells me she's going to find another leading man really quickly."

"Thanks for telling me," Sophia said. "Just the thought of her breathing the air in Moose Falls bugged the hell out of me."

Caleb felt the sides of his mouth twitching at Sophia's comment. "Ditto," he said.

"Caleb, I—" Sophia began, just as Caleb started to talk.

"Sophia, I need to say something to you," he blurted out.

"Okay," she said with a nod. "You go first."

"I know you're afraid and unsure of where we go from here, but for the first time in my life I'm not." He sucked in a little breath to steady himself. "I'm so in love with you, Sophia. You're it for me, and I can't imagine a life without you. I don't know exactly what that's going to look like except you and Lily will be right at the center." He tapped his chest. "Right here."

Sophia wasn't saying anything. *Why wasn't she saying anything?* He was in agony waiting for her to speak.

"I should have told you all this before, but I promised myself that I wouldn't say the L word until I knew that I was in it for the long haul."

Sophia's eyes were wide as she looked up at him. "And are you?" she asked in a low voice.

Caleb nodded. "Yes, I am. I want to be with you, Sophia. For always."

Sophia exhaled a deep breath. "Oh, Caleb. I love you too," she said, closing the distance between them and wrapping her arms around his neck. Relief and gratitude rose up inside him as soon as Sophia uttered the L word. He'd hoped she felt the same way as he did, and now he knew she did.

Sophia continued, "I think that I fell for you up in that attic, despite my best efforts not to." She blinked away tears. "And even before you said anything, I was planning to apologize, because I let doubt cloud what I feel for you."

Caleb brushed his lips over hers in a tender kiss. "And how did you come to that realization so quickly?" He shuddered. "The last time we spoke you were pretty determined to go your own way. Or at least that's what it seemed like." He placed his hand over his heart and made a face.

Sophia shook her head. "We can thank Hattie for that. She set me straight in no uncertain terms."

"Hattie to the rescue," Caleb said, grinning. "She's one special lady."

Sophia nodded in agreement. "So, what's next? Any updates on Yukon Cider?"

"I'm not sure how this is going to end and whether my brothers and I are going to run Yukon Cider or sell. But I know that I want to be right here in Moose Falls with you."

"Oh, Caleb," Sophia said, swiping away tears. "That means the world to me."

He leaned down and pressed a kiss on her forehead. "Whatever we decide as brothers, Hattie stipulated that we have to make the decision together. And, honestly, that's a gift, because it means that we're going to be a united front, no matter what we decide."

"That makes sense," she said, wiping away tears. "All for one and one for all." She was smiling now, grinning with happiness.

"But I know that I want you with me," Caleb continued, "wherever this journey takes us. I'm not prepared to give up my dreams, but I'm also not willing to toss Hattie's legacy away. It means the world to me to honor her in any way I can."

"Of course it does," Sophia said. "Hattie's done so much for Moose Falls and everyone who lives here. What she's built needs to be preserved, however you guys decide to accomplish that. Only the three of you can make that decision."

"You're a wise woman, Sophia Brand," Caleb murmured as his lips met hers in a passionate kiss. Sophia wrapped her arms around his waist and leaned in, the weight of her body feeling solid against his own. Just then the doorbell rang, and Sophia said, "Oh, that must be Ashton's mom dropping off Lily."

"Oh, no. She might see us kissing again," Caleb said with a groan. "This time you're going to have to explain it to her. Not it!" He held up his hands.

Sophia laughed out loud. "That's okay. I've got this. I'll

just tell her that this is what happens when two people love each other very, very much."

"I can't argue with that," Caleb said, pulling her against him for one last lingering kiss before she opened the front door and greeted her daughter.

EPILOGUE

A month later

"I've got this!" Caleb said, punching his fist in the air. He let out a deep breath he'd been holding, trying to shake off his nerves. After all, it wasn't every day that one popped the question to the woman of their dreams.

Landon raised a brow and looked Caleb over from head to toe. "Is that your proposal outfit?"

"What's wrong with it?" Caleb asked. He was wearing a black V-neck sweater and a pair of dark washed jeans. He let out a snort. "Only in movies do men wear tuxes to propose. I'm just going to be authentically myself."

Landon shrugged. "I guess it's okay. I thought you'd want the wow factor."

"Sophia is always wowed by me," Caleb said, earning groans from his brothers. "That's okay. She wows me too. Every time I see her beautiful face."

This time the Brothers Stone didn't let out a single groan. They knew he and Sophia had found the real deal.

"Are you sure you're all set? Because you know I wasn't completely prepared for my proposal," Xavier said, making a face. "I had to use a makeshift ring."

Caleb was on the verge of strangling both of his brothers. "Aren't the two of you supposed to be pumping me up?"

Xavier held up his hands. "I wasn't being negative. Just trying to teach by example."

"That was you," Caleb told him. "I was born ready. Beautiful round-cut diamond in an antique setting. Check. Asked Skip for his daughter's hand in marriage. Check. Got a little diamond necklace for Lily. Check. Memorized my speech. Check."

Landon and Xavier exchanged a loaded glance.

"What was that look for?" Caleb asked. "Come on. Tell me."

"Nothing," Landon quickly said. "We just wondered if you told Mom."

Ugh. He had completely forgotten to tell his mother about his plans to propose to Sophia. Daisy would be crushed if he proceeded without giving her a heads-up. Being so far away from her boys was hard enough. Caleb never wanted her to feel as if she wasn't a part of the fabric of their lives.

"Argh," Caleb said, slapping his hand to his forehead. "How could I have forgotten to loop her in?"

"You've had a lot on your mind," Landon said, patting him on the back.

"Why don't you FaceTime her now?" Xavier suggested. "She would love that."

"Good idea," Caleb said, reaching for his phone and dialing Daisy's number. In a matter of seconds, she picked up and Caleb saw her radiant face staring back at him.

"Hey, Caleb! I was just thinking about you," Daisy said, grinning.

"Of course you were. I've always been your favorite," he teased. His brothers were out of the camera frame, so his mother couldn't see them rolling their eyes.

"You know I don't play favorites," she said. "There's always been enough love to go around. How are things in Alaska?" she asked. "And the lovely Sophia? Are you still keeping her happy?"

"I sure hope so, since I'm about to ask her a very important question that will change both of our lives." He was getting a little choked up just saying the words out loud.

Daisy let out a gasp. "Caleb. You're proposing to Sophia?"

"I am, Mom. I've found my other half," he said, his voice sounding raspy to his own ears. Ever since he could remember, his mother had told him and his brothers that one day they would find their other halves. After his disastrous relationship with Abby and the subsequent fallout, Caleb had stopped believing in that possibility. Until now. Until meeting Sophia.

Tears streamed down Daisy's face, and she made no attempt to wipe them away. "I'm so proud of you, Caleb, for being courageous and giving love another chance. You could have given up on love, but you didn't. I think that I want to be like you when I grow up. You have my blessing, if you're wondering."

"Aww, Mom, you're going to make me cry," Caleb said, rubbing his eyes. Suddenly, Landon and Xavier were beside him, sharing the camera space so their mother could see all of them.

"Save the tears for the proposal," Xavier said, slapping him on the back.

"Xavier! Landon!" Daisy cried. "All of my boys together on this very special day. I couldn't be happier."

"We've got his back, Mom," Landon said. "One for all and all for one. Always."

Daisy blew them kisses and said, "Go get engaged, Caleb. The two of you deserve every happiness this world has to offer."

"Thanks, Mom," Caleb said. "Love you." The call disconnected amidst shouts of "I love you" and hand-blown kisses from their mom.

"Good deal," Xavier said, gripping Caleb's shoulder. "She's super proud."

"And happy," Landon said. "At the end of the day, if Mama's happy..."

"Then everyone's happy," Caleb and Xavier chimed in, all of them bursting into laughter. It was their truth. Making Daisy smile was always a huge achievement. She had always given so much, yet never asked for anything in return. Caleb hoped to be that solid for Sophia and Lily.

"Now I'm ready," Caleb said, rubbing his hands together. "What time is it?"

"Time to get things shaking," Hattie said as she hobbled into the room on Jacques's arm. She had a wide grin on her face. She was wearing head-to-toe pink, which happened to be her favorite color. In Hattie-isms this meant she'd given her blessing to Caleb and Sophia. "Jacques is on hand to take you to Sophia's place so you can whisk her away to the falls." Hattie clapped her hands together.

"Remember, Caleb," she added, "you're special. And don't you ever forget it."

Overwhelmed with love, Caleb embraced his grandmother. "Thanks for always being in my corner."

Caleb drove off with Jacques at the wheel of Hattie's white Bentley, the fanciest car she owned. He had it all planned out. Jacques would drive them to the falls, where Caleb would take her to the prettiest spot, then get down on bended knee and propose.

"You okay back there?" Jacques asked. "Today's going to change everything in your life, Caleb."

"You've got that right, Jacques. A whole new world for

me. Bring it on," he said, getting more excited the closer they got to Sophia's house. As the stunning Alaskan scenery whizzed past his window, he felt his enthusiasm building. By the time they pulled up to Sophia's house, he was practically jumping out of his seat to exit the car.

"I'll be waiting for the two of you," Jacques said, tipping his hat to him.

Caleb flashed him a grin and headed to the door. He had timed his arrival down to the minute according to when he'd told Sophia to expect him. He held his arms at his side and shook them to release his nerves. This was going to be a special day for him and Sophia. Of course she might suspect something was up when she saw the Bentley, but she might think it was tied in to her upcoming birthday.

He rapped on the door, turning around to send Jacques a thumbs-up sign. He began whistling as he waited. He knocked again, harder this time. After the third round of knocks the door opened up, revealing a weary-looking Sophia. She was wearing pajamas decorated with heart shapes, big fuzzy slippers, and a long white robe. Her hair was a bit messy, having been placed in a bun that was coming undone.

"Caleb?" she asked, appearing confused by him showing up at her door.

His heart plummeted. "Sophia. Did you forget about our date?"

Sophia's hand went to cover her mouth. "Oh, no! I'm so sorry." She looked past him. "Is that Jacques out there? In Hattie's Bentley?" Her voice was filled with awe.

"Yeah, I had something special planned for us," Caleb explained, trying to hide his disappointment.

"Come in, but don't get too close," Sophia instructed him. "I'm not feeling so hot."

"I'm not worried about that," Caleb said. He figured he'd already been exposed to her cold germs. "My immune system is pretty strong."

Once he was inside, she continued, "Lily got sick last night with a bad cold, and I must've gotten her germs. It was a rough night. I totally forgot about today, and I'm so sorry."

The sad expression that came over her face replaced all of his disappointment. She was sick, and he wanted to take care of both his girls. He swept his hand across her cheek.

"Have you eaten? Why don't you go sit on the couch and relax while I make you some tea and toast? Or anything else you might like. A burger? Fries? And I can run a bath for you with Epsom salts."

"You're incredibly sweet, Caleb. And I'll take you up on that, since Lily is sleeping at the moment, so I can take a breather." Her brow furrowed. "Why is Jacques here? What had you planned for our date?"

Caleb hesitated. What should he say? His heart was brimming almost to overflowing. Even though his plan had fallen apart, he still wanted to ask Sophia this monumental question.

"Tell me, Caleb," Sophia pressed. He could tell she wasn't going to let it go. When it came to things like this, Sophia was a total bloodhound.

"They do say in sickness and in health," he said, reaching into his pocket and pulling out the cedar box and holding it in plain view. A little gasp slipped past her lips as he dropped to his knees.

"Sophia, you've changed my life for the better. You're everything to me. Kind, compassionate, and loving," Caleb said. "I've never wavered in my feelings for you, Sophia. It just took me a little time to realize it was love. I want to be with you for the rest of our lives. I want you and only you.

Sophia, it would be the honor of my life if you would marry me." He popped the box open to reveal a stunning antique diamond ring that shimmered and sparkled to perfection.

"Will you?" he asked, waiting on pins and needles for her answer. So much hinged on this question. He felt a little out of breath.

She let out a little squeal. "Yes, of course I will, Caleb," she said, reaching down and tugging him to a standing position. He gently placed the ring on her finger, admiring how beautiful it looked.

"I want our life to be full of adventures, whether it's right here in Moose Falls or exploring the wilds of Africa," Caleb said. "And I know Lily already has a dad, but I'm committed to being a parent to her and always loving her."

"Oh, you've made me so happy," Sophia said, reaching up and placing her arms around his neck.

"We're going to make each other incredibly happy," Caleb said, smiling down at her.

"I think you're going to shock a lot of women by settling down, Caleb Stone. You've earned quite a reputation as a flirt," she said in a teasing voice.

"From now on, you're the only one I'll ever be flirting with, Sophia Brand," Caleb said, wrapping his arms around her waist and pulling her against his chest. He leaned down and placed a blistering kiss on her lips, signifying what they both already knew with absolute certainty. They were in this for the long haul, wherever their journey took them.

ACKNOWLEDGMENTS

I am grateful to anyone and everyone who has been reading and enjoying this Moose Falls series. I'm so thankful for my agent, Jessica Alvarez, and all of her fantastic advice and support. Grateful for my editor, Madeleine Colavita, for embracing this series from day one. Always appreciative of the Forever team and all of their support.

I have so many author friends (too many to name) who are always firmly in my corner cheering me on. I love my village.

Don't miss another trip to Moose Falls!
FOREVER IN ALASKA coming in Fall 2025

ABOUT THE AUTHOR

Belle Calhoune grew up in a small town in Massachusetts as one of five children. Growing up across the street from a public library was a huge influence on her life. Married to her college sweetheart and mother to two daughters, she lives in Connecticut. A dog lover, she has a mini poodle and a black Lab.

She is a *New York Times* bestselling author, as well as a member of RWA's Honor Roll. In 2019 her book *An Alaskan Christmas* was made into a movie (*Love, Alaska*) by Brain Power Studios and aired on UPTV. She is the author of more than fifty novels and is published by Grand Central Publishing and Harlequin Love Inspired.

Book your next trip to a charming small town—and fall in love—with one of these swoony Forever contemporary romances!

THE SOULMATE PROJECT
by Reese Ryan

Emerie Roberts is tired of waiting for her best friend, Nick, to notice her. When she confesses her feelings at the town's annual New Year's Eve bonfire and he doesn't feel the same, she resolves to stop pining for him and move on. She hatches a seven-step plan to meet her love match and enlists her family and friends—including Nick—to help. So why does he seem hell-bent on sabotaging all her efforts?

HOME ON HOLLYHOCK LANE
by Heather McGovern

Though Dustin Long has been searching for a sense of home since childhood, that's not why he bought Hollyhock. He plans to flip the old miner's cottage and use the money to launch his construction business. And while every reno project comes with unexpected developments, CeCe Shipley beats them all—she's as headstrong as she is gorgeous. But as they collaborate to restore the cottage to its former glory, he realizes they're also building something new together. Could CeCe be the home Dustin's always wanted?

Connect with us at Facebook.com/ReadForeverPub

AN AMISH CHRISTMAS MATCH
by Winnie Griggs

Phoebe Kropf knows everyone thinks she's accident-prone rather than an independent Amish woman. So she's determined to prove she's more than her shortcomings when she's asked to provide temporary Christmas help in nearby Sweetbrier Creek. Widower Seth Beiler is in over his head caring for his five motherless *brieder*. But he wasn't expecting a new housekeeper as unconventional—or lovely—as Phoebe. When the holiday season is at an end, will Seth convince her to stay…as part of their *familye*?

CHRISTMAS IN
HARMONY HARBOR
by Debbie Mason

Instead of wrapping presents and decking the halls, Evangeline Christmas is worrying about saving her year-round holiday shop from powerful real estate developer Caine Elliot. She's risking everything on an unusual proposition she hopes the wickedly handsome CEO can't refuse. How hard can it be to fulfill three wishes from the Angel Tree in Evie's shop? Caine's certain he'll win and the property will be his by Christmas Eve. But a secret from Caine's childhood is about to threaten their merrily-ever-after.